STRANDED

Blayne Cooper

Spinsters Ink
2009

Spinsters Ink
P.O.Box 242
Midway, Florida 32343

Printed in the United States of America on acid-free paper
First Edition

Editor: Cindy Cresap
Cover designer: Linda Callaghan

ISBN-10: 1-883523-63-X
ISBN-13: 978-1-883523-63-3

Acknowledgments

It takes a village to write a book, blah, blah, blah. It was
lly mostly me. But those who did help were great. Susan and
phanie, a heartfelt thank you, not only for your assistance,
t your support. Cindy, thank you for making my least favorite
rt of the writing process—editing—easy.

This novel is dedicated to the people who love me w
stranded. I love you back...on nearly a universal ba

Other novels by Blayne Cooper

Hard Times

Kellie and Lorna navigate through the oppressive, hidden world of life behind bars where the lines between right and wrong blur, sexual passion is forbidden but explosive, and love is the biggest risk of all.

Unbreakable

From their earliest years, five very different girls were as close as sisters—sharing everything, even secrets and lies—until their friendship and their lives were ripped apart by a devastating act of betrayal from one of their own. The bonds of love and friendship can be as strong as steel. But are they unbreakable?

The Last Train Home

A desperate quest to reunite a family takes Ginny Chisholm and Lindsay Killian from the slums of 1890s New York City to the farms of West Virginia and the bustling frontier beyond. This harrowing journey moves the young women from one mishap and adventure to another. It also leads them from friendship to a tender and unexpected romance.

Chapter 1

I know what you're thinking. Nobody likes staring into the three-paneled mirror of doom while trying on swimsuits. But did it really have to be *this* bad?

I jumped at the series of sharp knocks on my dressing room door.

"C'mon, Rachel, hurry up."

God, we were probably going to get kicked out of Macy's. Again. "I'm going as fast as I can."

"How long is it going to take to haul that swimsuit over your big butt?"

My sister Joanie. I'd have been mad about her rude comment if I hadn't said something even worse as she tried on a pair of very low-cut, and unflattering, jeans only an hour ago.

Slowly, I opened the door of my dressing room and tried to keep from cringing. "How bad is it?" I motioned down my body with a defeated hand as I stepped out. "Don't lie to spare my feelings."

She snorted as if the thought had never crossed her mind. And it probably hadn't. We don't have that sort of relationship. Joanie and I might occasionally lie to ourselves, but we never lie to each other. At least about anything that matters.

"Well." She tapped her chin thoughtfully. "It's better than the last one. But not as good as the turquoise one you had on a few suits ago. Oddly, it brings out the light flecks in your eyes." My eyes are a peculiar, very pale brown golden color that I worry looks more canine than human. "It also supports your massive boobs. Lift"—she demonstrated by clutching her own breasts—"and separate."

At five-six and 161 pounds, I was undeniably full-figured, which sounded way nicer than saying "a porker." But… "Massive boobs? You give me too much credit." I glanced in the mirror and turned my head from side-to-side. No double chin yet, thank Christ.

Joanie glanced down at her own chest, which wasn't insubstantial, especially considering her naturally slim physique. "Your thirty-eight double D compared to my thirty-four C? Actually, when compared to anything that's not bovine, they're massive."

I refused to laugh. "Jealous much?"

"Duh."

I frowned into the mirror. The reflection wasn't as brutal as the one in the stall, but only because it didn't provide multiple views of my ass and they'd toned the lighting down. Presumably, to scare you into buying what scared the hell out of you only seconds before. "I'm not getting this one or the blue one," I declared. "In fact, I'm not to going to wear a swimsuit at all. Like any sensible woman, I'm hiding my body in normal clothes." Take *that* Jenny Craig. "Plus, I'm never, and I do mean *ever*, eating again."

Joanie shook her head. "Stop complaining. You're getting an all-expenses paid trip to Venezuela and you're not taking a swimsuit? Are you crazy? The beaches will be hot and the men will be even hotter."

I tugged at the suit, lifting up my left boob. "I burn in five minutes, and you know it. If I go to the beach, I'll have to be under a hat the size of an umbrella the entire time." I ignored her comment about the men.

"There's this new invention. It's called sunscreen."

Joanie, who didn't share my peaches-and-cream complexion—or as she liked to say, necrotic skin tone—would never understand. She got tan. I fried like a drumstick at KFC.

"I prefer an old invention," I said. "It's called shade. Or preferably clouds *and* shade." I let the swimsuit strap fall, checking out the bounce factor. Joanie was right. Not bad, but not as good as the turquoise. "Anyway, this trip is mainly work, not a vacation."

"Uh-huh. And since when do disc jockeys get to travel the world? It's a reward for your great ratings. They're bribing you because your contract runs out soon, big sister. You rock."

I laughed a little at her enthusiasm. My lifelong cheering section was partly right. I'm half of the *Reece & Rachel Morning Show.* And six months ago, after a long and sometimes vicious public battle, Reece and I finally made it to number one in the ratings. And we've stayed there ever since.

I hurried back into the changing room. Joanie and shopping didn't mix, and I only had a few good hours with her before her attention to my prospective wardrobe would begin to wane.

My sister and my mother are the only family I have left. My grandparents passed away before I was born, and Dad, who I adored, had a fatal heart attack about a year-and-a-half ago. That's when my mom joined the workforce full time and started tearing through boyfriends the way most women do cheap pantyhose. I love her, and she loves me, but we aren't especially close.

She hasn't approved of most of the choices I've made since I was five years old and refused the Cinderella costume she bought me for Halloween. And I haven't liked most of the choices she's made since she turned sixty. So I guess we're even. For some reason I've never seemed to grasp, she and Joanie get along famously, and so Mom and I do most of our talking through her.

Joanie lives a good two hours outside of Denver. We speak on the phone nearly every day, and have confided in each other forever. But because of our crazy schedules and an independent streak that runs through us both, we don't see each other more than once or twice a month. Even at that, I'd had time to tell her what was going on. I just hadn't.

"I agreed to sign a new contract last week." I waited for the explosion.

"Last week? Rachel!"

"Don't have kittens."

"Does Mom know?"

Joanie hated being the last to know anything and would likely be on the phone with our mother before we left the mall. "I was waiting until all the legal mumbo jumbo was tied up before I told you. But my new contract isn't the best part. The best part is that the station has officially pimped me out."

"I always said you were a ho."

I yanked the suit down, the paper crotch-guard scratching my inner thighs. "A little respect please. You're not only talking to the better half of Reece & Rachel—"

She made a rude noise. "*Way* better."

"But you're also speaking to the new color commentator for the Denver Dragonflies."

"Huh?"

I frowned. "The new professional women's soccer team."

"Here? In Denver?"

"Don't you read the papers?"

"I have three children under six-years-old. If it isn't printed on the insides of my eyelids or on the last episode of *Dora the Explorer*, I don't know about it."

Keeping it simple, I said, "It's a new part-time job away from Reece and the pay is awesome."

Joanie let out a loud whoop. "If someone's going to bother to broadcast professional women's soccer, which, by the way, seems incredibly silly to me, then I'm glad it's you. Congrats."

She wasn't a soccer fan. And, in truth, neither was I. But I'd wanted to do something more challenging than banter with Reece, tell people about the traffic and announce insipid Top 40 singles for years now.

I'd done the play-by-play for my college basketball team, and a Triple-A baseball team early in my broadcasting career. True, that was a good ten years ago, but experience was experience. The fact that I've become somewhat of a local celebrity didn't hurt my chances either. My face, along with Reece's and that perfect-toothed, shit-eating grin of his, is on a billboard right downtown.

You can't imagine how nerve-wracking it is to know that your picture is being viewed by thousands of cars every day as they honk and spew their way down Broadway. Jaw clenched, I drive by the stupid thing every day myself on my way to work. And every day I wonder if today will be the day that someone spray-paints a nasty black goatee on me. Or a flaming red zit the size of Krakatau? The kind the photographer airbrushed out of the real photograph. Or maybe devil horns?

Okay, I must admit I kinda like the idea of devil horns, but that's not the point.

That billboard, and what it represents, is a big part of why I got this new job. The Dragonflies have yet to play their first game, but the team's owner is doing what he can to weave the new team into the fabric of Denver. Wisely, he's using well-known local Coloradoans to do it.

I emerged from the stall fully dressed and finger-combed my curly copper-colored hair into some semblance of order. It wouldn't help, but that never stopped me from trying. Everyone thinks naturally curly hair is great. But they're *so* wrong. It's a lot like owning a cat. It can be soft and shiny, but you don't control it, it rarely plays nice, and it most of the time it acts as though it doesn't particularly like you. It's a money pit and the best you can hope for is that it will behave and let you pet it once in a while.

Once again, I considered getting it cut into something shorter and sassier. And once again, I waffled. With a grievous sigh, I tossed Joanie the turquoise bathing suit and marched out of the dressing rooms.

It hit her in the chest and she smirked. "Told you."

Over my shoulder, I said, "Have I mentioned that you're watching my cat while I'm in Venezuela?"

Horrified, she stood there like a statue. "Oh, shit."

I walked for a moment in smug silence before Joanie appeared at my side again.

"Lunch?" she asked as she wound her arm around mine and began tugging me toward a Chinese restaurant in the food court that I knew she loved, and she knew I despised. "And with a new job, you're buying."

I smiled and began to prepare for our next battle.

"You will not," I ground out. "It's already been decided."

"The hell I won't." Reece leaned back in his chair and crossed his arms in a pose that meant his mouth would still be moving, but he was shutting off his ears.

I ripped off my headset and threw it on the table next to me. Luckily, it was one minute past eleven a.m. which meant we were officially off the air. "You will *not*. Jerry swore—"

Reece scoffed. "You think I'm going to let Jerry The Producer tell me what to do with my own show? Then you don't know me very well."

Oh, I knew him all right. "It's *our* show, and you're being a big baby, all because I have a new gig and you don't," I pointed out tartly. "Deal with it, Reece. But don't make me suffer while you do."

His mouth clamped shut. Bingo.

"And don't pout. You still make more money than I do, you jerk. And you hate sports and know nothing about them anyway."

The muscle in one of his cheeks began to twitch.

Bingo again.

As our eyes dueled, the appearance of a well-worn but disturbingly charming smile threatened to crack my composure. I didn't know whether to smack him or... smack him.

Reece is good-looking in a young, college professor sort of way. Tousled blond hair, worn just a tad long for business. Slightly rumpled corduroy jackets with leather elbow patches. Designer T-shirts with blue jeans. Sturdy brown loafers. He's the sort of guy who would rather cozy up with a piece of classic literature—only to sprinkle quotations from what he's just read into upcoming conversations—than watch football on Sundays.

Despite his natural good looks, he'd look like a full-on nerd if I hadn't been supervising his haircuts and pulling the pocket protector from his jacket every morning for the past eight years. Either way, he was absolutely nothing, in looks or personality, like the borderline shock jock image that he cultivated for our show.

I was the quick-witted straight man in our routine, which was exactly how I was in real life. The fact that Reece could act one way, and then five seconds later become a completely different person, should have been a warning sign not to marry him.

Then again, I was never very good at picking up on warning signs.

"I'm not doing reruns while you're gone, Rachel. I'm a big boy and can go on-air alone." But he was already losing steam because he knew I was right.

"There's plenty of old tape." I leaned back in my chair, relaxing now that I was sure of how things would turn out. "Take a nice vacation while I'm gone. How long has it been since you've visited your parents or brother?"

Reece crossed his arms over his chest as he considered my words.

Our morning show bickering, which consisted of affectionate ribbing with a hefty dose of stinging barbs thrown in, was radio show magic. There was enough genuine conflict and fondness to entertain and sometimes titillate, but not enough to turn most viewers off. We both gave and received, and we usually deserved whatever the other dished out. We were a team, and Reece without Rachel, or vice versa, just didn't work...at least in that format.

Which is the very reason I'd wanted to branch out.

Our personal relationship, however, was far less magical than our professional one. We'd been divorced for about a year and a half, though in public we downplayed that. Our friends and family knew, of course, and it had even hit the local papers when we split. But the public liked the "couple" vibe we displayed on air, and nobody wanted to mess with success. So on-air, except for the occasional gaffe where we asked about each other's houses or off-air schedules—something any real couple would already know—we blithely pretended nothing had changed since the divorce.

I take that back, something *had* changed. After we'd stopped being married, the show had gotten better, and I went back to liking Reece again. At least most of the time. When we didn't see each other every second of the day, we actually had something to say to each other. Our time together was fresher and more like the early days when we heated up the airwaves in smaller markets like Colorado Springs and Vail.

The station hadn't even had the need to use their five-second delay to bleep out profanity in...days. Okay, hours. But progress was progress.

We openly dated other people and he had a disgusting amount of success with the ladies while still keeping things low-key and fun. I, on the other hand, had endured exactly three dates that led exactly nowhere.

"You want me to check on P-Diddy Kitty while you're out of town?" Reece asked. His way of apologizing for being a jerk and giving in without actually acknowledging that I was right.

"Joanie's doing it."

His body went stiff at the mention of my sister's name. Half a head shorter than me, and cute as a button, she's probably the least intimidating-looking adult I've ever seen. Even so, she'd threatened to castrate Reece during my shitty divorce. And now, eighteen months later, he still wasn't sure whether the threat had been an idle one. I, on the other hand, was quite sure that Joanie had been serious. Despite being a year younger than me, she had been my protector growing up and hadn't relinquished the role since.

While I have a lethal tongue, I'm basically a klutz, and squeamish to boot. So as appealing as the thought of making Reece a soprano had been—and it *had* been—I'd probably have wound up with one less finger in the process. Considering that my fingers were as close as I was going to get to a boyfriend in the foreseeable future, I held them in very high regard and didn't take the risk. At least they never left the seat up or charged up my credit cards without me knowing about it.

"When do you leave on your trip again?" Reece asked, finding something very interesting about his fingernails. If he'd gotten a manicure again, I wouldn't be able to stop myself from calling him gay.

He knew exactly when I was leaving, but we were just getting to where we could engage in small talk off the air and not have it dissolve into something ugly. So I played along. "Tomorrow morning."

He paused and cleared his throat. "I'll miss you, Rachel. Things aren't the same here without you." Restlessly, he played with the headset in his lap, keeping his eyes firmly trained on his hands and his voice light. Displays of emotion weren't his thing. "Be careful, okay?"

Then he looked up and gave me a slightly embarrassed smile. God help him, he really would miss me. And against the odds, I would probably miss him too. I couldn't help but smile back. Even though he made me crazy most of the time, his words warmed me. It's weird how two people can be so right and so utterly wrong for each other at the same time.

We were living proof.

Chapter 2

The airport buzzed with activity. Like me, it seemed that at this very moment, everyone in Colorado was itching to be someplace else.

I wasn't sure who from the Dragonflies would accompany me on this trip, so I was wearing a lightweight skirt and blazer. It would be hell on the twelve-hour plane flight, but my attorney had warned me during my contract negotiations that the team ownership and management were as conservative as they come.

I didn't consider myself particularly conservative about anything, so this was my attempt at faking it. I could keep my political and social views to myself, if I had to. It was the first of what I suspected would be many concessions, something everyone goes through with any new job.

The world of sports broadcasting is a hard nut to crack. My competition for this job had been some very heavy hitters in local sports commentating. *Male* heavy hitters. And considering the format of the *Reece & Rachel Morning Show*, the team was taking a big chance on me. There was no way that was I going to mess things up by wearing a tacky Hawaiian print shirt and making a shoddy impression. I'd wait and scare the locals instead.

So with a hat the size of a VW Bug, a half dozen cheesy print shirts, and a swimsuit that could hold up to two cannon balls in a hurricane, Venezuela, here I come.

Despite being in my grown up clothes, I was also struggling to remind myself that this was a working vacation. I had a real assignment.

Miranda Gutierrez, a relatively unknown, but extremely promising, South American soccer player, was the latest Dragonflies recruit. She was all of seventeen years old and nearly six feet of lean muscle and dark good looks. The team had wooed her relentlessly and all but stolen her from the Los Angeles Meteors with a last-minute offer of big bucks.

Not that the Dragonflies had much to worry about. Once the general public got a good look at Miranda, the team would no doubt make a fortune selling jerseys with her name on them and products of all kinds with her image. I predict that every fourth-grade girl in Denver will want Miranda on her lunchbox—while every man under a hundred will want to eat *her* for lunch. Think Gabriella Sabatini but with pouty lips, a better haircut and a perky pink soccer ball.

There was just one catch. The future jewel in the new team's crown, the story goes, was petrified about moving to the States, and downright phobic about the media. Last fall, an overzealous, stalkerish Canadian reporter scared the crap out of her after an exhibition match in Vancouver. He'd ended up in jail and she'd ended up on the next plane home to Mama and Papa. It was Miranda's first and only experience in North America. Since then, she'd refused all interviews, something rumored to be giving the Dragonflies team owner an ulcer as big as his head.

So here I was, coming along on this trip to do a couple of lightweight interviews that would be played on the *Reece & Rachel Morning Show* instead of reruns, and more importantly, to make nice and show Miranda that Americans, particularly the press, weren't as bad as she feared. I might have overplayed the sweet side of my personality during the interview process… just a touch.

After my assignment with Miranda, I'd be set free to see the sights. Could someone on the Dragonflies staff do pretty much what I'd been asked to do? Sure. But it was my face on a billboard on Broadway, and then this wouldn't be a bribe that my station had worked out with the team to entice me to sign on for two more years of the morning show.

But the deed had been done and my name sat proudly on the bottom line. That meant two more years of Reece—who *still* made more money than me—before he'd had his morning coffee or bothered to comb his hair.

Venezuela had better rock.

I'd been at the gate for nearly forty-five minutes when the Dragonflies delegation arrived in a clump of chatting voices, bringing with them the strong odor of too much male cologne. They spotted me right away, waving in my direction, though they were all strangers to me. Stupid billboard.

"Ms. Michaels?" A beefy man, he stood well over six feet tall and had a head so shiny it reflected the fluorescent lights overhead like the hood of a car on a sunny day. He extended a large hand. He appeared to be about my mom's age, and his eyebrows were bushy and silver-white. "I'm Jacob Dane."

I gulped. This guy didn't work for the Dragonflies. He *owned* them.

I hoped my hand wasn't sweating when I reached out to shake his. "Pleased to meet you, Mr. Dane. Thank you for this opportunity."

He gave me a quick once-over, his gaze sharp, but not unkind. "You're welcome."

After a good look, he must have found whatever it was he'd been looking for because the introductions continued with him gesturing to another man who stood directly behind him. His voice was proud when he said, "This is my son, William. He's the—"

"Team general manager, I know." I smiled my most winning smile, fully aware that I went into radio, and not television broadcasting, for a reason. It's not that I'm ugly. In fact, I have it on good authority that I'm more than decent looking. My own mother would never lie about such a thing.

The main reason I didn't go into television broadcasting is that you can usually tell exactly what I'm thinking by the look on my face. It's always gotten me into trouble and through the years has been a source of constant embarrassment. And right now I was nervous enough for my stomach to be coiled tight and hands to be twitching. It had to be showing.

"It's a pleasure to meet you as well, Mr. Dane," I said, discreetly wiping my hands on my jacket.

Both men beamed. Thank God I'd just recalled seeing the junior Dane's face in a recent article in the *Denver Post*. I'm horrible with names, but I never forget a face.

William was a thinner, shorter version of his father, though he still possessed the final, stubborn vestiges of what once must have been a full head of coal-black hair. He gave me a friendly pat on the shoulder, his smile never faltering, dark eyes twinkling. I'd put him at about forty years old when he'd first walked up, but his toothy grin and smooth face caused me to look past his rapidly retreating hairline and reevaluate my guess. My gaze dropped for a split second before finding his eyes again.

He filled out his suit nicely, with nary the hint of a bulge around his waistband. That meant he was probably in his early thirties, making us contemporaries.

"I'm glad that you signed with us, Ms. Michaels," he said. "This is going to be a great year for Denver. And I'm excited that you're going to be a part of it." He pumped his fist in the air with the exuberance of one of those guys who paints his face and beer belly bright orange and always gets airtime on ESPN during a football game. "Go Dragonflies!"

Okay, a little gung-ho for my taste, but the guy actually seemed to be genuine in his excitement. "Go Dragonflies," I echoed gamely, though with slightly less volume.

Jacob Dane appeared to have forgotten about me because he was speaking in low tones to the woman at his left. She was holding two three-ringed binders that looked as though they weighed a ton apiece, but her attentive eyes never left Mr. Dane's as he spoke.

She had a pretty, but not stunning face, and a trim, athletic build. With straight, white teeth and an enviable complexion, she looked very much like a super-healthy version of the all-American-Got Milk?-girl-next-door. Somehow I doubted that *her* treadmill was currently being used as an expensive clothes hanger

The woman's thick, sandy-brown hair was captured in a soft, stylish bun that sat at the nape of her neck. She had golden highlights that had either cost a fortune or were nothing short of a gift from Above.

It took all my willpower not to hate her instantly.

Her glasses with tasteful frames sat atop her very straight nose. Clad in a perfectly tailored, peach-colored linen pantsuit, her heels were higher than mine, which I equated with nothing short of abject misery.

Poor thing. Being an executive secretary had to be a bitch.

One great thing about my job is that you don't need more than a couple of professional outfits. I usually wore sweatpants to work.

The secretary also reminded me of someone I couldn't put my finger on.

A quick glance at the Dragonflies group told me everyone, except for me, was wearing Dragonflies jewelry. Jacob had on cute insect cuff links that were studded with diamonds. The secretary sported small Dragonflies earrings with gorgeous topaz wings. And William wore a slightly bolder purple Dragonflies pin on his lapel.

I was one of them now, sort of, and dammit, I wanted something sparkly too.

As if reading my mind, the woman tore herself away from her boss long enough to awkwardly dig into the pocket of her blazer to hand me a slender jewelry box. Our eyes met and a soft smile blossomed on her lips. "Welcome aboard," she said. "We opted for the bracelet since we thought earrings might bother you when you wear an earpiece or headphones at work."

Her voice was a deep, smooth contralto, the kind that graces late night jazz stations and threatens to lull you to sleep while you drive. For some reason, I hadn't expected that, and I smiled back, wondering if anyone had ever told her she should be in radio.

"I'm Nora, by the way," she said gently, prodding me into alertness.

Her smile was both friendly and shrewd, like she had a secret, and suddenly I knew who she looked like. It was the actress on that television series about the poor wretches marooned by a plane crash on what looked suspiciously like Hawaii... Evangeline Lilly.

"It's nice to see that jewelry is something you'll wear," she continued. "I hate it when we give it to people who stick it in a drawer and forget about it."

Suddenly, I was mortified at my poor manners and the thought that I'd lusted after the jewelry so badly that it had been written all over my face. It wasn't like I wore a lot of jewelry anyway. I didn't. It's just that free things are way, *way* better than anything you had to buy yourself. Everyone knows that. "Thank you for the gift," I said to Nora, quite sure that she, and not anyone else, had been thoughtful enough to actually think about what would work best with my job.

Jacob gazed down fondly at her, deep creases appearing in freshly shaved cheeks. "So impatient. I was just about to introduce you, but as usual, you beat me to it. Ms. Michaels, Nora Butler is my invaluable assistant. William's my right hand and Nora is my left."

I looked at the woman's overflowing arms and felt a twinge of sympathy. "It's nice to meet you, Nora, but you can skip the handshake. I wouldn't want you to rupture something."

Both Mr. Danes seemed to remember their manners at the exact same time and they rushed to relieve Nora of her binders.

"I told you they were too heavy to carry," William chastised mildly as he set the binders in a chair that actually groaned under their weight.

Nora lifted an impertinent eyebrow. "And you were going to bring them instead?"

I smothered a chuckle. Cheeky. I like that.

William let go of a guilty grin. "Never. In fact, you know that I refuse to even touch them."

Jacob clucked his tongue, though his expression remained mild. "William, Nora, don't go making a bad impression on our newest team member." The words were said in a completely neutral tone of voice, but like children who'd been reprimanded for having too much fun in school, Nora and William instantly straightened, their smiles dropping from their faces the way leaves flutter from trees in the fall.

William recovered quickly, but the stress showed up on Nora's face in the form of tiny lines around her eyes. For a moment, I thought Nora and William might be siblings. But two people couldn't look more opposite, and there was no way any family could survive *that* much togetherness. I also recalled reading that Jacob Dane had only one child, a son. So I dismissed the thought.

Jacob glanced at his watch, then down at Nora. "Our flight is at the other end of the terminal, so it's time for us to go."

My eyebrows jumped. Go?

"But before we do, I wanted to give you and Ms. Michaels this." With a great flourish Jacob presented Nora with an envelope.

Nora looked to William in question and a helpless expression overtook his face.

Uh-oh.

"What is it?" she asked warily, turning the envelope over in her hands.

"Open it and see," Jacob said.

She did, with me doing my best to peer over her shoulder without looking like I was snooping. After all, Mr. Dane had said it was for me too.

First Nora's mouth dropped open, then mine.

Jacob laughed, and I instantly knew that he'd misinterpreted both of our reactions.

Inside the envelope were tickets to a ten-day, private, guided tour through the wilds of Venezuela. Three very expensive tickets. One in my name, one in Nora's and one in Miranda's. A quick scan of the brochure the tickets were stapled to promised a thrilling, but safe, "Adventure of a Lifetime."

Christ. Going to the mall during a clearance sale was exciting enough for me. This new job was going to play hell on my schedule during soccer season. I'd recently lived through a searing divorce on the heels of my father's death, the realization that unless I lowered my standards to guys found in biker bars or very dark frat parties, I'd all but given up the chance at a regular lover, and begun repairing one of the most important personal and professional relationships of my life. All that was adventure enough.

I squinted to see the dates on the tickets. Three days from now.

So much for any free time to shop and drink margaritas in my hotel pool. The trip would take every bit of my time in Venezuela and a few additional days that I hadn't planned for.

As shocked as I was, Nora looked even more stunned. And furious. She actually had to draw in a calming breath before speaking. "I don't see how I'll have time to—"

"Make time, Nora," Jacob interrupted, voice firm. "Get to know Miranda and help her have a good time and relax. But for God's sake, make sure she doesn't as much as twist her ankle."

Nora and William both paled at the mere thought.

"C'mon, it'll be fun," Jacob proclaimed in a booming voice that brokered no disagreement.

Nora's eyes, which were the interesting shade of early summer grass, turned to chips of mossy ice.

"I knew you'd love it," Jacob gushed, rocking back on his heels. "You deserve it, Nora. You've worked like hell to help get this team off the ground. Anything important has already been rescheduled on your behalf."

Oops. Nora just blew a blood vessel. Someone didn't like having her schedule messed with.

"And Ms. Michaels?" Jacob continued. He turned to me. "Consider this a little signing bonus. Besides, I thought Nora would have more fun if she brought along a girlfriend."

Friend? We'd just laid eyes on each other.

I hoped the Dragonflies had a good dental plan, because I could actually hear Nora's teeth grinding.

"Jacob, you shouldn't have," she said, the barest hint of steel in her voice.

Oblivious, he just kept on smiling. "William said you'd be surprised. He helped me pick the gift out."

She narrowed her gaze at William and he audibly gulped at the sight.

Time to nip this in the bud quickly. Besides the fact that

emotionally I wasn't up for any thrills, I was not an outdoorsy sort of gal. Bugs. Sweating. Dirt. I hated it all. And I had a feeling our "adventure" wouldn't take place in an air-conditioned Town Car.

It wasn't that I was opposed to hard work. Far from it. My hours at the station were brutal and I worked tirelessly to get *Reece & Rachel* to the top. And although I hadn't taken a real vacation in more than three years, this "adventure" had the potential for disaster. Peeing outside, and most likely down my leg, wasn't my idea of fun. Fun to me meant good friends, good food and relaxation. Not fighting the elements and my own lack of athleticism.

"The gift is amazing, Mr. Dane," I gushed, laying a hand on his sleeve and squeezing gently for effect. "But it's too much for me to accept." I added a note of regret to my voice. "Really."

"Nonsense. It's all set."

"But I already received a generous bonus from the radio station when I signed on with the Dragonflies. So, while this is very kind of you, it isn't—"

"Aren't two bonuses better than one?"

My brow puckered. "Well, yes. I guess so. But, I didn't pack the right sort of—"

"I won't take no for an answer."

No shit, I wanted to scream.

"William?" Now Nora sounded more desperate than angry. "You know how busy things are. This isn't the time for me to take a vacation."

Words you'll never hear me say to my boss at the radio station.

The younger Dane held up his hands in supplication. "I'm sorry, Nora." They shared a long-suffering look. "It's only too bad that I won't be able to join you."

I tried not to sound too eager. "If you're short a ticket, I'd be happy to give—"

"Well," Jacob began, his hearty voice stopping all other conversation on the matter. "We'd better get going. I'll expect photos of your trip, Nora. In fact, I can't wait to see photos from *each and every stop* on your adventure with all the participants."

Oh, this guy was good.

Then Jacob bent and gave Nora a robust hug and whispered something into her ear, his lips so close to her cheek that they almost touched. I caught the words "Your house," but that was all. My eyebrows were still firmly planted high on my forehead when a strand of hair escaped her bun and Jacob reached up and casually tucked it behind Nora's ear.

The out-of-the-blue act was startlingly familiar.

When Jacob straightened, William winked at Nora and a look of irritation, no, resentfulness, swept over her face before being swiftly hidden.

Ah, now I get it. Barf. Apparently, the lovely secretary does some moonlighting of a very personal nature for her boss, and Junior'd figured it out. How inconvenient. I spied Jacob's bulky wedding ring and my estimation of Nora Butler plummeted. While I'm certain there are worse ways to climb the corporate ladder, at the moment I couldn't think of any.

How sucky was this? I was walking into a soap opera. I could only hope that somewhere in all this someone was waiting to sweep me off my feet. Or at least have sex with me. And after more than two years without...the sweeping part had moved over into the optional column.

My attention was drawn back to William when he echoed his father's wish of safe travels before jogging after Jacob, who was already twenty feet down the terminal.

Nora let out a resigned sigh when they were gone and plopped down into a chair next to the binders. I could practically see the weight tumble off her shoulders with each of their steps. She scrubbed her face. "*Fuck*."

Okay, even though she was a home-wrecker, maybe we would be friends after all. I couldn't help but like someone who swore worse than I did.

I sat down next to her as she began intently rooting through her bag. "So it's just us going?" I asked, trying not to be bitchy because she was shagging the boss and I was going to fly twelve hours only to have to spend most of my time being eaten by mosquitoes, or bats or whatever the hell flew around in the Venezuelan sky.

"Just us," she said, giving me a weak smile. She pulled a pack of chewing gum from her purse and offered me a stick.

I never chew gum, but I took it anyway. She was obviously dismayed, and I found myself eager to do anything she wanted just to make her feel better. You'd think her boss-slash-geriatric boyfriend would know her well enough not to give her a trip she'd hate at a time when she didn't want to go. Yutz, should have stuck with Paris for the weekend or diamonds.

With a strong nudge, I reminded myself that her love life was none of my business. "So, if it's just us, why are Mr. Dane and Mr. Dane at the airport too?"

She leaned back in her seat and crossed her arms. "They have another meeting to attend in London first thing in the morning and then Brussels two days after that. So no South American sun for them." She must have seen the question in my eyes because she added, "Miranda is from some tiny town and the poor kid is scared to death to be moving to the States. She'll be coming alone as soon as she turns eighteen in a couple of weeks. I'm part of her welcome wagon, and I'm going to work to calm her parents' fears over the endless corruption, debauchery and depravity that awaits their baby once she starts hanging out with the team."

"Will there really be endless depravity, debauchery and corruption?"

"At the very least."

"Cool."

We traded unexpected grins.

Nora said, "Jacob was afraid if we sent too many people to South America it would freak the kid out even more. And then the trip to London popped up..."

I spared a wistful thought for the shade and cool rain of London. The theater. The museums. I even tried to feel sorry for Miranda, since Nora apparently did. But imagining the lucrative contract she'd signed while most kids were still babysitting or working at Taco Bell for their money didn't help.

I crossed my legs and Nora's gaze swept down to my feet, which were encased like sausages in a pair of low-slung heels. A tiny line appeared between her eyebrows. "Are those what you're wearing on the plane?"

For a second I thought she might be being catty about my shoes. Which would really suck because they were good shoes, but nothing like what a boss-slash-boyfriend could buy. Then I caught the look of interested concern she was giving me and decided to stop being such an ass. "Sadly, the answer is yes."

I leaned closer to her so no one else could overhear. She smelled nice, a mixture of clean soap with a hint of vanilla. And I made a mental note to ask her about her shampoo later. "I wasn't sure what big cheese might show up on this trip, so I wanted to make a good impression in case I met any executives."

She lowered her voice to match mine. "You did make a good impression."

"You think?"

She nodded confidently. "I do."

"Thanks," I said, genuinely pleased. "I'm glad at least someone thinks so." I took in her outfit, which looked at least as restrictive as mine. "What about you?"

She looked as though she wanted to say more, but she finally settled on, "It doesn't matter. I'm fine." Then she surprised me by saying, "Do *you* want to be more comfortable?"

"Well, sure. But—"

Her eyes took on a determined gleam. "C'mon." She was already on her feet and moving toward one of the kiosks at the end of the terminal at a frightening speed, her heels clicking loudly on the floor. Did all Dragonflies employees run everywhere they went? If so, in the future I might actually get the amount of exercise I claimed I did during my last physical.

I shook my head. "No way. Absolutely not. No how, no way."

Nora held up the shorts and T-shirt again and frowned. "Why not? They aren't that bad."

She looked truly puzzled as to why I didn't want to buy a pair of long, neon-orange Denver Broncos shorts and a semi-matching orange T-shirt—the only one in my size—that proclaimed "I'm with Stupid."

"How would you feel if I wore this and then ended up sitting right next to you?" I challenged.

"Lucky." Then, to my amazement, only her eyes smiled. I'd seen Tyra Banks do that on my favorite show, *America's Next Top Model*, but who knew a real person could pull it off?

I guess that was the end of the discussion, because before I could protest any further, she handed her corporate American Express card to the guy at the cash register. On our way back to the gate, she thrust the sack containing my new clothes in my direction. "Too bad we couldn't do something about the shoes."

Was she always this solicitous of near strangers? "You don't need to—"

She stopped me. "Please don't say it. It's truly my pleasure. Especially after the little surprise Jacob, I mean, Mr. Dane, sprang on you."

"It's a great gift," I said valiantly, hoping my smile wasn't as plastic as it felt.

"For some people," she said knowingly.

I relaxed a little. "Exactly. Just not me."

"I really am sorry."

I brushed away her concern. I would live. I hoped.

"Oh, and whatever you need to wear on our adventure," she sneered that last word, "I'll be happy to buy with the Dragonflies credit card. It's not your fault that you didn't know what to pack."

She was right, of course. But— "You won't get in trouble for that, will you?"

"I'll be fine."

She appeared to have that phrase down pat. Trouble was, and I couldn't put my finger on exactly why, I didn't buy it. But what could I do other than remember the manners my parents had tried to teach me and say thank you?

I spied a bathroom where I could go change—shorts with heels and nylons was a little too trashy-hooker-with-varicose-veins (or Dallas Cowboys cheerleader) to me, but desperate times called for desperate measures. I'd only made it a few feet when a gate agent announced the seating of all first class passengers. Steerage, my class of ticket, would come next.

Oh, hell. Now I'd have to bump and strain to change clothes in the microscopic bathroom on the airplane. With any luck, people seated near the bathroom would think I was joining the mile-high club. That is, until they saw me emerge alone. Then they'd just think the truth. Joy.

Nora adjusted the shoulder strap on her carry-on and removed her boarding pass from a side pocket. "Enjoy your flight and I'll see you when we land." She held my gaze for a few seconds before her eyes dipped... "I'm sure you'll look great in the Broncos clothes."

I blinked, and then glanced down at myself. Surely she hadn't been looking at my chest when she said that?

She took a step forward, and settled into her place among the sea of people who weren't talented enough to form a line the way our kindergarten teachers had shown us. "Oh, and, Ms. Michaels?"

She was flying first class? I want a boss to sleep with. One with hair, please. "Call me Rachel."

"If you call me Nora."

"Done."

"Rachel, those binders on the seat are yours. I thought you might have some time for reading on the plane. They contain information about the organization and, most importantly, the Team Code of Conduct. It applies not only to players, but to all employees, full or part-time, as well as contract workers. Mr. Dane wants everyone to review it as close to his or her hiring date as possible. There's a tear-out sheet for you to sign in the back."

"Okay," I replied, hoping there wasn't an obscure policy against stupid T-shirts on page eleven. 'Cause I sure as hell wasn't going to get past page ten of that monstrosity before I fell asleep. Of course, the four or five tiny bottles of vodka I planned on drinking on the plane weren't going to help the situation.

When she was gone, I dropped down into a chair, in no mood to fight to get to a seat that I'd already been assigned. Instantly bored, I sat in silence for a few seconds before thumbing through one of the enormous binders. I spied an organization chart that looked like a large pyramid and turned the binder sideways so I could read it properly.

My gaze lit on a name embarrassingly near to the tippy top. One I'd just become familiar with.

I closed my eyes and swore under my breath.

Nora was Jacob Dane's assistant all right. The Assistant *General Manager* of the team. And after Jacob and William, she was the most powerful person in the entire Dragonflies organization.

I groaned silently. She should sit next to me and wear my new T-shirt.

Chapter 3

A blast of hot, moist air tinged with the strong smell of jet fuel ruffled my hair as I moved down the stairs and stepped onto the blazing tarmac. My stomach roiled. The flight had been nothing short of wretched. We'd hit turbulence while we were still over the States and it hadn't let up for the entire trip. After the second hour I began to pray for the incessant rocking to stop. By the fourth hour I knew God was blowing me off and I simply wished for a quick death. When the tenth hour in the air rolled around, I began to consider being a little more proactive. If I rushed the cockpit it was always possible a zealous air marshal would shoot me and put me out of my misery.

But here I was safe, if not the least bit sound. My makeup, what little I had on, anyway, began to melt and I squinted, wishing I hadn't packed my sunglasses in my checked bag.

So this was Venezuela.

Not far from the ocean, I still wasn't feeling any of the much-lauded temperate Caribbean wind. The airport consisted of two terminals and a series of green-roofed buildings that were nestled in the mountains and ringed with lush vegetation. A smattering of palms dotted the edge of the property, and the scraggly grass was so green it looked like Astroturf.

I stretched my lower back, then rubbed my temples with the index finger and thumb of one hand, the binders-from-hell clutched against my chest with the other. My arm was already burning from the strain. Nora didn't just look fit. She was.

I stepped aside before the passengers trampled me. They chattered away in a language I didn't understand as they scurried past me to hunt down their luggage.

As my stomach began to settle, I set my watch ahead only one hour, though the trip had taken twelve. For the life of me, I've never been able to understand why flying, where you do nothing more taxing than read or nap, took so much energy. But it did and I was dead tired, ready to chuck my shoes, and crawl into bed.

But the day wasn't over yet.

It was then that I realized Nora wasn't among the crowd clustered near the plane. What a moron I'd been, assuming she was a secretary. I hadn't done or said anything irreparable, but I hadn't treated her with the same formality I'd accorded William and Jacob. That wasn't just stupid, it was rude. I tried to tell myself that it had been her passive deference to Jacob Dane that had led me down the primrose path of false assumptions, but that was a lame argument and I knew it. But even though I'd been thinking like a caveman, I could still find childish solace in the fact that I had been right about something (her shagging the boss) and was, at the very least, morally superior.

God, I'm a jerk sometimes.

I found Nora near the entrance to the building waiting patiently, her eyes tracking my every move with the intensity of a jungle cat stalking its prey. Oh, well, at least if I had a stroke from the heat, she'd know right away and could call for an ambulance. She didn't look the least bit green around the gills, and I envied her iron stomach.

As we waited for our luggage to arrive she lightened my load by silently taking one of the binders. "Thanks," I said guiltily, trying not to think about how, only minutes before, I'd been happy to find fault with her. Sometimes I was more asshole than jerk.

She took off her glasses and propped them on top of her head. I used to do the same thing to my Barbie, but the glasses always fell off when she and GI Joe teamed up to rescue Ken from whatever mess he'd gotten himself into. "Did you read through the Code of Conduct?" she asked.

I nodded dutifully, even though I'd only made it through a few torturous pages. God only knew why this was so important to everyone, but it was. I promised myself that I'd read the rest in my hotel tonight.

"Good. For verification purposes, please explain to me our e-mail policy that's detailed on pages fifty-four to fifty-six. In detail."

My eyes widened. "Umm…"

Impatiently, she began clicking her fingernails against each other. "Well?"

"I—I—I—"

Then her face broke into a girlish smile and she threw her head back and laughed. "I'm sorry, I couldn't resist. You looked so serious just then."

I let out a weak breath as I felt my heart resume beating. "That page fifty-four thing was a joke, right?"

Her grin was warm and much more relaxed than when we'd left Denver. It made her look closer to twenty than thirty and kicked "pretty" up a notch. "Of course."

"Oh, thank God," I said in a rush. "I read as much as I could, which wasn't much, I'm afraid."

"This isn't junior high, Rachel. I promise there won't be any pop quizzes."

She found her bag, a tasteful black one, of course, and said, "I hope that you at least signed off that you've read them."

I eyed her carefully. She *seemed* serious. "Yes," I said cautiously.

My obnoxiously bright purple bag was only a few away from hers and I struggled to lift it off the conveyor belt.

"Good." She set her bag down, opened the binder she was holding and flipped to the last page, the one that contained my signature. Then she tore it out. Afterward, she reached out to me, palm up, and wiggled her fingers meaningfully.

I passed her the other binder and she repeated the process, but didn't hand the binders back.

"You don't have to carry—"

I shut up when Nora, like a force of nature, marched over to the nearest garbage can and unceremoniously dumped the binders. She gave them a tiny wave. "Adios." Then, astonishingly, she did the same thing with her cell phone and her Blackberry. Afterward, she tugged a few pins from her hair and removed a band, setting it free, and sending it several inches past her shoulders.

I'd never seen someone figuratively and literally let her hair down the way Nora just had. It was a bit like watching a no-nonsense moth turn in to a colorful butterfly right before my eyes.

She pointed to a kiosk that held postcards, candy and every brand of cigarette imaginable. "If you don't have international calling on your phone, it looks as though you can probably buy a calling card over there."

I'd quit smoking ten years ago, but, with practiced ease, my eyes lit upon my old brand in an instant. I was, I knew in my heart, destined to fight my oral fixations for a lifetime.

"Is there someone you'd like to call to let them know that you made it?" Nora asked as we strolled over to the kiosk.

"My sister, Joanie. You?"

Her face was suddenly grim, and I wished I hadn't asked such an unintentionally personal question. "Not a soul."

I shuddered as our taxi drove through yet another slum, complete with packs of stray dogs digging through the garbage on the street, scrawny, barefooted children who should have been in school, and rough looking teenagers who made vulgar gestures at me as we drove by. If I'd wanted this shit, I'd have gone to Detroit.

The lingering scent of body odor and stale cigarettes inside the cab threw cold water on my romanticized remembrance of smoking.

Nora sat on the far side of the backseat, eyes closed, and relaxed.

"Umm... Nora?" I whispered, in case she was sleeping.

One eyeball opened. "Yes?" she burred.

"A really knowledgeable travel agent made our hotel

reservations, right?" I couldn't help the hopeful lilt in my voice. I wasn't sure I should be this honest, but the situation left me little choice. "'Cause if our hotel is in a neighborhood like this, I'm not even getting out of the cab."

Nora laughed and shifted to show me that she'd been leaning on the door lock to hold it down. "Me neither. I hope you don't mind, but I've been secretly plotting to use you as a human shield, if necessary," she said cheerfully.

I grinned, loving that she hadn't offered me some horseshit about how she'd protect one of her employees at all costs or how everything would be perfectly fine and I was just overreacting.

She pushed down her lock again and mumbled something funny about how, if she was successfully mugged, she was going to demand a refund on the self-defense class she'd taken years ago. Magnetic. That's what her personality was. A striking combination of competence and vulnerability. Poor Jacob Dane never stood a chance.

I tried to relax a little and did my best to ignore the spring that was poking one of my butt cheeks and the unknown sticky substance that was holding me to the seat by the other.

The taxi sped down the road far too fast for the rough street. I glanced outside and saw two women screaming at a red-faced man. No doubt, someone was about to be bitch-slapped.

Startled, I jerked back when a cool finger slid down my forearm to my wrist. I turned to see Nora intently examining the skin she'd just touched. "Sorry," she said, glancing up and self-consciously withdrawing her finger. "I was just wondering if you brought bug spray?"

My eyebrows lifted and, a little uncomfortable with the unexpected touch, I rested my own hand over the skin she'd just touched. "Excuse me?"

"I was just brushing it away."

I'm usually not this inarticulate. But… "It?"

"The—" With lightning quick reflexes, she squashed a rather large greenish-yellow bug against the window with her hand.

"*That* was on me?" I shuddered.

With a grimace, Nora wiped her hand off on the seat between us and nodded. "Ugh."

"I'll buy some bug spray as soon as possible," I vowed. "Hopefully, it will contain DDT."

"Good plan."

A few more streets passed, all as bleak and filthy as what we'd already seen, and real worry edged into Nora's eyes. She said, "My administrative assistant, Robert, booked the reservations at a place called El Matador."

I smiled and nodded. "That's good, right? Don't trust an impersonal agent to do what your trusted assistant can do himself?"

She chewed on her lower lip for a moment, then blurted, "Robert is the sweetest guy in the world, but an enormous bumble-fuck when it comes to planning and organization."

"What?" I screeched, giving her a shocked look. A professional at her level knowingly had an idiot for a secretary? "Look." I pointed out the window at a small child toting a rifle. "If we get a flat tire, we're dead."

"I'm pretty sure two of our four tires are flat right now."

"Shit."

She silently mouthed what I assumed was her own horrible obscenity. At least I hoped so. I grabbed hold of the seat in front of me as we plowed in and out of a vicious pothole.

"If Robert's so bad, why don't you fire him?" I asked unhappily, already making alternate accommodation plans for when we walked into our hotel just as it was being robbed by a gang of banditos. The airport wasn't the greatest place I'd ever been, but it had been crawling with guys in khaki military uniforms. I'd sleep there, on the floor, if I had to.

We still had another flight to Miranda's hometown, but not until tomorrow afternoon. And going back to the airport now would just save me another trip in a car devoid of shock absorbers.

Nora drew in a deep breath, her eyes narrowing a bit. "He... I can't fire him."

She didn't offer anymore information and I took her at her word. She *couldn't*, not *wouldn't* fire Robert. Maybe he knew about Nora's relationship with Jacob Dane and was holding it against her? Or maybe they were comrades in corporate espionage? Or maybe he was her brother and her mother didn't know about him and she was keeping her father's dastardly secret and all the while helping to support her dull-witted half sibling by offering employment?

Yeah, I watch the soaps. But who doesn't?

"Jacob likes him," she said, answering my unspoken question. "And I've worked too hard at building this team to let a little thing like a ditzy secretary stand in my way."

Chapter 4

Moonlight, and the occasional well-placed lantern, bathed the courtyard of our hotel in a golden glow. A soft breeze that still held a hint of the delicious roasted beef we'd had for dinner along with the tinkling sounds of Caribbean music wafted over us as we sat around a small wicker table in plush patio chairs. The murmur of conversation from the tables around us was drowned out by our own sporadic, but robust laughter.

We'd both swapped our business suits for shorts, T-shirts and sandals. And Nora had changed her hairstyle yet again. This time it was in a high ponytail that was officially "cute" and made her look more like a co-ed than a senior executive.

Eyes twinkling with mischief, she lifted her *Cuba libre* and clinked it against mine. "To Robert." This was the third time she'd offered that same toast.

"To Robert." I agreed heartily and took a healthy swig.

She drained her glass and sighed softly. "The man is a genius."

Grinning, I nodded. "A friggin' genius."

Straight out of an episode of *Lifestyles of the Rich and Famous*, our hotel was perfection. Large rooms featured natural stone, fine linens and enormous canopied beds with comforters so thick I was already eagerly anticipating jumping in and not being able to climb back out until morning.

But it wasn't like where I sat now was too rough a locale either. The patio was spacious and well designed, allowing for a communal experience but with plenty of privacy for each table. Palm trees softly swayed and enormous pots of lush flowers dotted the grounds. The glimmering pool alongside us was Olympic-sized and sparkled as though it had been filled with diamonds.

I expected to see Enrique Iglesias round the corner at any moment.

I asked, "Do you usually stay in places like this when you travel?" If so, I'd change my requirement of a lover with hair and steal Mr. Dane for myself.

Nora rolled her eyes. "Ha! I sometimes go out with our recruiting staff to size up important prospects. The last place we stayed for business travel was the Holiday Inn Express on our way to Possum Grape, Arkansas."

I shivered. Possum Grape? So much for the glamorous life of an executive. I was back to wanting a lover with hair.

She rubbed her eyes and I noticed for the first time they were a little red-rimmed and watery. We both should have been in bed hours ago, but we'd let the evening get away from us. "Everyone has been working so hard to get the team up and running," she said quietly as she drew her finger up the side of her glass, collecting the condensation.

"Only two more months until the first game."

She glanced up from her drink, suddenly concerned. "I'm not complaining."

"I know."

"It's just that…" She lifted one hand and then let it drop sloppily.

"Two months sounds like a long way off?"

A tiny, wry grin twitched at her lips. "And that's when the real work begins." Her smile began to grow. "Still it will be worth it in the end. I'm living my dream job. Well, almost my dream job. And how many people can really say that?"

I held up my glass for yet another toast. "To successful women."

Nora lifted hers in return and shook it, sending ice chunks

clanking around the bottom. "All gone."

I lowered my glass. "I forgot—"

Smoothly, she reached over and put her warm hand over mine. Then, using both our hands, she raised the glass to her mouth. She stopped just before the rim hit her lips, and lifted an eyebrow in question.

Damn, I wish I could do that.

I nodded my consent, and finally, the smile that had been inching across her face for the past few moments grew wide enough to stretch her cheeks and give me the barest glimpse of dimples I hadn't seen before. The candle on our table fluttered with a breeze that caressed every inch of warm, exposed skin, and cast a series of dancing shadows across her face, shrouding it in more sensuality and mystery than any woman had a right to.

Inanely, all I could think was, *Wow*.

She took a deep drink and I heard myself swallow at the same instant she did.

"To successful women," she said softly when she was finished.

When I didn't move a muscle, she gently withdrew the glass from my hand and set it on the table, all the while looking me square in the eyes. And I swear, somehow, that smile got even bigger.

Suddenly, I realized what I was doing and let out a strained laugh, my face heating. God, how embarrassing. I'd just been watching her drink, and I'd been mesmerized by it. One more drop of alcohol and I was going to go from pleasantly buzzed to outright drunk. My upper lip was already numb, and that was a sure sign I'd hit my limit.

If the thought of making a fool of myself in front of Nora wasn't enough deterrent, the thought of getting back aboard another plane tomorrow with a hangover was. "I've…umm… I've obviously had enough to drink. Sorry."

She straightened a little in her chair, affecting a more formal pose. "Nothing to be sorry about." She sighed. "Now what were we talking about?"

I left my drink on the table as we spent the next half hour

chatting about the weather and our hobbies as we continued to get to know each other a little better.

She seemed to take inordinate pleasure in the fact that she was a complete stranger to me and relaxed even more when I confessed that my Dragonflies research hadn't touched upon her at all. I guess in a small, family-run organization, everybody knows your business and it was nice to be starting fresh with someone.

As much as I was enjoying myself, my eyelids were beginning to droop and the same was true for Nora. I was only a few minutes from calling it a night when two men in cotton shirts, Bermuda shorts and sandals over black socks approached our table. I figured them for insurance salesmen at some big convention, and, except for the socks, they really weren't too bad looking. No unsightly facial hair or scrawny chicken legs. They were clearly older than us, but not by so much that they'd be popping Viagra.

I frowned. Not that Nora had a problem with old guys.

But best of all, unless they were going to outright ask Nora for a three-way that included both of them, the numbers were finally in my favor!

But did I want them to be in my favor tonight? While I was starved for physical attention, and, okay, an orgasm that was motivated by a real live person other than myself. I was having fun with Nora, and we were leaving Caracas in the morning. At best I could have a night of meaningless sex. Seconds ticked away as I tried to think of an "at worst," but when I did, it was compelling. Even trying to be careful, a one-night stand could leave me with some funky disease.

Yuck. That thought cooled my blood even more than the black socks had.

"Hello, ladies," the taller of the men said as they stopped at our table, his wingman taking a trusted position at his rear flank. Oh, shit. Up close he was sort of cute, and I felt my resolve begin to melt away like a sandcastle in the surf.

But before I could contemplate my lack of willpower, Tall Guy turned away from me and looked right at Nora. I could have been offended. Then again, it wasn't as if I could blame him. He offered Nora a gleaming smile that had, undoubtedly, helped him close many a sale. "Why is a beautiful woman like you alone?" He gestured around the courtyard. "On a romantic night like this?"

"I didn't feel like I was alone," Nora said slowly. Her playful gaze swung to me. "Did you, Rachel?"

I held in a smile. "No, not really."

"You see," Nora said, smiling back at me. "We both have plenty of company."

Wingman seemed to realize that his friend's opening line had sucked and surged in to fill the breach. To my surprise, he didn't focus on Nora. Instead, he stepped out of the shadows and looked right at me. "Excuse me, but if you wouldn't mind a little more company, I'd love to join *you*."

I beamed, and tried not to think about how he'd just abandoned his buddy. "That would be—"

"No." Nora's voice was flat. "Thank you."

"There's an empty seat right here," I countered in a rush, pulling out the chair and ignoring the glare she shot my way. I hadn't been going to invite Wingman to stay. But Nora didn't know that, and the last thing I wanted was her making my decisions for me. I was a big girl and even if I wasn't third in charge of anything, I was a professional too.

I shot her a glare that screamed, *I don't look like I do 5,000 sit-ups a day. Don't screw this up for me.* But she didn't seem to notice.

Tall Guy pointed at Nora's naked ring finger. "You're not taken."

She blinked at his audacity. "I'm very taken. I'm just not wearing a ring." Her voice rose several notches. "I'm a *nun* and you're flirting with one of *God's* wives, asshole!"

My eyes widened.

Then she crossed herself. Incorrectly, I might add.

Tall Guy blanched. "Oh, God. I mean, not *God*, it's just an expression…I mean, I was just…" His eyes darted from side to side as if he hoped the earth would swallow him up right now. And, again, I couldn't blame him. "Later, man," he mumbled to Wingman as he made his escape.

Wingman, who was still awkwardly standing next to me, winced. "You're not a nun too, are you?"

Twelve years of Catholic school completely prepared me for my answer. "*Hell* no!"

Nora scowled. "She's a raging dyke who hates anything with balls."

I gasped.

"Run!" she barked at the unfortunate man.

He jumped back a step.

"That's why she's in Venezuela," Nora continued ardently. "She's a fugitive from justice." She wrung her hands. "Oh, the things she did to her poor husband!"

Wingman's eyes were the size of saucers. I couldn't tell if he believed the ridiculous story or just thought that Nora was insane. Maybe a bit of both. Not that it really mattered. At this point we both were so riveted that we could only watch the scene unfold in a combination of horror and utter amazement.

Nora fanned herself dramatically, as though merely recalling my horrific crimes might send her crumpling to the ground. "I'm Sister Christian, the poor wretch's spiritual guide. God bless her pathetic, damned," she paused to leer, "*sinful* soul."

Holy shit. How drunk was she?

Wingman took another step backward, putting even more distance between him and Nora. But I had to give the man credit. He did manage to mumble something close to goodnight before practically running to join Tall Guy back at the bar.

"Jesus!" I hissed once he was out of earshot. "Why did you do that? Have you lost your mind?"

Nora leaned back in her chair, looking nauseatingly pleased with herself. "Nope. My mind feels fine." She picked up my glass, which now held about an inch and a half of melted ice and the dregs of my drink. "Would you like another?"

Disgusted, I tossed my napkin down on the table and rose. "I'm going to bed."

"Aren't you going to ask me to join you?" She batted her eyes at me. "Seeing as how you're a raging dyke and all."

I smiled sweetly and took the glass from her hand. Then I yanked the neck of her T-shirt away from her body and dumped the remaining contents down her bra. "You need to cool off."

She yelped loudly, but I didn't turn around as I marched toward my room, my vision as red as my cheeks.

"Is that a no?" she called after me.

Still able to hear the music from the patio, I stalked across the lawn toward my room. I was already feeling bad about what I'd done, but there was no way I was going to go back and apologize. No freaking way.

I was just slipping my room card into the slot when a hand parked itself on the wall next to my head. Startled, my heart abruptly pounding wildly, I whirled around and brought my fists up to defend myself from my unknown attacker. Not that I could do much. But at least I'd go down fighting.

"Whoa." Nora eased away from the door and raised her hands in surrender. "It's just me." She lowered her hands slowly. "I know you're mad enough to clock me one." She gave me a chagrined look. "But I wish you wouldn't."

"I'd never hit anyone." My hands were shaking with adrenaline and I tucked them under my arms.

Her lopsided grin told me she didn't believe what I'd just said anymore than I did. "Okay," I admitted. "I'm not going to hit *you*."

Sighing in relief, she tugged off her glasses and rubbed eyes that were glassy and bloodshot.

"Unless you deserve it," I added for good measure. She was on my shit list and I wasn't afraid to show it.

She crossed her arms over her chest. "And just what else would it take for me to deserve it? I should probably know... just in case."

Given the opportunity, I began angrily ticking points off on my fingers. "Embarrassing me in front of strangers. Ruining my chances for an exotic romantic interlude. Trying to make my decisions for me. Any of those things would qualify. Again."

She scratched her forehead looking a little confused. "I didn't do all those things."

"You most certainly did!"

She shifted, suddenly uneasy. "There's still a chance for a

exotic romantic interlude."

I snorted. "Yeah, right." I waved my hand in the direction of the patio. "Those guys are probably still running."

"Not with one of them." She moved a little closer and gave me a look that was so frank in its sexuality that there was no way I could misinterpret its meaning. The look was also so scorching hot that I felt the flash of heat all the way to my toes.

My eyes saucered. "Uhh..." I closed my mouth then opened it, only to close it again. I'm usually not that inarticulate, but mixed signals coming from my body and my brain had me close to short-circuiting.

A few awkward seconds passed before she breathed, "You're not interested." It was more statement than question.

Part flattered and part freaked out, I blew out a breath. I could deny that I was interested. But that would be a lie and I knew it. So I settled for telling her that I was sorry and the truth. "Nothing like that is going to happen between us, Nora."

She looked at me with something like disbelief and my ire spiked immediately. "Nothing like that is going to happen between us *in a million goddamn years*," I added.

"But I don't have a million goddamn years, Rachel," she said reasonably. "I have less than two weeks to convince you."

I was taken aback by her boldness, but barely had time to absorb it when the color drained from her face. "Uh-oh."

She wrapped her arms around her belly and bent a little at the waist. "I don't feel so good."

I glanced around desperately, but there simply wasn't a good place for her to barf that wasn't right in plain view of everyone's room, and by the looks of her, she wouldn't make it to her room, which was across the courtyard. Not that dropping to her knees and publicly retching wouldn't serve her right. But somehow I didn't want to be that cruel.

"Come inside," I said quickly, ushering her through the door and to the bathroom before she could get sick all over my carpet. Thank God the maid had left a small lamp on when she'd turned down the bed.

After an accidental visit to the walk-in closet, we found the right door. I flipped on the light and she parked herself in front of the sink, tightly gripping its edge with both hands as she swayed a little. In the harsh light we both looked worse than I'd even imagined.

The circles under my eyes were so dark heroin addicts had nothing on me. Why in the hell would someone who looked like her proposition me? True, it might take more than five minutes to find a willing lesbian in the middle of the night at our hotel in Venezuela. But after less than one day with Nora, I was pretty sure even that wouldn't be an insurmountable obstacle for her.

"I just need to splash some water on my face," she said, biting back a groan and giving her head a little shake. "And maybe to stand still for a minute."

I nodded and left the bathroom to give her some privacy. My own stomach didn't exactly feel like aces. I wasn't sure whether it was nerves, the lingering effects of the-flight-from-hell, or the alcohol. Probably all three.

To my surprise, she didn't close the bathroom door behind me, and I could see from my position sitting on the foot of my bed that she hadn't moved an inch. She just stared at herself in the mirror, studying her reflection with a look of distaste as though she was an eerie science experiment under a microscope.

Nora pulled her wet shirt away from her body and I winced at the result of my childish behavior. After a few minutes, I think we both realized she wasn't going to upchuck, though she probably would feel better if she did. She flicked off the bathroom light and came over to sit next to me. "I'm sorry I needed to barge into your room," she said quietly. "I've been sick to my stomach off and on since that horrible flight."

My eyes widened. "You've been sick?"

She nodded miserably.

"You could have fooled me."

Her smile was a little wistful. "I can fool a lot of people." She gave me a wishing look. "So, have you changed your mind about us yet? I'm not *that* sick."

"You're cracked in the head."

"No, I'm not. I just know what I want."

My eyes narrowed. "Wanting and getting are not the same thing, Nora Butler."

"Not if you don't try, they aren't," she shot back.

"I'm not a lesbian," I said flatly, my blazing eyes, daring her to contradict me.

She merely shrugged as though that meant nothing. "So?"

Okay, I hadn't expected that. "You're my boss," I said, trying another tact. "*I* don't shag the boss."

She flopped backward on my bed, sinking into the decadent comforter. "I have much more to lose than you do. And even if I didn't, I would never hold your painful rejection of my sincere advances against you." She lifted her head a little to look at me. "Did I mention pain?"

I wanted to grin, but gritted it out. "You'll survive."

"Maybe. Besides, this has nothing to do with your job. And I won't risk mine. I want to have a fling and forget about real life, and you're the person I want to fling with. You have an employment contract with the team anyway. You're completely safe."

Obviously concerned, she sat up a little, bracing herself on her elbows. "You believe me, don't you?"

Despite my better judgment, I did, and I told her so. "But that doesn't change anything."

She relaxed again and turned earnest eyes to me. "I don't want to marry you, I just want to have sex with you. Preferably more than once. I want it to be really good and we might need a few tries to perfect things."

I was fascinated by the brutal honesty most men never dared. Her voice was deep and dusky and I liked listening to it far more than I should have. God, was I really so lonely that a few flattering words could have me rethinking something so fundamental about my life? I shook my head to clear it. "Bu—I mean—why?"

She blinked. "What do you mean, why? Why wouldn't I? I just do."

I sat on my hands and prayed that my voice didn't betray me. "But I don't."

Nora looked as though I'd just dumped cold water on her for the second time. "You're involved with someone?"

Reece flashed through my mind. We were certainly involved

with each other, but not in the way that she meant. "No."

"The thought of sleeping with a woman turns you off?"

I hesitated, not sure that I was willing to go there with a virtual stranger. Even a pretty one who was lying boneless so close to me that I could feel the heat pouring from her body and soaking into mine. Worst of all, she was infinitely more compelling than the men in the black socks could ever hope to be. "Umm...No. That doesn't turn me off."

"Then it's me." Her expression turned sour. "Great. *I* turn you off."

"God, no!" Okay, I didn't mean to say that so loud. I was reminded again that we'd both had too much to drink. I wouldn't let that happen again.

I fell back beside her on the bed, descending into its softness with a sense of self-indulgence...and frustration. What was I supposed to say to her? I'd never gotten enough romantic attention to have to say no this vigorously before.

To be honest, I loved pleasure of all kinds. And that put sex at the *very* top of my list. I've heard more than one woman talk about it as though it was some sort of marital obligation. And I'd agreed with that. So long as it was Reece's obligation to me.

"I can't, Nora. Please just take my word for it. It's not going to happen."

She yawned, and then scrubbed her closed eyes with her fists, making her look like a little kid. "Damned party pooper," she mumbled.

I couldn't stop my chuckle. Did she have to be endearing too? Was God punishing me with an itch I couldn't scratch? I examined her relaxed face closely. "I couldn't see it before, but you really *are* drunk, aren't you?"

She scowled and spread her thumb and index finger only a fraction of an inch apart. "Only a little."

"Do you always proposition women you've just met?"

"I don't proposition anyone."

Except me...and the very married Jacob Dane. Then, before I could tamp it down, resentment flared inside me. I didn't like what that feeling did to me and I didn't like what it made me think about Nora. "You need to go."

"You're right," she said quietly as she stood.

I thought she might lurch sideways, but she stood ramrod straight, chin up, and shoulders back.

When I sat up, she reached out very slowly and ran her thumb over my cheekbone. I should have jerked away. I really should have. But resolve failed me, and instead, I closed my eyes and leaned ever so slightly into those warm fingers.

Was that my sigh or hers?

Her hand dropped from my face. "I need to go get some rest so I can work on convincing you that you should be in my bed. Or that I should be in your bed." She shrugged one shoulder. "I'm flexible."

She was ignoring what I'd said as though it hadn't happened. "I can only imagine how flexible you must be," I said tartly. I shot to my feet and jabbed a finger in her face, forcing her to cross her eyes to look at it. "Maybe some people find your sort of persistence attractive, Ms. Butler, but I don't."

"Nuh-uh." She waggled her finger at me the exact same way Sister Mary Catherine had in the third grade. And a different Mary Catherine had in the sixth grade. And a third Mary Catherine had in the ninth grade. You get the idea. "You're lying again. Oh, Rachel." She shook her head woefully. "You're a terrible liar."

My jaw clenched tight. "Get. Out."

She moved purposefully to the door, but, maddeningly, she lingered there. She hiccupped, then clamped her hand over her mouth. "'Scuse me. By the way, seeing as how we're going to be lovers soon, would you mind not calling me Ms.—"

I threw my pillow at her and she was too slow to duck. It smacked her right in the face with a loud thwack. "Get out!"

"Okay." She peeled the pillow from her head, pushed her hair out of her eyes and gently tossed the pillow back on my bed. "I can take a hint, ya know."

"Hardly." I was tempted to say more, but she finally appeared to be ready to leave. And she really did need to go...before I did something incredibly stupid. Like change my mind about ordering her out of my room.

When she was gone, I rested my forehead against the cool

wood of the closed door. I thought about the day, amazed that I'd met her only hours ago. What I didn't want to think about was how tempting her offer had been. In fact, I didn't want to think about anything remotely close to that. I wasn't ready.

I headed to the bathroom, shucking my clothes as I went. Nora had left her glasses on my sink and I fingered them for a moment before curiosity got the best of me and I put them up to my eyes to see how bad her eyesight was. Christ. I got an instant case of vertigo and yanked them off, only barely managing to set them down gently. She must be blind as hell without them. She was probably wandering aimlessly around the courtyard right now.

Well, too damn bad for her.

I gazed into the mirror again and wondered what she'd seen there as she'd stared so intently.

I knew what I saw when I looked at her, but somehow I was sure it wasn't the same thing.

Chapter 5

The next morning I sat alone at a table on the hotel patio as I drank my morning coffee. Like a starlet hiding from the press, even on this overcast day, I kept my head down and my dark sunglasses on. Only I wasn't famous, just mortally embarrassed, dehydrated and jet-lagged.

I checked my watch. Before the night had gone careening to hell in a 747, Nora and I had had plans to meet here at eight a.m. It was eight forty now and so far she was a no-show. Not that I could blame her.

Last night I'd been a little harsh, a lot juvenile and had very likely alienated someone important to my employer. Not bad for my first day of work. Dad always said I was an overachiever.

Had she deserved getting a drink dumped down her blouse, thrown out of my room and hit in the face with my pillow? Hell yes, she had. But that still didn't make it right. If I followed that logic Reece should have been dead a hundred times over…and Joanie only a few times less.

A sudden thought filled me with dread. What if she'd left me alone in Venezuela? I rubbed my eyes and dropped my napkin over my empty coffee mug.

I was about to go back to my room and figure out what I should do when Nora cautiously approached the table. She was wearing her dark sunglasses too, and she eyed my cup warily, as though I might toss it at her head at any second. She was dressed casually again and looked just a tiny bit disheveled despite it being first thing in the morning.

"I'm sorry I'm late." Her voice was raspy and her pallor wasn't good. She motioned to the empty seat across from me. "I slept through my wakeup call."

God, she looked as embarrassed as I felt.

"May I sit?"

"Please."

"Listen, Rachel..." She paused to clear her throat and I began to squirm in my seat. Short of having our parents at the table while we did this, I didn't think this could get more awkward. "About last night—"

"I'm sorry," we said in unison.

She smiled tentatively, and, instinctively, I mirrored the gesture.

"You don't have anything to apologize for," she said seriously. "My behavior was horrible and I'm more ashamed than you can imagine." She found something very interesting about the tabletop. "I don't proposition strangers and I don't make them say no a half dozen times. I don't know *what* I was thinking."

My smile vanished.

She glanced up and caught the expression on my face. "That's not what I meant. I just meant that I shouldn't have pushed you. I'm sorry." She swallowed so hard I could hear it. "If you want to file a complaint against me with the team's HR department, I'll understand."

I gasped. "I don't want to do that! I won't be working directly with you, and I'd be surprised if I ever even see you again after this trip."

"Thank God." Tension exploded from her body like water bursting through a dam. "I would jump off a bridge if you did go to HR." She grinned wryly. "I was just being polite." Nora extended her hand. "Friends?"

I breathed a tremendous sigh of relief myself. As I grasped her hand, I tried not to think about how soft her skin was. She'd planted a wicked seed in my mind, and it was going to blossom into something that consumed me if I didn't stop it this instant.

Professional relationship only, I repeated several times to myself. "Apology accepted. If you don't mind me asking?"

She nodded.

"What *were* you thinking?"

She sat, took off her sunglasses and gently gnawed on one of the stems. "It's sort of hard to explain."

"Try me."

Her face colored. "You're going to think I'm... Well, I don't know what you're going to think."

I just waited, doing my best to be patient.

After what felt like half an hour, she said, "Last night I felt... free. It was the first time I've felt that way since I don't know when. It was as though if I didn't act on what I wanted, just this once, I would die." She pinned me with her eyes. "And what I wanted was you."

When she saw my smile falter she quickly added. "You're beautiful, Rachel. That's not a come-on, okay? It's just the truth." She stopped talking when the waiter came over and filled her coffee cup. She asked for cream and stirred it slowly without saying another word, giving me time to process what she'd just said.

Elbow on the table, I rested my chin on my open hand and debated letting her off the hook for her behavior. "Aren't you going to mention my tits?" I said once we were alone again.

She began choking on her coffee.

"Guys *always* mention my tits."

"I am *not* a guy." But, given permission, her gaze dropped. I'll give her credit though, her eyes didn't loiter below my neck for more than a couple seconds before they lifted to meet mine. "Now that you mention them—"

I held up a hand. "Do yourself a favor, Nora, and quit while you're ahead."

Her eyes twinkled just a little. "Deal."

"Oh, I almost forgot." I dug into my purse and passed over her glasses. "Here."

"Yes! I thought I'd lost them." She expertly slid them into place. I guess the stereotype existed for a reason. They made her look more intellectual, like a slightly naughty librarian. God help me, but it was hot.

"Change your mind about me now that you can actually see?" I wished I hadn't said it as soon as the words left my mouth.

She frowned deeply and scooted her chair closer to mine. Then she dropped her voice so low that only I could hear her. "Why would you say something horrible like that? I was wearing my glasses last night, remember?"

I knew my insecurity about my weight was nearly as unflattering as the pounds themselves, so I changed the subject and brightly asked, "How long until our flight leaves?"

Her jaw worked for a few seconds as she decided whether she was going to let things lie, and to my surprise, she graciously backed off. "Our flight leaves at noon. But I was warned to be there really early. Are you ready?"

The very thought of flying again after yesterday's trip made my stomach lurch. "No."

"Me neither." We shared sympathetic looks. "Let's get it over with."

I glued on a brittle smile. "Nothing could be as bad as yesterday, right?"

Her hopeful smile was every bit as fake as mine. "Absolutely."

The flight to Mérida wasn't as bad as the one to Caracas. It was worse.

"I'm walking back to Colorado," Nora exclaimed as we collected our bags.

"Can I walk with you?"

"Sure. It will give me someone to talk to for the four months it'll take us to get home."

I chuckled weakly, but was dead serious about not flying. There had to be a train or boat or something that could get me back to the States. At this point, a mule would do.

A fantastic looking young man wearing a pair of grubby jeans and a muscle T-shirt that fit like a second skin met us at the baggage claim. He had thick curly hair, the sort you want to run your fingers through, and large eyes framed by sinfully luscious lashes.

"Go Dragonflies?" he said, his enthusiasm only tempered by a hint of question in his thickly accented voice.

Nora took charge. "That's us."

"Go Dragonflies," I echoed loudly, causing her to turn and laugh at my unexpected outburst. The tension between us on the plane had sucked as much as the turbulence, and I couldn't take it anymore. I liked her and I really did want to be successful coworkers and, hopefully, friends. So I figured it was about time I got with the program and made that happen.

He grabbed our bags as though they were filled with nothing but air. "You come?" His big brown eyes filled with question and we both nodded like besotted schoolgirls. Beaming us a smile that belonged on a toothpaste commercial, he indicated that we should follow him. "I drive."

Nora leaned close to me as we walked to the parking lot. "I think he rehearsed those words."

I smiled. "Probably."

"I honestly prefer your curves, but I'd follow him anywhere. He's too beautiful to ignore."

I sighed dreamily, my gaze firmly planted on his backside. "If Mr. Dane ever *really* wants to give me a bonus..."

She laughed and we shared easy smiles. "I'll see if this guy is available."

Except for a few potholes that our stud driver, Paulo, navigated with exaggerated care, the three-hour trip to the Gutierrez ranch was surprisingly nice. As I lightly dozed, the scenery that whizzed past changed several times. Grassy plains morphed into dark woods that were as much jungle as they were forest. Then the tangled trees gave way to scrub-brush covered hills.

The countryside was rugged and beautiful and with every passing mile the population dwindled. When I grew bored, Nora kept me entertained with tales of her days as a raucous college soccer player. Who would have guessed that behind the sexy little bun and glasses lurked a wicked sense of humor? Soon the time and miles began to fly by.

Though I had to pry the information out of her as though

it were a state secret, I discovered that she hadn't just been an adequate soccer player in her youth. She'd been an alternate to the US Women's Olympic team in Atlanta in '96. I couldn't believe she'd even want to keep that tidbit to herself. If it had been me, I'd be so proud that I'd introduce myself by saying, *Hi, I'm Rachel, and I was an Olympic alternate.* But apparently the ruthless self-promoting gene runs stronger in the Michaels family than it does in the Butlers.

What I hadn't had to pry out of her was her obvious love of the game. She spoke about the sport with the same creepy affection-slash-addiction that actresses had when discussing Botox. The Dragonflies were truly lucky to have her.

When Paulo started pointing to the local sights and babbling away in Spanish, I assumed we were almost there and I dragged my eyes off Nora, to pay more attention to my surroundings. The small town closest to the ranch consisted of a decrepit gas station, a school the size of a 7-11, a half block of small shops that looked mostly closed, and a bustling cantina.

"Miranda played soccer at the local school?" I asked Nora, wondering how much competition there could be in a town that had more stray dogs than people.

She shook her head. "Not since grade school. She's spent the last six years at a fancy, private girls academy in Valencia and finished a semester early."

"Girls school, huh?"

"Yeah. I guess that's why her parents are worried about what she'll encounter in the States." She affected a wide-eyed innocent look that would do any ingénue proud. "She'll be thrown into a wicked world that contains members of the—gasp—opposite sex."

I smirked a little. "Just because it's a girls school, doesn't mean it's sheltered. I went to an all-girl high school, and trust me when I tell you, the girls there were just as boy crazy, if not more so, than the kids at the local high."

"All those girls in those cute plaid skirts and they were only boy crazy?" She looked truly bereft. "Shit."

"Awww…far be it from me to kill the fantasy. I'm sure there were some who were girl crazy too."

"Like you?" she asked, unable to hide the twinkle in her smile.

"Nope. I only had eyes for a boy in the neighborhood named Teddy Travis. I waited for him to ask me out for three years, but it never happened. Alas, I spent the night of my senior prom crying in my bedroom. And bathroom. And kitchen."

A pause. "Well, that story sucked."

I laughed again. "I suppose it did."

She turned to look out the window and softly said, "Rachel?"

"Yeah?"

She looked back at me. "Teddy screwed up big time."

"That was..." A pleasant sense of confusion left me a little tongue-tied. "That was really sweet. Thank you."

Her smile was so wide it crinkled the corners of her eyes. "No problem. Now tell me about this interview you're doing with Miranda. I understand that even though you're going to be in the same room, you'll both call into a central number and then it's going to be recorded? How's that going to work?"

A little thrill chased up and down my spine as it always did when talking about my work with someone who was truly interested. Not for the first time on this ride, I found myself wishing she were sitting beside me instead of the seat in front of me.

By the time we arrived at the Gutierrez home, I was expecting something like the squalid shacks we'd seen outside of town and thankful I'd had a recent tetanus booster. But once again, I was surprised. The family clearly wasn't wealthy by American standards, but the modest ranch was obviously well cared for and prosperous. It even contained most of the amenities of home.

Paulo showed us into a spacious kitchen, where Elena, Miranda's mother, fussed over us as though we were long lost relatives. She spoke slightly broken, but intelligible English and gushed about her daughter and husband, who were due home from a quick trip to town, any minute.

As Paulo disappeared with our bags, Elena passed us plates that overflowed with warm corn tortillas, shredded goat meat, salsa verde and manchego cheese. She ushered us out to a covered patio behind the house and told us she would introduce Miranda as soon as the girl arrived. We tried to convince her to stay and relax and join us, but she was hell-bent on returning to the kitchen.

The evening sun had slid behind a tall barn, but it was far from dark when Nora and I found ourselves alone together. But this time it wasn't uncomfortable.

"We finally made it," Nora said, stretching her legs straight out in front of her. She inclined her head in my direction. "Was the trip a little more than you bargained for?"

A little? "No, it was a lot more than I bargained for." But, to my own amazement, with the breeze kissing my face, my keister in a comfortable chair and interesting company, I wasn't the least bit sorry. We chatted about our recent car trip from the airport for a few more minutes before I couldn't resist the food on my plate any longer.

"Have you ever eaten goat before?" I asked, looking down at it. It smelled fantastic, but I was still a little leery. I loved food, but I wasn't particularly adventurous about what I ate.

"Nope," she said, taking a big bite. "And I'm not now. I'm pretending it's chicken." Her eyes rolled back in her head. "Oh, my God. It's the most amazing chicken I've ever eaten."

My mouth began to water. "Good enough for me." But just as I was about to take a bite, I heard a muted scream that seemed to be coming from one of the barns.

Nora and I both stilled. We listened carefully, and sure enough, we heard another scream, this one just a little louder than the last.

I set my plate down on the ground, my heartbeat accelerating. "What should we do?"

"Someone might be hurt," Nora said, worry showing on her face. She adjusted her glasses. "We'd better check it out."

I nodded and we set off toward the barn, walking as quickly as we could. There were actually several barns on the property. This one was obviously the oldest and didn't reek of livestock. I was sure a stiff wind would send its rickety walls to the ground and I was suddenly reminded of every horror movie I'd seen as a child. The killer always lured his victim somewhere like a dank basement or rickety barn. And the dense heroine would carelessly go there, running headlong into her violent destiny, which she would find at the end of a pitchfork or scythe.

"Shouldn't we get Elena?" I whispered, keeping my voice down as we approached. There was no way I was giving away my position to Jason or Freddy Krueger until the last possible second.

"We could, but what if it's Elena that's in there and she needs help right now?"

God, I hated it when she was all mature and sensible. Not wanting to admit my fear, I braced myself and followed her to our doom. About halfway there, she crouched and picked up a large stick that she gripped like a baseball bat.

"Hey," I whispered, nudging her hard. "I don't have a weapon."

Apparently more than willing to give it up, she held out the stick. "If you really want to hit someone with this, be my guest."

I grimaced as I pictured the brutal act. I really was more of a lover…okay, a big talker, than a fighter. "Never mind. I'll just stand behind you and stay out of the way."

She rolled her eyes. "Gee, thanks."

The sounds coming from the barn were nearly constant, but Nora paused outside its closed door. "Maybe we should look in the window first?" she said in a low voice.

Ah. A fellow coward at heart. I liked her more with each passing moment. "Good idea," I whispered back.

Cautiously, we peered inside the nearest window. Or we tried. It was so dirty I had to wipe it several times before we could see inside. And what did see, was not at all what we expected.

Leaning against a wooden post, was a shirtless Paulo, who was drinking straight from a bottle of what looked like tequila. Miranda, who was gorgeous and on the very cusp of woman-hood—I recognized her from her photo in my team literature—was standing braless, with her blouse mostly unbuttoned before him, her dark hair cascading down her back.

After looking her up and down possessively, Paulo passed

her the bottle and slowly peeled down his tight blue jeans to reveal a pair of snowy white butt cheeks that contrasted with his tanned torso and chiseled thighs. *Yummy*. Some girls have all the luck.

Miranda groaned her approval and slugged back a long drink as though she were an old pro.

"Christ," Nora murmured as Paulo chased Miranda around the barn. Though he tried, he couldn't manage to muffle her screams of girlish delight. After several laps he caught her, pressed her against a support post, grasped both of her wrists with one of his large hands and lifted them over her head until she was forced onto her tiptoes. He nuzzled her neck briefly, and then attacked her parted lips so hungrily that my temperature began to rise.

It was masterful domination without the slightest hint of violence and Miranda swooned. Okay, I swooned too. But who could blame me? They looked like they had just stepped off the cover of a trashy romance novel. Young. Taut. Flawless.

Nora backed away from the window and scrubbed her red face with both hands. "I don't think we should be watching this."

We both turned around and slid down the barn wall until we were sitting down on the soft grass.

"They're better than cable," I whispered, slightly stunned and disturbingly aroused.

"*Way* better," Nora said, her voice so thick I wondered just how dedicated a lesbian she really was. Of course, she'd never said she was a lesbian at all. That had been my assumption. Maybe she was just a very adventurous straight chick.

"Hey," I muttered, coming to my senses now that I wasn't on visual overload. "Isn't she just seventeen years old?"

"Well, yes, but only for a few more days."

We couldn't help it. We peeked in again. Miranda was now topless, straddling Paulo, torturing his chest with her teeth and fingers. She looked a little wobbly, but I wasn't sure whether it was the alcohol or Paulo's prowess that had her swaying.

Nora rubbed the back of her neck with the palm of one hand. "She's hardly an unwilling captive."

I gaped at this newest scene. "This is the girl whose parents are afraid to let her come live in Denver?"

Nora nodded unhappily. "I think it's the other players who should be worried."

"No kidding."

Nora pushed away from the barn. "Let's get out of here. Things look like they're about to get serious, and I'll never be able to look her in the eye if I watch her having sex."

But, somehow, it didn't feel right to leave them like this. I gnawed on my lower lip, torn between being a voyeur, a responsible adult or a live-and-let-live sort of gal. "She's still pretty young, Nora. What if this is her first time?"

Nora gave me a look that said I was crazy. "Did you mount the guy like he was your pony and pinch his nipples during *your* first time?"

Okay, Miranda was no virgin. "But what about her father?" He had to be home now if she was. "I doubt he would approve of a ranch hand with his daughter. He might go bonkers and shoot him."

"That'll teach her to be a little quieter."

"Nora—"

"Rachel, they're not free-basing in there. They're just fooling around. And Paulo is not my responsibility," she pointed out. "Let's hope he's a fast runner and that Mr. Gutierrez is a bad shot."

"Nora!"

She threw her hands in the air. "What?"

"Fine." I lifted my chin. "Never mind."

She narrowed her eyes as she pondered what to do, then she began to walk away.

"I'm sure you wouldn't work for a team that discriminated against pregnant players, anyway. So no matter what happens, everything will be all right."

She stopped dead in her tracks, then wheeled, lips tight. "Pregnant?" she spat as though she equated that state of being with a rousing case of leprosy.

I nodded. "They didn't look like they were slowing down to be careful to me." I really didn't want to ruin Miranda's fun, and

God only knew that Paulo was a specimen made to be enjoyed, but she was only a teenager, and one who was about to leave Mr. Venezuela for a new life, probably for good. Then there was the alcohol. Half the bottle was already gone. I'd been there myself, only with a guy far less tempting, and it was a recipe for disaster.

"Hopefully, those uniform shorts the girls wear are really stretchy," I continued. "I'm thinking someone young and fit like her could play well into her seventh or eighth month."

"Miranda!" Nora howled at the top of her lungs. "Where are you? Oh, Miranda-a-a-a!"

I had to clamp my hand over my mouth to hold in the laughter as I looked in the window. Miranda practically flew off of Paulo, whose pants were stuck to one leg. He spun in several circles before he scurried into a large pile of hay and burrowed inside like a rat escaping the barn cat.

"Miranda!" Nora bellowed loud enough to wake the dead. "Where ar-r-r-r-re you?"

This time I couldn't stop my laughter. The girl was buttoning her shirt as fast as she could, but she was tripping over her own fingers. "Give her a second so you don't cause her to pass out, will ya?"

"Is he hidden yet?"

"Oh, yeah. He's probably dug halfway to China by now."

My eyes bugged out when I realized that was all the time Nora was going to give them. She marched over to the barn door, threw it open and pasted on an enormous smile.

"There you are. I'm so pleased to meet you," Nora gushed. She grabbed Miranda's hand, ignoring the fact that the girl's unzipped skirt was falling off her slim hips, and practically dragged her out of the barn. "I think it's time for dinner. I'm sure I heard your mother calling you."

Wow. When Nora decided to take charge, she didn't mess around.

Miranda looked helplessly at me and I could only wave as they moved past. Then she focused on Nora and rattled off something in Spanish that I was sure was incredibly nasty. For the first time since I landed in Venezuela, I was glad I didn't speak the language. Though it did remind me that I wanted to learn some new curse words while I was here.

I could see it when comprehension dawned for Miranda. She said only two words as she tried desperately to pull up her skirt with only one hand, jumping up and down as they marched along. "Go Dragonflies?" she asked.

Nora continued to drag her back to the house, picking bits of hay out of Miranda's dark mane with her free hand. "That would be me."

I didn't bother to introduce myself. Somehow I could tell this wasn't a good time to interview her. Instead, I silently filed in behind them, wondering if I would catch a glimpse of Paulo in what was sure to be a mad dash from the barn.

Then, and quite without permission, my eyes lit on Nora's bottom as she walked. I couldn't have stopped my broad grin if I'd tried. The view from back here wasn't too shabby either.

After a long, private talk with Miranda and a few hours of surprisingly comfortable socializing with Miranda's parents, it was time for bed. It was Elena who escorted us to our quarters. It was easy to see where her daughter got her good looks. Elena's dark hair was streaked with gray and she was well into middle age. Still, the woman could easily turn heads herself.

"I'm so glad you came to us," Elena said, exhaling loudly after the long day. "I did not care for the men who came before and only spoke of contracts."

She opened a bedroom door and ushered Nora and me inside the small, but well-appointed room. A bedside lamp had been left on and it bathed the room in a soft, golden glow. "I could see my baby in America surrounded by those who wanted to use her legs for soccer and the rest of her body for their own pleasure." She wrinkled her nose. "At least with women I know she'll never have to worry they will be thinking those sort of disgusting thoughts."

I shouldn't have felt guilty when she said that. Not at all. But somehow I did, and I forced myself not to look at Nora. I knew if I did, I wouldn't be able to hold in my grin.

"I'm glad we came too, Mrs. Gutierrez," Nora said solemnly,

saving me from myself. "I'm thrilled to have your daughter playing for the Dragonflies, and want you to know that I take your concerns for her well-being very seriously."

Nora's confidence filled the room as completely as the air. "I will personally make sure that she settles in with a good crowd. I've already made arrangements for her to room with one of our more senior players, Rosa Andrews. Rosa has a reputation for being levelheaded and smart. Spanish is her native language, and she's already asked me if Miranda might be interested in attending mass with her."

Relief flooded Elena's eyes.

Nora took the older woman's hand and patted it gently. "Everything is going to be okay."

The self-assurance in Nora's voice and the look of pure gratitude shining on Elena's face riveted me to the conversation. Neither I, nor Elena, had the slightest doubt that Nora meant every word she said. It had been a long time since I'd had a moment of pure faith in someone, and I relished it.

Without warning, Elena pulled Nora, and then me, into boisterous hugs. "Gracias," she whispered in my ear, and my part in this quickly became very real.

I was suddenly glad that we'd interrupted Miranda's tryst. She'd have a lifetime ahead of her where she was old enough to make choices for herself. Hopefully, at least some of which would be free from the influence of tequila. But even though it had been me who'd prompted the interruption, and I'd admitted as much to Miranda, it was Nora who had taken the brunt of the girl's rancor. Miranda wouldn't even speak to her now.

Elena explained that our clothes had been put in the closet along with our bags. Next, she motioned to the bed. It was full-sized, covered with a lovely pale cotton quilt, and meant for both Nora and me. Great. It was going to be like going to bed with a piece of cheesecake on the nightstand and expecting it to all be there in the morning.

I thanked Elena for her hospitality, and Nora closed the bedroom door behind her.

We both flopped backward on the bed at the same time, and I threw my arm over my eyes. How many hours could one day have?

The bed creaked as Nora glanced my way. It was late and her voice was quiet. "Will sharing be a problem?"

I should have said yes. I know I should have. But to be honest, I just didn't want to. I let my arm rest at my side. "No problem for me. You?" Was that a note of challenge in my voice? No. No. No.

"I'll be good," she vowed, her fingers shaping the Boy Scout promise. "You won't even know I'm here…lusting after you."

I chuckled. My ego hadn't been so thoroughly indulged since, well, ever, and I wasn't above enjoying it.

"You were great with Miranda," Nora said, adjusting her pillow.

I cringed. "I don't know how you can say that. She's pretty mad at you. I tried—"

"Don't worry about it. She's embarrassed, and with all that pent-up sexual frustration she needed to be furious at someone or explode."

"Yeah, but I was the bad guy, not you. I'll talk to her again tomorrow."

"Don't. You need to have a warm, friendly interview. And I need to be an authority figure even though I'm not old enough to be her parent. Everything worked out just the way it needed to."

I grinned evilly. "Except for poor Paulo. He might have needed medical intervention after being left so…"

Nora stuck her leg straight up in the air. "Stiff?"

We both giggled and let our laughter dwindle down slowly, dragging out the silly moment as long as we could. Then her eyes met mine and warmth flooded me as I felt a surge of attraction.

Acting more casual than I felt, I turned away and clicked off the light for privacy even though we were still in our clothes. The curtains were pulled back and a full moon lit the room. Though I really didn't need it to picture Nora. I'd had hour after hour to just look at her today. I found myself intrigued by her long, tapered fingers and graceful neck. Her ears were perfectly shaped and her jawline held just the right amount of strength without being masculine. She was smart and kind too, her generous tip at breakfast having made our waiter smile like it was closing time.

And she was as untouchable to me as the stars.

I was quiet for a few minutes as I contemplated my ill-advised crush. Then I shifted and saw Nora studying me carefully. Of course, one look at my face, even in the shadows, and she knew what I was thinking.

Her gaze fastened on mine and my heart began to race.

She cleared her throat gently. "Do you mind if I ask you something?"

I turned more fully to face her, buying myself a few precious seconds by being extra careful not to roll over on her hair, which was splayed out on her pillow and had pooled in a small space between her pillow and mine. "Sure," I said, and heard the quiver in my traitorous voice.

"You said you were attracted to women, but—"

"That's not what I said."

She blinked a few times. "Close enough."

I bit my tongue, but only because she was mostly right.

"So what is it about me that you find so objectionable? With those guys at the hotel, you were willing to at least meet them. And I'm guessing that means you were open to the idea of..." She paused and made a vague gesture. "Getting together, if things worked with one of them?"

Feeling a little slutty, I nodded.

"If you're just not into me, that's okay. But sometimes you seem... Well, when you look at me it seems..."

I willed my face not to heat. "As though I'm attracted to you?"

She blew out a long breath. "Yes."

Dammit. I was pinned better than the tail on the donkey. "I am," I admitted. "Sometimes."

Her brow creased and she got out of bed and opened the bedroom window, bringing in the scent of wet grass and flowers. She leaned outside, letting the breeze toss her hair. With her back to me, she said, "Then I don't understand why you won't give me a chance. Anything that happens here won't affect your life back home. I promise."

I grabbed her pillow and clutched it to my chest. It already smelled like her shampoo. "That's part of the problem."

She turned to face me, confusion written across her strong features. "You're looking for a long-term relationship?"

I squeezed the sides of my head. "That's the *last* thing I'm looking for."

"Then we're back to you just not being interested in me."

"That's not it. Come sit down, okay? This might take a few minutes."

"I'm going to change into my pajamas first." She smiled gently. "I'll handle rejection better when I'm wearing something comfortable." She motioned for me to continue talking and turned her back to me again to strip out of her shirt.

"Okay," I began, feeling a little adrift. She had a gorgeous back and so I closed my eyes so I wouldn't be distracted. Too bad that only lasted for about three seconds. "First of all, it's me, not you." My eyes widened. I did *not* just use the oldest rejection line in the book.

She gasped. "You did *not* just say that."

"In this case, it's really true."

"Uh-huh," she murmured doubtfully.

Oh, damn. She was wearing sexy panties and a matching bra over that great body. Hot. Hot. Hot. I bit my lower lip.

"Rachel?"

"Hmm?" I muttered, completely distracted.

She glanced at me over her shoulder and gave me a puzzled look. "You were saying?"

My head snapped up. "Oh, yeah." My brow furrowed. "Umm...what was I saying?"

A sexy grin began to take shape on Nora's mouth. "I have no idea." She pulled on a large pair of comfortable looking cotton shorts. "But take your time."

I gave her the chagrined look of the truly-well-and-busted and decided it was really stupid to be shy about much of anything at this point, though I did manage to close my eyes again. "Okay, here goes. I *can* be attracted to women. I think they're sexy and all the stuff that goes with that." I paused and gathered my nerve. "When I was twenty-two, I even had a romantic relationship with a woman that lasted a couple of months."

I nearly jumped out of my skin when Nora landed on the bed next to me, causing us both to bounce up and down.

"Now we're talking," she said, a laugh bubbling up from low in her throat. She took my pillow since I was still holding hers. "Define romantic, please."

"Hearts. Flowers. Cunnilingus. Clear enough?"

"A demonstration might help."

I just stared.

"What? You asked."

"After my relationship with her, I—"

"You can't even say her name?"

I gritted my teeth. "After my relationship with *Lola*—"

"Your girlfriend was a stripper?"

I sighed and refused to join her in laughter, though it wasn't easy. I knew she was just trying to lighten the mood to put me at ease. And to my chagrin, I was forced to admit that it was working. "She wasn't a stripper. She was an accountant. Blame her parents for the name, not her."

"Okay, okay. Keep going."

"After my relationship with *her* ended, I met Reece and fell in love. I haven't been with a woman since. And to be honest, I haven't really considered being with one."

Her smile slipped away. "Did she break your heart?"

"No," I said, obviously surprising her. "We just didn't fit together. And it ended because it wasn't right for us. It was... intense. More intense than I wanted. You'd think because I'm a woman that I would understand another woman. But I didn't... not at all. There was too much drama, too much laughing, too much crying, too much...of everything!"

Her gaze sharpened. "You're fascinating, you know that?"

Now it was my turned to be surprised, though the intense look on her face told me she was telling the truth. "If you say so."

"What you had was just one relationship, Rachel. You have to know every woman is different. It wouldn't be just that way with someone else."

"I know that. I do. But I understand men. I get them. The

difference between us works and we fit." I blew out a breath. "I wouldn't be having this conversation with a man at all."

Nora's forehead creased. "Is this conversation bad?"

"I—I… It's hard."

She nodded. "Do you want to stop?"

My first reaction was to say yes. But even though the subject was uncomfortable, the company wasn't. "No."

"Was the sex with Lola bad?"

Okay, this wasn't going to help my case. "No," I said softly. "It was awesome."

She tucked a pillow under her chin and her voice dropped to a whisper. "We could have the awesome part without the crying and drama."

How could I put this so that she would understand? "I loved my ex-husband with all my heart and we had a serious, deep relationship. But I also know that I can sleep with a man for nothing but fun. I can have a fling and keep my head. I can have a holiday romance and keep my heart. I don't think I could do that with a woman. It feels different to me. I wanted to crawl under her skin! I wanted more emotional connection even when more was too much. It won't be different with a different woman because for *me* it's the same. And right now, more than ever, I need easy. I need non-complicated. And that won't ever be with a woman. Not for me."

I darted a glance at Nora, who had rolled over onto her back and was staring at the ceiling, a look of deep concentration on her face. If that convoluted explanation of why we weren't naked and sweaty together hadn't thrown a wet blanket over her ardor, nothing would. "Still awake?"

She didn't answer for a long time and I started to get angry. I'd told my innermost thoughts and feelings to someone I barely knew. She'd better not have actually fallen asleep.

"I think you're wrong," she finally said.

I counted to ten before answering. "About what?"

"I think you got your heart broken twice."

A sliver of surprise lanced through me and I opened my mouth to protest.

"No. It's okay." She pulled the thin bed sheet over her legs and reached for my hand. "I can't blame you for being gun-shy." She gave my fingers a good squeeze before letting go. "Thanks for telling me, Rachel. Good night."

I felt a little shell-shocked, like I'd just broken up with someone I'd never been with in the first place. It also didn't feel like our conversation was over, but I don't think either one of us could think of anything else to say.

"Good night, Nora."

But as tired as I was, sleep was still a long way off.

Chapter 6

The next day dawned bright and sunny. Birds chirped, Elena chatted away happily, and the house was filled with the delicious scent of fresh-made coffee. With nary a headache in sight, I was rested and over the jet lag that had plagued me the day before. I was also looking forward to a great interview with Miranda. All in all, I should have felt wonderful.

Instead, something felt dreadfully unfinished.

I knew that the reasons I gave Nora for not wanting to get involved had been the stone-cold truth. But as I covertly watched her include Miranda in the conversation at the breakfast table even as the girl blatantly ignored her, I had to admit she appeared even more attractive to me than she had the day before. If I had every reason not to take her up on her offer, why was my brain having a hard time convincing my hormones that my reasoning was sound?

"What do you think, Rachel?"

I jerked my head up from where my gaze had been glued to Nora's elegant fingers to find everyone at the table staring my way. My eyes widened a bit. "Umm…"

"What time do you think would be a good time for the interview?" Nora asked for what was obviously the second time. Her words were gentle and deliberate, spoken as though she were talking to a dull child. "And where do you want to set up?"

"Errr…." I said.

She gave me a confused look and I could only offer a tiny shrug. I was confused too. I looked at my watch. "How about at nine o'clock?" It was eight o'clock now. My gaze flitted around the room. "I can use that phone." I pointed to a chunky wall-mounted device that reminded me of the utilitarian phone I had growing up. "And Miranda can use my cell. I have a calling card."

Miranda leaned forward in her chair, absorbing every word I said as though her life depended on it.

"The interview is going to be broken down into lots of smaller chunks when it airs. I'd like to ensure we get a good hour of tape, so we should probably talk for an hour and a half. Piece of cake." I really only needed forty minutes of good tape, but it's always better to toss tape than be stuck with something you can't use.

"That long?" Miranda sounded petrified. "I do not think I have that much to say."

"What about her English?" her mother piped up, clearly concerned. "Will people understand her or laugh at her accent?"

I looked at Nora, but she just gazed back at me, an expectant look on her face. This was my area of expertise.

I smiled gently. "No way people are going to laugh. Her English is flawless and her accent is…" I just stopped myself from saying *hot*, "…not going to be a problem. I don't know where you sent Miranda to school, Mr. and Mrs. Gutierrez, but her grammar and diction are better than mine."

Miranda didn't have the husky voice that Nora did. Instead, hers was delicate but also vibrant and clear with just a hint of the exotic. "Listeners are going to *love* her."

Mr. Gutierrez puffed up his chest a little, while Elena and Miranda just appeared mortally relieved. Apparently, they were the worriers in the family.

I turned to Miranda. "You don't have to worry about having enough to say." I let some of the confidence I felt fully emerge. "That's my job, and I'm good at it. You just need to relax and have a good time. I've got a million easy questions to ask and we'll follow up on the ones that turn out to be the most fun." I lifted my eyebrows. "Okay?"

The last traces of her terror melted away. "I can do that."

In a sudden whirlwind of activity, Miranda's father politely excused himself saying he needed to check one of his flocks. Then Elena ushered Miranda out of the kitchen to have her change her clothes for her interview.

That part didn't make any sense to me.

"So," Nora said over the rim of her coffee cup, "Are you ready for our adventure to start this afternoon? Tonight we stay in some sort of lodge. Then hiking, I think, and rapelling and zip-lining next week."

Wasn't traveling to a faraway land in the company of someone you wanted, but knew you shouldn't have, adventure enough? I sighed and decided to be honest. "I'm really not. I'll do my best, but I need to give you fair warning that I'm not an outdoorsy person. I've never even been camping. A picnic at the local park is about as back-to-nature as I get."

Nora thought for a moment, then set her cup on the table, a sense of purpose blazing in her eyes. "Then stay here. You don't need to go, and I'll take full responsibility for that decision."

I blinked. There had been nothing ambiguous about Jacob Dane's order. So why the sudden change of heart? "How are you going to do that?"

She gripped her cup a little tighter. "I just will."

"Are *you* still going?"

She nodded again, her face every bit as grave as it had been in the Denver airport. "I don't have a choice, but that's my problem and not yours. I'll deal with it, Rachel." She lifted a challenging eyebrow. "I'm good at my job too."

"I don't understand what's changed." I frowned. "Won't you get in some sort of trouble if I don't go?"

"I'll be fine."

I was starting to hate those words. I'd doubted them before. But now, somehow, they seemed like an outright lie. "If you're going, then I'm going too. No one needs to cover for me."

She scowled. "But—"

Miranda interrupted us by bounding into the kitchen dressed in a modest skirt and silk blouse, her mother still preening her hair as they entered.

"Tsk." Elena slapped Miranda's hands away from the plates and said something in Spanish that made it clear Miranda didn't need to clear the dishes and take the chance at dirtying her clothes.

Looking defiant, Nora pushed her cup away and leaned back in her chair. "Rachel, you don't need to do this."

An ugly thought suddenly popped into my head. She wasn't trying to do me a favor. Once I really made it clear that I wouldn't have sex with her, Nora didn't want me around. Anger flared inside me. "Oh yes, I do."

"You don't. I can make Jacob understand."

My voice dropped to its lowest register. "*I'll* be fine."

I hadn't meant to snap, but I couldn't stand feeling like she was trying to distance herself from me. Just because sex was off the table didn't mean we couldn't be friends. Hell, it meant that we really could be.

Nora stormed out of the room, and Miranda gazed back and forth between us, giving me a curious look.

I ignored it as I rolled up my shirtsleeves. "I'll help your mother with the dishes."

At one o'clock that afternoon, a tall van that was more like the size of a small bus pulled up in front of the Gutierrez ranch. Through the bedroom window I could see the driver as he exited and approached the front door.

He was our tour guide, the rugged man from the travel brochure.

He was more barrel-chested than he appeared in his photo, though he was clearly in good shape. He wore desert-weight army fatigues on the bottom and a black, long-sleeved camp shirt on top. His sleeves were rolled up past the elbows, exposing heavily tattooed forearms, and his hair was trimmed painfully close to his skull and was the same jet-black color as his bushy unibrow. His stained hat vaguely reminded me of Indiana Jones's.

I loved the fact that he looked as though he could kick ass

and take names. Hopefully, any large reptiles we met along the way would feel the same way I did.

I was about to turn away to fetch my suitcase when I saw Nora jog out to meet him. I sighed as I watched her speak to the man, using her hands to make her point as she spoke and laughing easily at something he said. *Why did she have to be so damn pretty?* I thought sullenly.

I know I was the one who put the kibosh on anything happening between us, but she'd opened a door in my mind that was going to be hell to close. I couldn't stop thinking of what *could* happen, if I'd only let it.

Nora dug in her pocket and handed him what looked like a wad of cash. My heart sang. She was paying him to beg off sick. We hadn't spoken since breakfast because I was still furious over her plan to ditch me. That, of course, didn't mean she couldn't cancel the whole damn trip.

A surge of relief left me feeling spent. I grabbed a novel that I'd purchased in the Denver airport and lay down on the bed to read, or maybe even take a short nap. I promised myself that Nora and I would talk later and we'd get past our most recent argument.

I was nearly asleep when a light knock on the door caused me to jump.

"It's just me." Nora's voice was quiet. "Are you decent?"

It hadn't been more than fifteen minutes since I'd been admiring her from afar, but somehow the very sound of her voice made me want to lash out. The feeling that had accompanied the sting of her rejection was as familiar and well worn as an old sweater. "If I say no will you go away?"

She flung the door open and walked right in carrying a stuffed to the gills backpack. Unceremoniously, she dropped it on the floor next to the bed with a loud *thunk*. "This is for you. We're leaving in fifteen minutes." Then she turned and marched out of the room.

"Well," I grumbled to the empty room, trying not to wince at her obvious anger. "There's no need to be rude."

My stomach was in knots, but I told myself it was because the trip hadn't been cancelled and not because she was mad at me. Unfortunately, some lies are easier to believe than others.

I tugged over the pack and found that it contained clothes and camping gear. There was mosquito netting, a hammock, a knife, freeze-dried food and fishing line and hooks. Then there were the mystery items. First-aid items that I didn't know how to use. Something that I supposed was to start fires, though it just made me want a smoke. I turned some packets over in my hands. Iodine tablets for…iodine deficiency?

I felt more like I was going to battle than camping.

Nervous as a whore in church, I checked the tags on the clothes. I was notoriously hard to fit, and Joanie had all but given up on buying me anything that I didn't try on first. How embarrassing was it going to be if I couldn't button my shirt or zip my pants? But everything was in either my exact size, or sized so generously that it wouldn't matter. Even the socks would easily allow for my narrow, but long feet. Someone went to the trouble of doing this just right. And there was no doubt as to who it was. Bitch.

There was another knock at the bedroom door and Nora's quiet voice floated into the room. "Rachel, no matter what else you think, this morning I was just hoping I could get you out of doing something you weren't interested in. Don't be mad, okay?"

I had always been more hurt than mad. With me, it's sometimes hard to tell the difference.

"Is… um… is everything okay?"

Something in the bottom of the bag caught my eye, and I pushed aside a shirt to find a smashed flower tied to what looked like a hastily written note.

Hoping this makes roughing it a little less rough.
—Nora

Slightly befuddled, I felt my face ease into a smile as I pressed the bloom to my nose. I couldn't be on the cusp of lusting for her *and* liking her and still stay sane. I just couldn't.

"Is everything okay?" she repeated.

As I gazed intently at the closed door, I sighed. "I have no idea."

The send-off that Paulo gave Miranda, once her parents disappeared back inside their house, was memorable to say the least. To be honest, it made me not only feel wistful, but a little bitter, something that shouldn't happen to anyone, much less a thirty-four-year-old. But it had been a long time since someone looked like they were going to die from missing me before I'd even left.

That night we stayed in a great little hotel that was on the way to our hiking destination. The accommodations were modest, but the service was so attentive and friendly that I began to feel a little stupid for dreading the trip so much.

Our guide, Lucas, was knowledgeable, but gruff, and he excused himself once we checked in and were shown to our rooms, saying he would be back to pick us up at nine the next morning.

Miranda had been shooting Nora daggers all day. And although Nora was taking it in stride, it was starting to piss me off.

When Miranda made a show of ordering wine with her dinner, both Nora and I looked at each other in question. We really hadn't planned on being babysitters. "Do you know the drinking age in Venezuela?" I asked Nora quietly.

Scowling, she shook her head, and by unspoken consent, we decided to let it drop.

"So, Ms. Butler," Miranda said a few minutes later, causing us both to look up from our meals in surprise, "There is something I need to tell you." She paused a moment and gulped down the rest of her drink. God, she looked nervous and painfully young.

Nora and I shared a panicky look and I knew we were thinking the same thing. *Please don't let her say she's pregnant.*

Nora swallowed hard and set her fork down. She looked as though her appetite had flown out the window. "Yes?"

"Paulo and I were secretly married last weekend."

"Oh, fuck!"

The wait staff turned to stare at our table.

"Nora," I said under my breath. Fighting was just going to make things worse. "Easy."

Her furious gaze swung in my direction. "What? She's only *seventeen*. Shagging Mr. Stud was wrong, but *marrying* him is okay?"

"I didn't say that." I leveled a glare at Miranda, whom I doubted had any idea of what she'd gotten herself into. Stupid kid. "That was more than foolish."

"Idiotic," Nora added.

Miranda's expression was hurt, but also willful. "I will be eighteen by the time we get back from looking at monkeys in the jungle. There will be no reason to change things then."

"There'll be monkeys?" I asked, horrified.

"I know what you're thinking. But soccer does not control whom I marry. Love does."

Nora pointed at her own chest with her thumb. "You think *I* care who you love or who you marry? You can marry your boyfriend, your girlfriend, or one of your sheep for all I care."

Miranda glared.

"What I *do* care about is that despite my well laid plans, you now have no place to live."

Miranda's smug smile slid away. "Wh…What? My mother said you—"

"Your new roommate didn't sign on to live with your new husband and, I wouldn't think of asking her to."

Miranda swallowed hard, but managed to keep her chin high. She was as stubborn and spirited as a wild colt. Oh, boy. This trip was going to be *extra* fun.

Nora was visibly trying to control the frustration that made her want to strangle Miranda. Her face was flushed, her voice was raspy, and her eyes were throwing off more sparks than an arc welder. *Sexy as hell*, my disobedient mind whispered.

Nora let out a groan as though she'd thought of something new and horrible. "Forget whether your underage marriage is even legal. Think about the fact that Paulo doesn't automatically get to live in the States just because you're married. Neither of you are citizens. We're going to have to get immigration involved to make sure he can live in the country legally. That will likely take weeks, if not months to iron out."

Miranda's resolve began to crumble, but Nora showed no sign of stopping. "And now I have to have every bit of marketing and press that we'd intended to use to introduce you to Denver retooled. Believe it or not, *child bride athlete* was not the angle we were going to promote!"

Miranda looked as though she might cry. She turned to me, her eyes begging for my support.

No way. For most of today the girl had either pined piteously for Paulo or chattered away as though she hadn't a care in the world. That, in combination with the shabby way she was still treating Nora, reminded me of just how immature seventeen was.

"Nora's right, dumbass," I informed her in no uncertain terms. "Getting married the way you did was thoughtless. And now a lot of other people are going to have to get involved to get your mess under control. And your poor parents..." Oh, Jesus. When had I started channeling my mother? Next would I order everyone to go run to the bathroom to go potty in case there wasn't a convenient place later?

Miranda openly blanched. Then, in the flash of an eye, she wrangled her defiant mask back into place.

Thank goodness Reece and I had put off children the way most folks put off starting a diet. Monday had always sounded like a promising date...until the day actually came.

Nora's low voice was full of concern. "Miranda, are you pregnant?"

Her face twisted from a combination of embarrassment and revulsion. "Of course not!"

"Thank God." Then Nora caught a good look at Miranda's expression. "Don't give me that look. We saw you in the barn with Paulo, remember? It's a fair question."

Miranda's face burned. "You know nothing. You saw nothing."

Nora arched an eyebrow, and I could almost see the smoke streaming from her ears.

Uh-oh, things were about to get messy.

I jumped when Nora stood and gave her own bottom a sharp

slap. Then she gyrated a few times as though she was riding a bucking bronco. "Giddie up, girl!"

Miranda's blush darkened. The wheels turning in her head were nearly audible as she calculated just when she and Paulo were interrupted. "And just how long *did* you watch us?" Her glare swung to me, but I lost my nerve and looked away. Then her blazing gaze shot back to Nora. And stayed. She struggled with her English for a few seconds before exclaiming, "Pervert!"

Nora and I both flinched but didn't offer any denials.

Disgusted, Miranda stood and swiped angrily at the tears forming in her eyes. "That's what I thought. I cannot trust you at all." Then she stomped off toward her room.

When we were alone, Nora let her face fall into her hands. "That went well."

I couldn't disagree so I just kept my mouth shut.

"Was I too hard on her?"

I let out a long breath. I was a little out of my realm. My own relationship with my mother was far from perfect. And P-Diddy Kitty had never married. "You were a little rough. But, then again, you didn't call her a dumbass." I shook my head. "But what she did was retarded."

"She could have had Paulo come to Colorado to visit during soccer season. I would have helped her out. I'm not immune to the pull of young love. She didn't have to get married." Nora leaned back in her chair and closed her eyes. "I can work everything out. I can." She sounded as though she was trying to convince herself as much as me.

"Jacob Dane is going to freak, isn't he?"

She snorted. "Utterly and completely. Our recruiting staff already had a hell of a time convincing him to invest in such a young player. Recruiting for him has been a nightmare. Last month he nixed a prospective goalie from Ohio because she admitted to drinking a few beers at a party when she was sixteen years old. *Five* years ago."

My eyebrows disappeared into my hairline. "With standards like that I shouldn't even be allowed in the stands."

"You're not a player, so you're allowed to have an actual past. Jacob envisions his team as Ivy-League-college-graduate-good-girls who would be shining examples of athleticism and feminine morals. Inserting a dose of reality has been difficult to say the least."

"Maybe he should invest in show dogs instead of people. They're less likely to disappoint."

Bleakly, she looked at her plate and nodded. "I'm finished."

"Me too. And don't worry about Miranda. We'll think of some way to spin this." I shrugged one shoulder. "Besides, nobody cares about women's soccer or soccer players, anyway."

Nora just looked at me.

Brilliant, Rachel. "I mean… Well, I'm sure *some* people—"

She chuckled softly and waved away my worries. "No, you're right. And that's another thing I need to work on, just not tonight. C'mon, I'll walk you to your room."

As we pushed in our chairs, she gently bumped her shoulder against mine. It was an unexpectedly friendly gesture that warmed the pit of my stomach as thoroughly as cocoa on a blustery day. "I don't mind that it's *way* out of my way," she said breezily.

I grinned. Our rooms were next door to one another.

Nora ducked her head. "Thanks for backing me up with Miranda."

"Of course. That's what friends are for."

She glanced up, surprised by my choice of words. "Is that what we are?"

I let a little of my feelings show. "I hope so, Nora." The toothy smile she gave me made my heart skip a beat.

"I thought we made a pretty good team. Bad cop and worse cop. I like it."

I thought about what had happened. "We'll be an even better team when I pull all my weight. This was the last time."

She dropped a tip large enough to cover the entire table next to her plate. "Last time for what?"

"The last time that you take all the heat from Miranda over something that was my idea."

"But—"

"Nuh-uh." We climbed a few stairs that led out of the tiny restaurant. "I got my interview, which was great, by the way.

Despite her being a weenie tonight, she was sweet and funny on the phone. She's a good kid, I think, who made a very bad decision. Anyway, it's time for me to act like a responsible grown-up and not hide behind your skirts."

She rubbed the back of her neck with one hand as she thought it over. "I don't like it."

I did my best to look mean. "Learn to live with disappointment."

"If this is your responsible grown-up, I'd rather she not come out and play until later. Like when we're faced with Miranda's wrath again, or a python."

I groaned weakly. "At this point, I might prefer the snake."

We climbed another set of stairs and finally turned down a long hallway. The golden lights were low and inviting. Nora said, "No complaining now. You had your chance to escape this trip, but wouldn't take it."

I gnawed on my lower lip. "I know. And I'm sorry I lost my temper this morning. Sometimes I have a bad one, but it shouldn't have been directed at you."

What I left unspoken was the reason for my ill temper. With startling speed, Nora was becoming something that I craved, but couldn't have without a dangerous price. She was walking freakin' chocolate. *Godiva* chocolate.

She nodded thoughtfully and her expression softened. "I hurt your feelings."

I blinked a few times, unsettled at how on target she was.

"I'll do my best not to do it again."

Goddammit, now I wanted to stop and play tonsil hockey with her right here in the hallway. "Are you always this nice?" She wasn't fighting fair.

"I know you might find this hard to believe, but I really am a nice person."

She didn't know how dead wrong she was. I didn't find it hard to believe at all. "So the hard sell campaign to get me into bed is over?" I tried to sound off-handed. It had to happen sometime, but that didn't stop my wounded ego from singing "Swing Low, Sweet Chariot" in the deepest voice possible.

A tiny, guilty grin made Nora's face appear as mischievous as a child who'd gotten away with peeking at her birthday presents before her party. "The hard sell wasn't working. Now you're just going to have to decide you can't live without me on your own."

I sighed aggrievedly, but inside my heart was tap-dancing. There really is no doubt that I am one sick puppy. "Using honesty and your real personality as a lure?" I shook my head a little. "Diabolical."

She chuckled. "I know. But slow. The days before we leave Venezuela are ticking by. And I can't be expected to come up with new clothes for you again where we're going. The store doesn't deliver to deepest, darkest Venezuela." She gave me a serious look. "I checked."

I could feel the beginnings of a blush. Inwardly, I rolled my eyes at myself. "Thanks not only for the clothes, but the flower. I meant to tell you earlier. It was the nicest thing someone's done for me in forever. And I haven't gotten flowers in…a long while."

An unhappy crease appeared on Nora's forehead.

She was actually angry on my behalf. It was ridiculously endearing and I grinned.

"What's funny?" she asked.

"I was just thinking of why I last got flowers. It was a beautiful bouquet from my sister, congratulating me on losing a hundred-and-eighty-five pounds during my divorce."

"Holy shit."

We were practically the only guests at the small hotel, and we walked through the quiet hallway to our rooms without seeing another soul. When we arrived at my room, I leaned back against the door and my lips quirked. "She was referring to my ex-husband."

A burst of sudden laughter made Nora smile broadly. "I think I might like your sister."

I considered that. The intense, but personable, Venezuelan version of Nora would probably be fast friends with Joanie. But the Denver version, the one who was sleeping with her boss and pasting on a happy face in the wake of his ridiculous professional demands, might not fare as well.

Our conversation died away and we stood outside our rooms, not knowing what to do, or say, next. I had a flash of my younger self being dropped off on my porch after a date, the boy standing there awkwardly, damp hands in pockets, an anxious expression on his face, and me wishing he would just hurry up, take the reins and kiss the ever-lovin' hell out of me.

My stomach fluttered nervously when I realized this situation didn't feel very different.

Nora mirrored my pose against the door, forcing us to turn our heads to face each other. She was close, far deeper into my personal space than I would normally allow. She smiled reassuringly and the tension in my stomach shifted to something pleasant. Delicious. Anticipation.

I started to fall into pretty green eyes that darkened with each passing second. Adrenaline rushed through me and a throbbing sensation settled between my legs.

At the same time, we turned our bodies until we were fully facing each other, but still leaning against the door with our shoulders.

Nora inched forward ever-so-slowly, giving me every chance to move away. Warning bells screamed in my head. *Stop! Don't start this!* But wild horses couldn't have uprooted me from my spot. My toes curled in my shoes and her mouth paused a fraction of an inch from mine, her breath sweetly caressing my face.

"It'll be okay," she whispered hotly.

In a lustful daze, I nodded and let my eyes slide closed, trusting what I felt instead of what my rational mind told me. I laid my hands on her upper chest, ready to push her away, but enjoying the heat of her body more. I wound my fingers in her shirt to tug her closer and—

The thundering boom of a slamming door across the hall ripped us from the moment, and I jumped back.

Miranda looked back and forth between us, puzzlement causing her to go slack-jawed.

Shit, shit, shit. "Wh-what are you doing?" I pointed at her bags accusingly. There's no defense like a good offense.

"I am leaving," she spat, her eyes shooting pure venom at

me, at Nora. "I will call my Paulo on the phone downstairs."

"You're not going anywhere." Nora's voice was deceptively calm. "It's late and even if he left right now, he couldn't be here for hours and hours." Her brows drew together. "So why are you ready to go right now?"

Miranda tossed her dark hair over her shoulders. "None of your business."

"Jesus Christ, stop yanking her chain and just tell us," I exclaimed, losing patience quickly. There was no way I was going to put up with days of this bullshit.

"Fine," Miranda said, a little wounded. But if she wanted an ally against Nora, she was going to have to keep looking. "The hotel owner's son said that he would drive me."

I put my hands on my hips. "Drive you hundreds of miles?"

Nora nudged me and whispered in my ear. "Is she talking about the creepy looking guy who took our bags?"

I pinned Miranda with wide eyes. "Do you even know him?"

She shrugged lightly. "We met when we checked in."

I covered my eyes with one hand, understanding a little better why her parents were worried about her living in the States.

"No way," Nora said. "No goddamn way. You're underage, you're away from home and you're my responsibility. I'm not having you run off with some guy, only never to be heard from again." She used her key to open her own room. "You're staying with me tonight. *All* night."

Miranda looked as though she'd swallowed sour milk. "Not after what I just saw, I'm not."

Nora ground her teeth together. "Then you'll stay with Rachel."

Miranda dropped her bags and waved her hands in the air as she spoke. "I am not sleeping anywhere near either of you... you..." It appeared she finally hit upon a word she didn't know in English. Pervert was such a good one I guess she didn't want to use it twice.

Nora took a step closer to her. "Pick a room."

Miranda unlocked her own room, snatched up her bags and

disappeared inside without another word.

"I know she's just a kid, but she is such a pain in the ass," I said in a disbelieving voice. She'd been so nice at her house.

"Tell me about it," Nora grumbled.

"What are we going to do?"

"About which problem? What she saw? Or her trying to escape our evil clutches?"

"The last one, I guess." Since we couldn't do anything about the first.

Dismayed, Nora said, "We're on the third floor, so I hope she won't jump. I guess I'm sleeping outside her door. As much as I'd just like to say *adios*, I can't let her run off with some weird guy she just met." She clucked her tongue a few times. "I'm going to call my family when I get home and apologize for my high school years."

"I'll take second shift."

"You don't—"

I held up a hand. "I know I don't. But neither do you, not really. She's not a little girl. If she ran off after we told her to stay put, nobody could blame you. The truth is, neither of us want something to happen to her. So come wake me when you can't take it anymore."

She looked at me long and hard to see if I was serious. "Thanks," she finally said softly, looking relieved.

I knew she wouldn't come get me, so I vowed to set my alarm.

"And Rachel?"

I yawned and wondered why the days in Venezuela were forty-eight hours long. "Yeah?"

Her voice dropped to a purr that sent a thrill skittering down my spine. "You owe me a kiss."

Chapter 7

The next morning our tour guide, Lucas, arrived bright and early, looking eager to begin our trek. As he waited, he shifted from one big foot to the other, a cigarette perched between his lips, his bulky body at odds with the dainty china and fragile furniture in the hotel restaurant. I supposed that he was most at home under the open sky or a jungle canopy, which actually made me feel a little better about this whole trip. I wouldn't let some Nancy-boy city slicker, like Jacob Dane, for example, lead me into the unknown, no matter how stubborn I was.

Both Nora and I looked as frayed as old afghans. Miranda, on the other hand, was rested and gorgeous, her dark eyes burning with an excitement I would have thought impossible just the night before. *She can't help the fact that she's young and pert*, I sternly reminded myself. *So I really shouldn't want to wring her skinny neck for it.*

Nora had talked her out of calling Paulo to come and get her. And through Miranda's watery, tight-lipped expression, Nora had tolerantly explained that since he hadn't been called the night before, he *still* couldn't be here for hours, the van was leaving now, and there was no way she would leave her alone at the hotel for half the day.

So here it was, well after lunch and the three of us were zooming along a narrow dirt road that ringed the edge of a steep mountain. There were no houses or farms here, only tangled, wild forests so green and lush that I wondered why I hadn't heard about them before. Even through the hazy, dark clouds, the view of the primitive land as we ascended the mountain was amazing, if a little eerie.

It was early in the Venezuelan rainy season, and we'd been driving through light showers all day, the pitter-patter of the rain tinkling rhythmically against the van's metal roof and lulling me into a state of near sleep.

From my spot in the very back of the van, if I managed to open my eyes long enough, I could see Miranda, dressed for hiking as she sat next to the driver, absorbed by the man's every word. Nora was parked in the seat behind her, stylish glasses firmly in place as she read over some information on local climate and terrain.

A clap of thunder boomed overhead, causing everyone to go silent for a few seconds.

"Not to worry," Lucas said calmly, giving us a slightly amused look. He peered out his side window and eased off the accelerator as we splashed through a series of deep puddles. Mud and rocks flew everywhere and the van lurched a little to one side. But he righted it quickly and then carried on as though nothing had happened.

Absently, it occurred to me that it must have been raining all night here for it to be this soggy.

Lucas inserted a cigarette in his mouth, but he didn't light it. "The rains usually don't last all day. Our rainflies will keep us dry tonight and our fire will keep us safe and comfortable."

"Oh, I'm not worried," I murmured, running a hand through my curls. The humidity had wrecked havoc on them this morning and I had no choice but to pull them back in a ponytail and try to pretend like it didn't look as though a bird's nest was tied to the back of my head. "I'm not thinking about it at all."

"Maybe it's all just a bad dream, right?" Nora murmured for my ears alone, her eyes never leaving her book.

I smiled and allowed my eyelids to flutter shut again. "It's not *all* bad." It's all right to have a teensy bit of flirting between friends, right?

The sound of Nora's throaty chuckle was interrupted by Miranda's bloodcurdling scream as the van's back tires lost traction in the mud and we went careening sideways.

Before my next breath, the world turned upside down and we began to free-fall down the side of the mountain. My heart leapt into my throat at the same second my stomach hurtled through the floor.

I've heard people say that accidents happened so fast they didn't know what hit them. In my limited experience, that's bullshit. Every terrible sound, every sickening smell, every glimpse of horror and beyond was paraded before me in a macabre show all done in slow motion.

After what seemed like forever, the van slammed into the ground so violently that I thought it would tear in two. But our momentum wouldn't allow us to stop, and we took flight again, only this time we started to roll.

The taste of warm blood filled my mouth, making me choke, as we spun again and again, occasionally hitting a tree or outcropping of rocks that sent us spinning in a new direction and rattling the fillings in my teeth. The scent of copper, diesel and warm, wet soil filled my nose.

Like Dorothy on her trip to Oz, I watched in confused fascination, and barely contained horror, as objects around me took flight. Camping gear slammed against every surface, and I realized I could no longer tell up from down. Then the frame of a backpack exploded against the side of my head, making everything go fuzzy and millions of tiny stars dance before my eyes.

But it was still daytime outside, wasn't it?

My seatbelt cut into me, stealing my breath as we spun again and again, my head slamming against the back of my seat more times than I could count. Something else large flew by me and hands that I couldn't identify reached to grab me, increasing my horror tenfold. "Nora!" I screamed, but the sound was lost in the chaos of crunching metal and shattering glass.

Tree branches lashed against the van, snapping off and punching through the windows like lances in search of a victim.

Oh, God, I was going to die and I wasn't nearly ready.

Then everything came to a halt so abrupt that I don't know how long it took for my brain to register the fact that we weren't spinning anymore...and that I was hanging upside down by my seatbelt. Like a rag doll's, my arms dangled loosely over head. My eyes fluttered open slowly as rain pelted my face and hot blood dripped from my head and through my hair onto the ceiling of the van.

What in the hell had happened?

The van creaked loudly one last time and then there was no sound except for the steady staccato of the rain. I held my breath, and willed my body to stop quaking, afraid that the slightest sound or movement from me would send us on another trip down the mountain. Then I began to choke on my own blood.

I coughed a few times, and tried to spit to rid myself of the acrid taste, blinking when two teeth flew out along with a mouthful of blood. "Ugh."

It was hard to breathe and I couldn't tell if it was because of the seatbelt digging into my waist or if I'd done something horrible to my lungs. Then I realized again how quiet it was. *God, what if they're all dead?* "N-N-Nora," I screeched, my voice panicky and high. "Nora!"

I jumped when a warm hand cupped my cheek and the van moaned again, the sound of metal scraping against metal sharp in my ears. "Shh... It's all right. I'm here," she said.

I was so glad to hear her voice I nearly cried.

I reached out with a shaky hand, my eyes meeting hers. She looked like she'd been run through a garbage disposal. Her clothes were torn and soaked with mud, which was also caked in her sandy-colored hair. And her beautiful face had a dozen small cuts that were all sluggishly bleeding, some with slender shards of glass sticking in them.

Nora leaned toward me and the van suddenly tilted to one side. She fell sideways and I screamed in pure terror.

"It's okay. It's okay," she murmured after we stopped moving, her eyes wide with fright. "We need to do this carefully." She glanced around, inching her way closer on her knees.

My stomach twisted and I spat out more blood. Weakly, I said, "I'm gonna be—"

"No," she commanded. "You can't be sick now."

Amazingly, my body obeyed, and I took a few deep breaths to still my pounding heart. "How bad are you hurt?" I asked shakily. I needed to keep talking and focus on something other than myself or I was going to puke.

"I'm—" There was a long pause. "I'm alive."

I let out an explosive breath and tried to ignore the throbbing in my head. "That good, huh?"

Again, there was no quick answer, but I could feel a hand on my seatbelt, struggling gently to release it with one hand. Her other hand was clutched to her chest.

I blinked away some rain mixed with blood and glanced toward the front seats of the van, but so many branches were crisscrossed in my path, and it was so dark up there, that I couldn't see more than blurry shapes. "Nora, I'm not going anywhere. Go check on Mir—"

"I will," she assured me. "The second I get you out of here."

The tremor in her voice scared me nearly as badly as the fall down the cliff had. "Is...is she okay?" It was so quiet up there. "Maybe she and the driver are unconscious." I was pretty sure I'd been spaced out for at least a few minutes myself.

Her fingers stopped dead and I heard her swallow. "I can't tell. The front of the van is crushed, Rachel."

A tremor of shock ran through me. "How crushed?"

"Almost flat."

"Oh, God," I whispered, my head swimming. "Then check her first. She's—"

"No." Nora's eyes were so fierce they were nearly glowing. She closed them for a few seconds, and consciously gentled her voice. "We're hanging on to the side of this damn mountain by some spindly tree branches and a prayer. We need to get out of here before we crash to the bottom."

"Nora—"

"I said no," she snapped. "Look at the front of the van."

"I can't—" With tender fingers, she wiped the moisture

from my eyes. I tried, sighing loudly, but I couldn't see past the broken tree branches and mangled metal before me. "Tell me what you see?"

"My glasses were smashed to bits. But what I see is an unholy mess." She lowered her voice to a whisper. "If Miranda or the driver are still alive, *and* by some miracle I can get either of them out of here, there's no way I can do it without the van slipping. Do you want to be trapped inside when it does?"

Jesus. Jesus. "Then you get out now and I'll unhook myself." There was no doubt that I was going to rock this place when my big ass hit the ceiling of the van.

She shook her head vigorously, sending wet hair scattering around her shoulders. "N—"

"Don't you fucking dare tell me no another time!" I squeezed my eyes closed in pain. Yelling made it feel as though a thousand knives were stabbing me in the shoulder and chest.

"Then don't *make* me say it," she said just as fervently. She wrapped her hand around the buckle of my seatbelt and jiggled it a few times, but nothing happened.

"I think you're going to have to cut me out," I groaned. "It's stuck."

"Crap. Okay, there's a knife in each of our packs, right?" Lucas had run down the list of necessaries when we first started our drive this morning. "I'll be right back."

It took what seemed like forever, but she finally returned with a sturdy looking pocketknife. She pinned me with a serious look tinged with sympathy. This was not only going to be scary as hell, it was going to hurt. "I'm going to start cutting. Are you ready?"

Already dizzy and disoriented, I tried to brace my hands against the ceiling. "I don't want to hit you when I fall."

"I won't give up on you, if you won't give up on me." Our eyes met with sizzling intensity. "Deal?"

We stared at each other for what felt like a thousand years, but couldn't have been more than a few seconds. "I pr-promise." God, why was I still spinning? "But—"

"You won't fall on me."

I girded my mental loins for the pain that was sure to follow.

"Please don't let me kill us all," I mumbled. "Okay."

With only a few strokes of the razor-sharp blade, she cut through the seatbelt, my body weight speeding the process along. I did my best to cushion my fall, and Nora did the same, but I ended up landing right on my head. My entire body exploded in abject misery.

The van rocked back and forth, creaking like an old boxcar moving down the track, and we both held on to each other for dear life. When it finally stopped, my shoulder still screamed in pain, and there was a good chance I'd wet my pants from relief.

Blinking the rain out of her eyes, Nora looked around as though she was surprised we were still alive. "We're almost out of here."

How in the hell was it raining inside? "Almost," I whispered, even more surprised than she was. I flitted my gaze around and I was shocked by the utter devastation. Most cars at the salvage yard looked better than the van. I desperately wanted to roll my aching shoulders but I was afraid of the extra movement. *Don't think about it*, I ordered myself. "Now what?"

"We get out of the van and check on Miranda." Unshed tears sparkled in Nora's eyes. "Maybe she's not..." Her words faded away.

I clenched my jaw and nodded, doing my best not to fall apart. *Too young to die. Too young to die*, kept running through my mind. "Kiddo, we'll be right back to get you," I called to the front of the van, deciding to cast my lot with hope.

We both waited, breath held, praying we'd hear something, even a moan or cry. But we were answered only by the steady sound of the rain.

Then I felt something familiar in the watery mud under my knee and hope surged. It was my cell phone, sodden, gritty... and crushed.

"I don't think there's a signal out here anyway." Nora gave me a bleak, but determined smile. She motioned for me to go first. "Let's go."

Getting out of the van was a torturously slow affair accomplished on hands and knees and made easier by the fact that the back third of the van had been mostly torn away. On the way out, we each dragged a loaded backpack with us. One pack had a bent frame, and the other was torn open and some items were obviously missing, but we needed the small first-aid kits that Lucas had mentioned were inside.

When I was finally free of the van, I lurched forward, my palms digging into the sodden earth. I greedily sucked in a lungful of wet air. It felt so good to be outside, even with the warm rain, which had picked up its intensity, and was beating down on me. The downpour quickly rinsed the blood from my face, though I felt my forehead carefully and realized I had another burning cut in my scalp that was still bleeding.

Nora emerged out of the rubble right behind me and unceremoniously shoved her backpack in the mud puddle alongside me. We caught our breath for a few seconds and then our eyes met and we nodded.

"Miranda. Lucas," I called out. "We're coming." But it wasn't as easy as just saying it. The trek was impossibly steep. We were both still dazed and Nora, who was clearly suffering, was moving so slowly that it hurt just to watch her.

A mass of mangled branches that the van had torn off on its trip down the mountain stood in our way and it took a good ten minutes of carefully climbing and cursing to reach the driver's side door.

The front of the van appeared even worse from this angle, and to my horror, Lucas's limp arm protruded from a sea of glass and strips of torn metal that used to his side window. Through the tangle of debris, that's all we could see. Not that it mattered. Nobody could survive being flattened like a pancake.

I knew I should say something, but I barely knew the man, and I couldn't keep from imagining what we would find on the other side of the van. With a shaking hand, I reached out to check the pulse in his wrist. I half expected the skin to be cool and clammy to the touch, but it was warm and soft...and he was very dead.

I glanced sideways and saw that Nora was as white as a sheet. "Let's sit you down," I said quietly as I wrapped an arm around her waist to steady her. There wasn't a good spot to sit down where we were, so I guided her a few feet away to a rotted log that could serve as a bench.

"I'm fine." She sat down with atypical gracelessness, nearly falling off the log.

She didn't resist when I smoothed the wet hair from her face and lifted her chin to look squarely into stormy, pain-ridden eyes. "No, you aren't." I began to look her over and groaned when I found that the lower half of one leg and the corresponding sneaker were stained solid crimson. Fear made my heart clench.

Shit. I berated myself for not taking care of her the very second we got out of the van. But between the rain and mud, and the fact that the world still felt like it was spinning upside down, I hadn't noticed how bad it truly was. "No wonder you're dizzy. You've lost too much blood."

For once, she didn't argue with me. With clumsy fingers, she untied a bright blue bandanna that had been holding up her hair and cinched it around a gash in her leg, wincing when I gently covered her hand with mine and pressed harder into the wound. "Like this, okay? We need to stop the bleeding."

"Right," she grated, her jaw clamped shut so tight I was surprised any sound emerged at all.

"I'll go check on Miranda." We both knew that meant I'd confirm to her that she was dead. "Be right back."

"Are you sure?" She motioned with her chin toward the van. "I could…"

"I'm sure. When I get back, we'll fish out the first-aid kit and get you fixed up." I only knew the bare minimum when it came to emergency medical treatment. But even I understood that if we didn't stop her bleeding very soon, she would be in big trouble.

"I'll fix you up, too," she offered valiantly.

I smiled a little. As hurt as she was, she was still thinking about me.

"Rachel—"

I bent over and smoothed the wet hair from her eyes. "I won't be long," I said, not giving her another chance to talk me out of looking. Then I pressed my lips to the top of her head. Despite everything, her hair still smelled clean, and was baby soft. I brazenly allowed my lips to linger, surprised to find the act gave me every bit as much comfort as it was intended to offer.

She instantly wrapped her arms around my waist and gently hugged me close. It hurt like hell and I wouldn't have traded it for a bucket of gold. Tears pooled in my eyes and I turned to find Miranda.

The rain continued to pour as I gingerly stepped around the van, trying not to jostle any of the branches that were holding it in place while still managing not to fall down the mountain myself. When I finally reached the other side, I grabbed hold of a large root to hold me in place. My boots slipped hopelessly in the mud, and I suddenly found myself fighting to stay upright.

Without warning, the van tipped to one side and I yelled as I scrambled out of the way on my hands and knees, my bones biting into the rocks and sticks beneath me. "Miranda," I choked out in horror as what tied the van to the earth simply gave way and it began to slide. Stupidly, I surged forward and grabbed hold of the nearest piece of metal, quickly realizing that I only had seconds until it took me over the cliff with it.

I dug in my arms and heels, losing a big chunk of the skin on my elbows in the process, but that didn't as much as slow it down.

"Rachel!" Nora screamed, her voice breaking from the force of her yell.

At the last possible second the sliding door I was holding broke off in my hands, sending me reeling sideways into the mud and knocking the wind out of me again. I dug in my heels and grabbed onto two handfuls of strong grass and held on to keep from sliding down farther, watching in stunned disbelief as the van crashed through a stand of bushes and then free fell what had to be another hundred feet, finally disappearing into the lush forest floor with a ghastly crunch.

I doubted there would be enough left of Miranda, Lucas or the satellite GPS that was attached to the dashboard of the van, to identify.

"Fuck!" I screamed, coughing a little from the action and covering my face with trembling, filthy hands.

Chapter 8

I sat down heavily next to Nora and stretched my legs out in front of me. The packs we'd left outside the back of the van were now neatly tucked up against her. I instantly wanted to chastise her for retrieving them instead of resting and keeping pressure on her wound. But I wasn't her mother or her keeper, so I made myself let it go.

She patted my knee and, craving the contact, I rested my hand on top of hers to keep it there. If she noticed at all, she didn't let on. I squeezed her hand gently, relishing the feel of her skin next to mine.

When her gaze swung up to mine, it was raw.

Nora hoarsely asked, "Did you see her before..."

I shook my head. There was nothing more to be done for Miranda and so I marshaled my supreme powers of denial and decided to focus on something that I could impact, if only a little. "How's your leg?"

"Bad...But...uh...I think it stopped bleeding."

Thank God.

Nora pointed to the packs, then lifted the hand that was still resting on my knee. I felt the loss of her touch immediately. "I found some good bandages, but I can't wrap it with one hand."

When I remembered the hand she had clutched to her chest

and its twisted fingers, my stomach roiled. "I'll do it." I began to root through the first-aid kit, a worried scowl on my face. "I…I think you're supposed to keep cuts clean and dry."

She snorted, but as if on cue, the rain tapered off to nothing. Nora raised her eyes to peer at the thick blanket of clouds and lifted her eyebrows. "*Now* our luck changes?"

"Shh…Don't tempt fate." I carefully unwrapped a heavy gauze pad and an ace bandage. The wound on her leg was several inches long and sickeningly deep. It obviously needed to be stitched, but I didn't have the tools or the talent needed to accomplish that.

I did my best to clean the wound, swallowing back the acrid bile that rose in my throat as I worked. Other than an occasional, involuntary hiss, Nora remained stoic and silent as I picked bits of sharp glass, grass and jagged splinters from her leg and then face. When I was finally finished, I nodded a little, exceedingly proud that I hadn't passed out or blown chunks. Florence Nightingale, I am not.

Selfishly, I had saved the worst for last. "Okay, let's take a look at your hand," I murmured, keeping my tone light and conversational when I really wanted to sob on her behalf.

At my words she held her hand closer to her chest. When I glanced up and saw a tear trail down her cheek, my heart caught in my throat. For an instant she looked like a hurt little girl trapped awkwardly in an injured woman's body. "I swear I'll be careful." And at that moment I knew I would have sworn anything to change the look on her face.

Her lower lip trembled and her gravelly voice was as wispy as I'd ever heard it. "Promise?"

"Promise," I intoned solemnly.

She swallowed hard and extended her hand. Two of her fingers were twisted in horrible, unnatural positions and clearly broken in several places. "Oh, Nora," I whispered, forgetting everything else. "I'm so sorry."

Her mouth formed a thin, grim line. "You need to pull them straight and splint them."

I was afraid she was going to say that. I carefully let go of her hand, feeling faint. "But I don't know how."

"I've seen it done a couple of times. I'll talk you through it."

She'd seen it done? Didn't she work in an office? "Where would you see something like that?" I wondered out loud.

She looked at her shoes and hesitated a moment before replying, "On TV."

"Are you fucking crazy?" I exploded, every bit of my frustration, fear and pain suddenly infusing my voice. My chest felt like it was on fire. I wouldn't be yelling again any time soon.

"No, but I've had better days." Her eyes were nothing but slits. "Are you going to help me, or am I doing it myself?"

I ran my hands through my hair, loosening a handful of curls. "I don't want to hurt you or do more damage." My tongue found the spot on the side of my mouth where I'd lost two teeth and I cringed at the renewed taste of blood.

"It's only until we get rescued, right? Then a doctor can redo it." Her chest heaved, and it was clear she was starting to lose her battle against unbridled tears. "Please, Rachel, I can't leave them like they are now. They *kill* me every time I accidentally move one, and I can't splint them while they're crooked!"

No. No. No. I moved closer to her on the log, searching her face, and finding only steely resolve. A million reasons why I couldn't do this ran through my mind. I sighed. "Are you sure?"

"Don't ask me again, okay?" Nora released a tremulous breath. "I'm about to chicken out."

She gave me the gruesome instructions and I followed them to the letter, a nervous sweat collecting on the back of my neck as I gathered sticks the size of her fingers, pulled the twisted appendages straight and aligned the jagged bones. She swayed in her seat as I bound her fingers to the wood.

I had just finished tying off the last bandage when she bent at the waist and began a series of gut-wrenching dry heaves. I smoothed her hair and then held it to one side, crooning nonsense words of comfort to her the entire time, and feeling like the biggest asshole alive for causing her more pain.

"Thanks," she croaked when she could finally speak, giving

my leg a soft squeeze with her good hand.

I gave her a cynical look. "Don't thank me. I probably just did something horrible to your hand."

"Do we have any water?" she rasped.

I scrambled over to one of the packs and passed over a full canteen.

After she drank her fill, she insisted on reciprocating the amateur medical treatment and awkwardly bandaged the wound in my hairline. My neck, back and shoulders felt as though the bones were rubbing together wrong, but there was nothing she could do about that other than administer some pain relief tablets from the first-aid kit. I chewed them greedily, willing them to start working right away.

Thunder boomed, causing us to look up, but for now, the rain had moved away.

We sat side-by-side on the log, taking a moment to gather our wits and apply a thick layer of mosquito repellant that I'd found in one of the backpacks. It stung like hell, but then again, so did the biting bugs who'd already joined the party and were determined to make our nightmare even worse.

The color was starting to return to Nora's cheeks, but dread still sat stagnant in the bottom of my belly. "What are we going to do?"

Squinting, she fixed her gaze up the mountainside. "I can't tell without my glasses. Can you see the road at all?" She blinked hard a couple times, thick lashes fluttering, the clear whites of her eyes contrasting sharply with her dirt-smeared face. "Jesus, how far did we fall?"

I craned my neck. "Far. All I see are rocks and trees."

"Which probably means that no one from the road can see us either."

I turned in the opposite direction. "Same with the van." It had been swallowed up by the trees at the foot of the mountain and was completely hidden from view. I rubbed my shoulder, looking for any bit of hope to hang on to. "Was there a railing or fence around the road that we might have broken through? Maybe someone will see where we went off the road?"

Nora moaned. "There was no fence. Just mud puddles and

then the edge of the road and a cliff."

My stomach dropped as I truly grasped our situation. We weren't due to be someplace else until late next week. No one would miss us, and even if they did, they had no way to find us. Tarzan couldn't have climbed back up the mountain to the road, and below us was only a steep trudge into a forbidding forest-slash-jungle in one of the most uninhabited areas of Venezuela… and the unknown.

Nora nudged me with her arm. "We're screwed, aren't we?"

If I could have found my voice, I would have agreed.

We sat in silence for nearly an hour, the warm breeze drying our faces and hair and bringing with it the scent of bruised grass, rich earth and worms. I don't know what Nora was doing, but I spent my time stewing, hurting and worrying with the force of ten Jewish grandmothers.

It was Nora who broke first. "There are no good choices here, Rachel, but we need to make *one*. We can't sit on a stump and wait to die."

Calling me a deer in the headlights would have been putting it mildly. "I don't know what to do."

"I have an idea, but I want to hear yours too."

My heart hammered. "I-I-I…."

Concern etched the faint lines of worry on Nora's face. "What's the matter?"

Overwhelmed, I let my face fall into my hands. "What do you want me to say? I can't even get the clock on my DVD player to stop blinking twelve and you want me to decide how we're going to keep from dying out here? I can't balance my hopeless checkbook. I don't know what the right answer is!"

She sat there, in shocked silence, no doubt, while she decided how to reply. Hopefully, it wouldn't include the word "flake" or "candy-ass."

Elbow on knee, she braced her chin with her hand. "I don't know what the *right* answer is either." She considered me with what looked a lot like contempt. "I guess we can each head off in her own direction and hope that one of us finds a way out of here and can send help to the other."

My head snapped up. She really was a whack job. "Different directions? I don't *think* so. I'm going to be stuck on you like a bad tattoo. No way you're getting rid of me."

Her smile was easy and just a tad sly. I'd been had. "I feel the same way. But if we're going to go together, we plan together."

A plan? I *never* want to make the hard choices. If I were good at working through problems would my marriage have ended up in the crapper? Would I have waited years to do something other than banter with Reece and take phone calls from stupid teenagers who wanted to dedicate songs to their even stupider friends? Would I need control top panty hose? Duh. Of course not. Avoidance and denial were my tactics of choice.

But one look into tempestuous green eyes let me know loud and clear a chicken-shit attitude just wasn't going to cut it. Not anymore. They also showed me something else. Something I hadn't seen in forever.

Someone *needed* me.

Nora might be a strong, capable woman, but she needed me to be one too. And the thought of my being dead weight when she needed me most was not only sobering, it made my skin crawl. "I think we should head to the van. We've got Miranda's and Lucas's packs with us, but that means ours are still in the van and full of supplies. And, depending on its condition, we might be able to use the van for shelter. No doubt it will rain again tonight."

Dead silence.

"Well?"

Her shoulders sagged and so did my spirit. "Thank God you didn't suggest we climb up this stinking damned mountain. Your plan rocks, Rache." Chagrined, she added, "I was going to suggest we set one of the packs on fire and hope that someone sees the smoke."

I winced, but actually felt a little proud that I'd come up with something more useful than destroying the only supplies we had.

Her glower would have been comical in any other situation. "I *told* you I didn't have the right answer. We should probably get going before it gets dark."

Darkness. Complete and total darkness. And this place was so utterly alive with the unknown it was shocking. Inwardly, I quaked. "I think—"

Nora froze, her attention on the mass of tangled bush and branches behind me. She cocked her head, listening intently.

My blood pressure spiked. "What?" I whispered, afraid to turn around. Then I heard it, too. Something was slowly making its way through the bush. Something big.

Nora quietly bent and slid a wicked-looking machete from the holder on the side of Lucas's backpack. The blade glimmered even in the gray light of the afternoon, and I felt like we were in some bad movie that wouldn't end.

Then I learned something about Nora that I would never forget. She was not only bat-shit-crazy, she made Dirty Harry look like a little second grader. A *sissy* second-grade girl. She didn't wait for whatever it was to burst out of the bushes and eat us. Determinedly limping, she moved to meet it *first*.

I grabbed her arm and held on tight, digging in my heels, much the way I did with the van before it fell down the mountain for the second time. "Jesus Christ! Do you want to die? Stop!"

An evil sneer on her face, she lifted the mother of all knives, ready to slaughter.

"Wait. Oh, shit, you nutcase," I hissed, holding on for dear life. "Wait!"

"Why?" she snapped, whirling around, sweat beading on her upper lip as she forgot about what was going to burst through the bushes. Furious, she faced me. But at least she lowered the knife. A little.

I looked over her shoulder and my eyes widened, then stung. When my mouth fell open, I inhaled a half a dozen mosquitoes. "Because you're about to murder Miranda," I choked.

Chapter 9

At the sight of her it was a though a thousand pound weight had been lifted off my shoulders, and I could tell that Nora felt the same way. Both our cheeks were wet with tears when we hugged her and pieced together what had happened.

What nobody ever tells you is that one out of a thousand times, it really does pay to be a stupid kid and break the rules. And this was one of those times for Miranda. Not wearing her seatbelt had saved her life.

Her face and arms were relatively free from injury, and so we guessed that she'd been thrown through the already shattered windshield as the van rolled. She sat alone and confused for longer than she could describe and then set off walking, only to hear voices a few moments later.

That was when she found us.

She was already black-and-blue from head to toe, worse than both Nora and I, and I felt like I'd been the ball in a pinball machine. Her shirt was shredded like the Incredible Hulk's and she had an uneven gash that began at one shoulder blade and ended in the small of her back. The wound looked painful, but shallow, and blood loss didn't appear to be an issue. But the goose egg on the side of her head, her lack of memory of anything other than the van sliding in the mud and her docile demeanor, also had me wondering if she'd suffered a concussion.

But she was talking and walking, albeit slowly, and so I couldn't help think that she'd be okay. Unfortunately, okay was a far way from safe. None of us would be truly safe until we were rescued.

Miranda glanced around her as if realizing something for the first time. "Where are Lucas and the van?"

My stomach tightened at the question and I glanced at Nora, trying to convey with my eyes that we needed to be sensitive about breaking the news.

She cleared her throat gently. "Lucas is dead, and the van fell off the mountain again and crashed at the bottom."

I glared at her. "That wasn't tender!"

"In case you hadn't noticed, Rachel, this isn't a Valentine." She tightened the bandage around her crushed fingers, cursing under her breath. "There really is no need for bullshit."

I knew that she was hurting, but who wasn't? "Since when is being nice bullshit?"

"*Mierda.*" Miranda rolled her eyes at us both. "If Paulo and I ever fight like the two of you, I will ask for a divorce."

I started at the comparison.

"What are we going to do?" Miranda asked as she peeled a long piece of grass off the side of her face.

Nora sheathed the widow-making knife. "We're going to try to make it to the van before it gets dark and retrieve the rest of the supplies." She lifted one of the packs and bit her lip to keep from crying out. "This is yours, but I don't have a cut on my back, so I can carry it."

Miranda studied Nora's drawn, pale face. As important as it was to move forward, with each passing moment it was more and more obvious that Nora wasn't going to make it very far today. Miranda glanced at her watch, and then down the mountain. Sounding more like a sage native than a saucy teenager, she said, "More rain is coming soon. We should try to find some shelter and rest near here for the night."

Nora froze for a second, and I thought she might argue. But, instead, she looked at me in question. I nodded and shrugged off one of the packs, rolling my shoulders to help the atrocious stiffening that was already setting in. I leaned toward Miranda and kept my grateful smile to myself. "Thank you," I whispered, my estimation of the girl rising.

The sound of far-away thunder boomed.

"What do we need to do to stay here?" Nora asked as she sat again and wiped her face with the back of her hand, smearing a little of the residual blood from her numerous nicks. "Fire or shelter first?"

We all three looked at each other in question, waiting for someone to say something smart.

Oh, shit. None of us knew a damn thing. This group might have risked death going to a campground together. Here, we were doomed. I took a step forward and promptly fell on my butt, sliding a good six feet before I grabbed hold of a bush to stop my progress downhill. "Maybe we should try to find flatter ground," I said, groaning loudly as I pulled my sodden ass out of the stinking, soupy mud. "Any more rain and we're going to end up like the van."

Nora squinted hard. "How about we go that way?" She pointed to her left. "It looks darker over there. And more trees means more cover from the rain, right?"

I wasn't sure the woman could see more than twenty feet without her glasses, but I couldn't argue with her reasoning. Left was as good a direction as any.

I hefted Lucas's pack. God, what did he have in there? I prayed it was a ham radio with the idiot's guide on how to use it.

Nora lifted Miranda's pack, her face as hard as stone as she settled it on her shoulders. She let out a long sigh when she caught sight of Miranda, who had set off in a purposeful march. "Miranda?"

Impatiently, she turned around, dark hair whirling behind her like a short cape. "Yes?"

"Your other left."

Without a backward glance, Nora began to hike in the opposite direction as Miranda.

It was going to be a long day.

Turns out I was wrong. It wasn't going to be a long day.

It was going to be a long day and a *long* night. We'd hiked an impossible, zig-zagging journey for almost two hours, though I doubt we made it more than a third of a mile. It wasn't quite full dark, but that was coming fast and we weren't nearly ready.

Crouched over a small pile of twigs and leaves that Miranda had gathered from the innermost branches of a nearby tree, Nora wiped perspiration out of her eyes with her wrist. "Let's try again." She released a few heavy breaths. "Last time."

Miranda nodded. "Okay, okay," she murmured, then switched to a stream of vehement Spanish.

I stood watching, shifting uncomfortably from one foot to the other. I'd tried for over an hour with Nora, and Miranda wasn't having any better luck than I had.

There was a flash of flame and smoke and, eyes glued to the scene, we all held our breath, just as we'd done two dozen times before. But as quickly as it had sparked to life, the tiny flame died.

Nora dropped her head and let the kindling fall from her hands. "No fire." Bleakly, she gazed up at me. "Sorry."

Miranda stood, wincing and grasping her lower back as she moved away.

"It's not your fault," I said, letting my hand rest on Nora's shoulder. There was no use in using all the gas in the lighter if everything was too damp to burn.

"Help me up," Nora asked, and I grasped her good hand and tugged her upright. "Thanks."

Miranda rejoined us, a contemplative look on her face. "We don't need to worry about the lighter running out. I have two more in my pack."

"You smoke?" Nora asked, clearly surprised.

"I'm quitting," Miranda said quickly, a flicker of shame in her eyes. "Paulo doesn't like it."

Nora waved her hand out in front of her, apparently too tired to complain that her star player had such an unhealthy habit. "Whatever. Right now I'm just glad we have the lighters."

Miranda visibly relaxed. "Do you want to keep trying? I'll help." It was obvious she was trying to make amends with Nora. Unfortunately, Nora didn't seem to notice.

"Not tonight," Nora said, leaning against a tree. "I think we just need to rest. Are either of you hungry?"

There were nine dry meals in each of the two packs, along with fishing equipment none of us knew how to use. I laid a hand against my belly. "My stomach is still in knots. I think I'll pass."

"Me too," Miranda said.

I began to unhook one of the sleeping bags from the bottom of the pack. "We can unzip the bags, lay them flat and put them together. Then we can string the rain tarp over us." *I hope.*

Miranda looked horrified. "We can't sleep on the ground!"

Oh, Christ. What now? That sinking sensation in my stomach was becoming a permanent fixture. "Snakes?"

"That's not what I was thinking, but that's one of the problems."

"Tarantulas?" Nora said, looking ill.

"Those too."

"What else?" I asked, totally sure I didn't want to know.

"Ants."

Miranda said the word so gravely that I wanted to burst into hysterical laughter. "Ants?" I could live with that. "We have those in the States. They ruin picnics and bother sunbathers." Confidence filled me. "We'll live."

She looked at me like I was an idiot. "These are stinging ants. They attack by the thousands and their bites burn like fire." Miranda shivered. "If you get enough bites, you will *not* live."

"Oh, *those* ants," Nora said, throwing her hand in the air.

Then I remembered what I'd seen in my pack when I was back at Miranda's parents' house. "A hammock." I'd thought that was an odd, mostly frivolous addition to the rest of our very pricey, serious survival equipment.

"There's one in mine too," Miranda said.

But that made a total of two hammocks, and there was no way we could put three people in two of those.

"We can take turns," Nora's features were barely distinguishable in the now waning light.

Miranda clicked on a flashlight and trained it on her own face from below, lighting up her cheeks with an eerie orange the way Joanie and I did when we were little. "I'm not tired yet. You both go first."

"I don't believe you," Nora bitched.

I gave Miranda a grateful look. She really could be a good sport when she put her mind to it. "We can argue about who takes the second hammock after we get them set up."

Miranda and I stretched the hammocks out between two sets of trees and went to work tying them. I had no idea how high off the ground they were supposed to rest, but I supposed it didn't matter so long as we could climb in and our rear ends stayed off the ground. Once the hammocks were hung, we all stared at each other, and waited for someone to take the plunge.

"You both first," Nora said, the lines around her eyes visible even by flashlight.

"I hit my head earlier." Miranda rubbed the spot with a grimace and moved away from the hammocks. "I do not think I should sleep right away."

I liked the idea that Nora would get some rest, but not the fact that I was going to sleep before a kid. "Miranda—"

She held up a hand. "My back only stopped bleeding a few minutes ago. I can't bear the thought of lying on it right now."

Stunned, I rushed over to her, Nora hot on my heels. I took the flashlight from her hands and trained it on her back. Her shirt was wet with sweat and something darker. The shirt was fashionably snug to begin with. Now the part of it that wasn't shredded looked like a second skin.

"Shit." Nora's voice was as hard as any worried parent's. "Why didn't you say something?"

"I don't know," Miranda snapped, looking hurt. "You look like you're going to pass out any second. Why haven't *you* said anything?"

Then, in charged silence, they glared at each other, arms crossed over chests, both knowing the other was right.

I groaned inwardly when I realized something about my companions. They were not only too much alike, they were like Reece and me. I could tell by the way they looked at each other, full of true concern when the other wasn't watching, that on some level, whether they wanted to or not, they already liked and cared about each other. But there was also something fundamental about their personalities that when mixed together acted as a repellent.

Oil and water.

I picked gently at the back of Miranda's shirt. The material was sticking to the cut, and I was afraid of what would happen if she left it on for the night and then tried to remove it in the morning. "How do you feel about going topless?"

"Topless?" she repeated the word slowly and without a hint of comprehension.

Nora looked at her back and made a hissing sound through her teeth. "You need to take your shirt off until your back starts to heal."

I wondered if she'd protest, especially considering her reaction to sharing a room with Nora or me after our ill-fated, near-kiss in the hotel hallway. But, without a bit of self-consciousness, Miranda simply stood, unbuttoned her tattered blouse and tossed it aside. It was so dark that the second it left her hands it disappeared from sight like the subject of a magic trick.

Miranda turned to look over her shoulder at her back. "Ouch."

I did my best to keep from commenting on all the dried blood and the fact that removing the shirt the way she had hadn't done her any favors.

Apparently, Miranda had decided that there was no need to copy Nora's earlier stoic display as she received what little I could offer in medical treatment. She squealed, cried and groaned every time the mood struck her. My hands shook like a drunkard's, and I thought I might go insane before I was through.

Nora took the flashlight from me and when our fingers brushed together I felt a sudden and unexpected rush of relief down to the bottom of my soul. *Thank God the crash didn't kill her*, was all that ran through my mind.

She trained the light's beam on the long gash, and our eyes met unhappily as more of it was revealed. Miranda was bruised everywhere and the skin around the cut was red, puffy and angry-looking. Could infection set in this quickly?

Miranda's bra was nothing more than a torn rag, which I whisked aside as I began to clean the wound with some antibiotic cream from the first-aid kit.

I made a motion with my hand that pantomimed a talking mouth. Nora nodded and cleared her throat. "So you never did tell us why you snuck off to get married in the first place. Your birthday is only in a few days. Couldn't you have just waited?"

I rolled my eyes. That wasn't exactly a neutral topic, though Miranda seemed to take it in stride.

"Papa wouldn't approve of Paulo and me no matter how old I was. And," she paused guiltily, "we thought it would make it easier for him to come to the States with me."

I squeezed more ointment onto my fingertip. "Your father would disapprove because Paulo is a laborer?" My dad never cared for Reece, but he always said it was because Reece was a bonehead.

"Of course not," Miranda exclaimed as though I'd insulted the hell out of her. "Papa had nothing when he was young also." She smiled proudly. "He respects how hard Paulo works."

"What's the problem then?" Nora asked as she kept the flashlight on my work but managed to lean against a tree. I was pretty sure she was about to drop.

Miranda jerked wildly when I touched a particularly sensitive area, and, already being wound up tighter than a stopwatch, I reacted just as crazily. "Shit," I muttered, jumping back, my heart thundering. I nearly crapped myself. If we lived to be rescued, I was pretty sure I was going to have white hair by the time they found me.

"Sorry," Miranda said in a childlike voice.

"S'okay." I forced a chuckle. "I thought it was a snake or something."

At my words Miranda and Nora began to scan the ground, then tree branches around us, sending the beam of light up into the trees. As if on cue, I heard the flutter of little wings. Something was flying around up there, and I was certain I didn't want to know what it was.

A drip of perspiration slid down my face and settled on the

tip of my nose. Irritated and itching from the heat and dirt and my wet clothes, I shook it away. "Nora?"

"Oops." She refocused the beam. "Sorry."

She sounded just like Miranda and that made us all laugh despite ourselves.

"Back to Paulo," I reminded Miranda as I screwed the cap on the ointment tube and considered what we could put over the cut. We didn't have any bandages that were big enough. The bleeding had stopped again, but there was no way she could sleep face down in a hammock. It was too dark to think about making any sort of a real shelter, and she couldn't stand up until we were rescued.

Miranda swatted at the insects that had decided she was the tastiest treat in the woods.

"Maybe instead of her going topless we can cover it with something loose?" Nora said, taking the time to scratch one of her own newly acquired mosquito bites.

As Miranda chattered on about the love of her life, Nora and I dug through the packs.

"How about this?" She lifted an extra large microfiber T-shirt that had been Lucas's. It would swallow Miranda, but that was sort of the point.

"Perfect." I slathered mosquito repellent over Miranda's neck and back.

"Paulo's eyes are so *beautiful*," the girl gushed.

Nora and I could only nod dreamily. It was true.

"They're like yours, Rachel," she continued. "Only a little darker."

Startled, I stopped what I was doing. "What do you mean?"

Miranda shrugged. "I mean your eyes are striking like his."

"Sexy," Nora added in a voice meant for my ears alone.

I felt my face heat along with a pleasant sense of confusion. I thought my eyes looked odd, not striking or sexy. But I was more than willing to be convinced.

As I slid the shirt over Miranda's head the scent of clean laundry assailed me, and for reasons I couldn't explain, I felt tears well.

I wiped angrily at my face, feeling as out of control as a

pubescent girl. What in the hell was wrong with me?

"You're trapped in the jungle in the middle of the night," Nora said, reading my mind. "You're *supposed* to be freaked out."

Miranda's head bobbed.

Oh, yeah.

Nora limped behind me and nearly rested her chin on my shoulder. Her sigh sent warm air dancing over my skin. "Are you okay?" she whispered, her lips close to my ear.

I nodded and forced a tight smile. "Next you get in one of the hammocks."

She drew in a breath to protest, but I wasn't in the mood. "Stop being a pain in the ass and lie down." I gentled my voice, but only because when she was this close my knees wanted to melt. "You've lost a lot of blood, and tomorrow we need to figure out a way to signal someone, or get to the road, or *something*. We need your help, Nora. And that means you can't pass out on us. Please."

I felt her lips against my cheek in something that might have been a kiss before she withdrew. "You win," she murmured. Her voice was filled with pain, and my stomach clenched nervously. She needed a doctor sooner and not later.

My gaze moved to Miranda, but she was intentionally making herself busy doing a bunch of nothing and not looking in our direction.

The skin Nora had touched tingled, and I had to force myself not to lift my hand in wonder and feel the spot. I turned and took the flashlight from her, putting it between us and training it upward so I could see her face but not blind her.

She smiled in a way I hadn't seen before. Shyly. "But don't think that's the kiss you owe me."

Reflexively, I smiled back and said the opposite of what I was feeling. "Not in a million goddamn years, remember?"

A tiny, hopeful grin edged its way across Nora's face. "We'll see."

It is not easy to get a person with a bad leg and broken fingers into a hammock. But after some wrangling and cursing and even slightly frantic laughter, she was finally in. When she relaxed, she let out a long-suffering breath that I understood completely.

Miranda was quiet as we stretched the rainfly over both hammocks. Next, I rolled over a rock, and then a log that was big enough to sit on, completing our makeshift campsite.

When we settled on our seats she pointed at the flashlight. "Should we save the batteries?"

I hoped she couldn't hear me swallow before I croaked, "Sure."

We were under a thick stand of trees and the sky was heavy with clouds. I thought I knew darkness, but I didn't. I'd never been particularly afraid of the dark as a child. That was Joanie's cross to bear. Then again, it had never draped over me like a hot, thick, impenetrable blanket.

"How are you doing?" I whispered to Miranda. I couldn't even see the outline of her body, though I knew she was sitting only a few feet away.

I heard her sniff a few times. "I'm okay," she said, despite the wobble in her voice. I could tell she was digging in her pack and then there was the sound of her drinking from her canteen.

Somehow, she found my hands and passed it to me. When the lukewarm liquid flowed over my tongue I realized just how thirsty I was and the urge to gulp it down was nearly overwhelming. But I had no idea how to find fresh water or use the water purifying iodine tablets from our packs. So I took slow, measured sips. I'd never even licked all the way to the center of a Tootsie Pop, but I was intent on making this last. If nothing else, being trapped in the wilderness was a lesson in moderation.

Far sooner than I wanted, I made myself set the water canteen aside.

As worn out as I was, I wasn't sleepy, and so Miranda and I began to talk, our voices mixing softly with the constant hum of insects, and the sound of rustling leaves, and the dull rumble of far-off thunder.

"I can't believe this."

The softly spoken words pulled me from a vivid nightmare that was almost as horrible as what our real lives had become.

I cracked my eyes open, blinking at the muted sunlight and taking in the vibrant tones of green all around me. The jungle, or forest, I couldn't quite tell which, pulsed with life. Bugs, birds and the breeze knocking together branches and rustling leaves combined to form a symphony so loud I was a little surprised that I'd slept through it all.

"Nora?" I croaked, my mouth cottony. I glanced at the other hammock and saw Miranda swaying with the breeze and snoring like a buzz saw.

I frowned as I tried to sit up. "Nora?" My body screamed in pain as every hurt, big and small, came roaring back to the center of my world. "Damn..." I flopped back down and nearly fell out of the hammock as it rocked dangerously. Then I caught sight of something from the corner of my eye.

Exasperated, I let my face press against the nylon hammock strings. It was like looking out from behind prison bars. "Why are you on the ground?"

"I was hoping to be older when I had to say this," she began, her body sprawled over a mass of tree roots in a twisted, uncomfortable angle. "But I've fallen, and...Jesus Christ. I've fallen and I can't get up!"

If we aren't the very definition of a mess, I don't know what is. "Are you hurt? 'Cause if you're not, I'm going to laugh at you."

A murderous eyeball rotated my way.

I stuck out my tongue. "Are you hurt *more* than you were yesterday?" She wasn't on the verge of tears as she had been yesterday, so I was pretty certain of her answer.

Her "no" came out as little more than a frustrated grunt.

"I'll help you as soon as I find a way out of the hammock." I tried to move carefully in deference to the ache in every bone in my body. But these weren't like the pretty, white rope hammocks that were more like beds and sometimes found on people's patios. These were stretchy, and the ropes were thin, and when you got inside it swallowed you up like the nylon version of the Venus flytrap.

I wiggled and jiggled and struggled, and Nora did the same thing as she tried to get up. Unfortunately, after several minutes, our biggest accomplishment was breaking a sweat.

Eventually, we both had to laugh. Crying just took too much damn energy. "How do you get out of these things?" I murmured, tugging at the mosquito netting that I'd somehow got twisted around me.

"I have no idea. Miranda helped me get out a few hours ago when she got in."

I must have been dead to the world because I hadn't heard a thing when they'd made their switch. Then I found an opening in the netting and poked my arm out. "Maybe I can...Yeow!" I turned the wrong way and the hammock spun, dumping me flat on the ground with a loud thump. The ground was warm and moist. Ugh. I coughed a few times. "Maybe I can kill myself if I try hard enough."

"I'm sure we'll both get lots more chances to do that." She blew a lock of sandy hair out of her face.

"Hang on." I groaned a little as I stood and my back cracked so loudly even Nora winced. Then I gave her a hand up, which wasn't nearly as easy as it sounded.

Finally, she was steady on her feet and she bent to dust off her pants. She'd been a busy woman.

Her face had been wiped clean, though the tiny cuts there still looked red and painful. Her hair was fashioned into a single braid that hung just past her shoulders, and she'd changed into what I could only presume was an outfit of Miranda's. The pastel blue T-shirt hugged every curve in a way that really should be illegal. If she didn't speak, she could have easily passed for one of Miranda's schoolmates. And try as I might, I could no longer even picture her dutifully toting around the Dragonfly company handbooks as though they were Gutenberg Bibles.

I also couldn't picture her with Jacob Dane, and the very thought of their affair made my stomach churn. She was smart and pretty and it was so obvious that she didn't need to sleep her way to the top that I wanted to grab her by the shoulders and shake her and tell her so. Frustrated with my miserable train of thought, I continued to simply watch her, forgetting about the things that were none of my business and that I couldn't change even if they were.

Her navy cotton cargo pants weren't as clean as her shirt,

but I was relieved at the lack of visible blood. What lay beneath the bandage was more than bad enough. Once we found some more water, I'd do a better job of cleaning her cut and maybe slather on more antibiotic cream.

"Thanks, Rachel," she breathed tiredly. "I'd been down there for a long time."

I opened my mouth.

"Before you ask, I didn't want to wake Miranda." She lowered her voice. "The poor kid let me sleep half the night while she leaned against a tree. She deserves some rest."

I narrowed my eyes at the sleeping soccer player. "She told me she was going to wake me up after two hours. She promised."

Nora lifted an eyebrow. "She's a teenager. If her mouth is moving, she's lying. But in this instance it was to help me."

We stood face-to-face, and her gaze turned concerned. "What?" I asked nervously, adjusting my unruly ponytail.

She didn't hesitate to brush a bit of dirt from my cheek and her tender touch made a lump rise in my throat. *God, maybe I really am a lesbian.* Because right now, I could feel the pull of attraction between us as though it were a living, breathing thing. I wanted to wrap my arms around her, bury my face in her hair and stay there. What I couldn't tell is whether I wanted her because I was interested in *her.* Or I wanted her because I knew I shouldn't have her.

"Rache, you have two black eyes and a swollen lip."

My hand went to my face. "Really?" It did feel puffy.

She nodded slowly.

"So I look pretty scary, huh?"

Nora smiled disarmingly as she cast about for something to say besides the obvious. "You look like you were thrown off a mountain."

I allowed my mouth to drop open in faux shock. "What a coincidence." Then despite my very prudent drinking habits, nature made one of her more persistent demands known. "I... um...I need to go and..." I gestured toward the bushes.

"Say no more." She blanched. "Please."

The look on her face reminded me of the one time I'd asked

Reece to pick up tampons at Wal-Mart. Making it clear she should have starred in *Aliens* instead of that big wimp Sigourney Weaver, Nora had been willing to charge into the bushes with a big knife to fight off an unknown attacker, but was squeamish when it came to bodily functions? Weird.

"There's toilet paper in both packs," she told me. "Apparently, Miranda didn't trust our tour guide. She brought two extra rolls."

"Two? I think I love her!"

Nora grinned. "And here I thought the way to a woman's heart was through her stomach."

"That's a man's heart. The way to *my* heart is to keep me from having to use a leaf to take care of personal business."

"I'll make a note. But that's not the best thing we discovered last night while you were snoozing." She dug into her pocket and held up a full prescription medicine bottle. She shook it happily.

I voiced my greatest desire. "Painkillers?"

Smiling so wide I thought her face might split in half, she said, "They were in a side pouch of Lucas's pack and say they're for back pain. Thank God one of us can read Spanish."

No wonder she wasn't screaming in agony over her hand. "Are you stoned?"

"Eh." She wiggled her healthy hand good-naturedly. "I was happier a couple of hours ago, but they're still taking the edge off the pain. I broke my ankle in college and what the doctors gave me then wasn't nearly as good as this. It must be really strong." Then she yawned. "But they make me sleepy."

I considered Miranda's snores. "I take it you shared."

"Of course." She uncapped the bottle. "Your turn. Open wide."

I did and she threw in a pill. "There is a God." I swallowed dryly, hoping they were muscle relaxants *and* painkillers. Hauling my ass through the mud to the van today was going to suck. I had put what we'd find when we got there completely out of my mind. It was either that or run off into the woods screaming.

After hunting down a private place to relieve myself that was still close enough to the camp that I wouldn't get lost, I came back to find Nora digging through Lucas's pack. She was placing items on a log and sorting through them with one hand.

Miranda was still dead to the world.

I glanced at my watch. Since no one would know we were gone for days and our only real goal was to make it to the van, there was no reason to wake her yet.

"I thought you did this last night. Whatcha looking for now?" I asked as I crouched down beside Nora, biting my lip at the pain in my lower back. I was going to make some chiropractor, dentist, but mostly a pharmacist very rich when I got back home.

"I found the pills right away and quit looking to save the flashlight batteries. Now I'm after a toothbrush."

I felt so disgustingly grungy that a good teeth brushing, especially around the hole in the side of my mouth that the accident created, which still tasted like blood, would be heavenly.

"I already found one." She held up a very used brush and I frowned.

I *so* did not want to have use that.

"But I'm hoping he has some new ones in here. He's got a lot of extra good stuff in here. I guess in case one of us forgot to pack something basic."

I began to help. Who knew what other useful items our *Señor* boy scout had in there?

Nora had trouble dumping out the contents of a small toiletry kit, and so I reached in and shook loose a few items that fell onto the log. Our eyes both widened spying the object of our desires. We looked at each other for a split second, then we dove for it.

"It's mine!" she whispered loudly. "I was looking for it."

"It isn't yours," I hissed back as I snatched it up. "And I saw it first."

We began to wrestle for it without getting too rough. We were too hurt for that. But even with her holding back, I could sense how strong she was. Suddenly, I squealed. Shocked, I sat up straight and covered my chest protectively. I blinked a few times. "Did you just pinch my breast?"

She pointed at her own chest with her bad hand, the toothbrush held triumphantly in her good one. "Who me? Would I do that?"

"I think you *would* do that." I growled. "You're going to pay for that."

She flipped her braid over her shoulder and smacked her lips together. "But I'll be paying with fresh and clean teeth."

"Amazing…"

Our gazes swung up to find Miranda watching us with an astonished, but amused look on her tanned face. "It's just like… how do you say? Female mud wrestling?"

I blushed to the roots of my hair, and, scowling, grabbed Lucas's crusty, used toothbrush. If I didn't think too much about it, maybe I wouldn't hurl as I used it.

"And how would you know?" Nora shot back to Miranda, her face every bit as red as mine. "You've only been married for a few days. Isn't it a little early to be watching pay-per-view with your new husband?"

Miranda looked at me with raised eyebrows.

"Pornographic movies," I clarified for her.

"Ahhh." Miranda smiled audaciously. "Who said I was with Paulo?"

And that wiped the smug look right off Nora's face.

I just shook my head. Duh. She really should have seen that coming.

Miranda's dark eyes slid closed. "Can I sleep more?" She let out a long breath. "I'm so tired."

"How's your head?" Nora asked, all traces of teasing gone.

"It hurts." She forced her eyes open again. "I can go…if you're ready." Her eyelids drooped of their own accord. "But I'm sleepy."

Nora looked at me in question.

I shrugged. "Let's just make it to the van well before dark." But Miranda wasn't really looking for permission. Her breathing was already slow and deepened as she drifted back to sleep, the damp morning breeze tousling her hair as her hammock swayed.

Nora began to open the new toothbrush without a hint of

shame over stealing it from me. I guess all is fair in love and dental hygiene.

I lifted my chin defiantly and squeezed something contained in a silver tube with Spanish written on it on Lucas's toothbrush. "I hope this is toothpaste and not Preparation H."

Nora adjusted her seat on a tree root and reached out, curling her fingers in a "gimme" motion. "Do you want me to try it first?"

"It's too late to feel guilty now."

She smiled wanly. "The timing works just fine for me."

I sniffed the tube and a minty scent filled my nostrils. "I'm pretty sure it's safe."

Nora passed me over a canteen and I drew in a deep breath and closed my eyes. I brought the toothbrush to my mouth... and paused. *Don't think about it. Don't think about it. Don't think about it.*

"Rachel, you're thinking about it."

I opened my eyes and glared at her. "Would *you* not think about it?"

"Hardly," she snorted. "Wanna use mine after me? I really will share. I just didn't want to use Lucas's. Mine won't be new, but it won't be as old and nasty as that one." She wrinkled her face. "I have one under my sink that I use to scrub out the treads of my sneakers that looks better than that."

I was dying to take her up on her offer, but pride is a bitch on wheels. "No, thank you." I stuck the brush in my mouth and started to scrub, feeling slightly gratified when Nora made a retching noise and had to look away. "It's toothpaste," I said, some foam escaping from the new hole in the side of my smile.

My brow knitted. "Hmm...."

She swatted a mosquito from her cheek. "What?"

I wrinkled my nose. "The toothbrush smells like stale cigarettes."

The blood drained from her face. "Ugh."

I turned my head and spat. "You know the worst part?"

"Your toothpaste mustache?"

I smiled sarcastically. "'Fraid not. The toothbrush doesn't just smell like cigs, it *tastes* like stale cigarettes...and possibly beer."

Her skin was as green as a leprechaun's as she wrapped her hands around herself and groaned. "You're right. That's the worst."

"Oh, no," I said innocently, sticking the brush in my mouth and scrubbing even harder. "Thadt's nod thugh worthst pard."

"Please don't tell me."

I spat again and chuckled evilly. "The worst part is that I *liked* it."

Nora shook her head miserably. "It's not here. Shit! Where the hell is it?"

We'd been walking for hours and there was no sight of the van. Somehow, we'd gotten so turned around we couldn't even tell which cliff we'd gone down. Everything looked exactly the same: green trees, ferns and vines, rocks protruding from the mud, and cliffs that disappeared into the forest.

"Let's rest," I suggested, utterly at a loss as to what else to do.

"And eat some of that pouched crap in the packs," Nora added.

Miranda put a few more paces between herself and Nora. Nora's mood had gone south ever since her pain meds had worn off.

"Right." I spoke slowly, doing my best not to flame her sudden anger. "Time for a rest."

Miranda tugged a few large leaves from a tree and then tossed them down to sit on. She dropped heavily to the forest floor and pulled out her canteen. It was half empty. She took a healthy swig and then passed it to me.

"No." I shook my head. "Drink more." I was getting a headache from what I thought was dehydration, which meant we were being too conservative with the water. I wasn't going to let Miranda shrivel up and croak with water left in the canteens.

I dropped down next to her and used the pack I was carrying as a backrest.

She took a few more large swigs, nearly swooning, then passed the canteen bottle back my way. I did the same and handed it up to Nora, who hadn't bothered to sit down.

Miranda reached into her pack and pulled out three food bags. "Veal patty with fruit sauce? Chicken A La King?" Her accent made that sound exotic and delightful. "Or beans and franks with…nut bar?"

"I'm going to murder Jacob." Nora plopped down next to me. "I'm not going to hire it out. I'm actually going to do it with my bare hands." She made a choking motion with her hands.

I smiled cruelly. "Get in line, Nora." I reached out to Miranda. This was the first time since before the accident that I thought I might be able to keep some food down. It wasn't that the knots in my stomach had eased. If anything, my anxiety was growing with every passing moment we couldn't find the van. It was more like I was finally hungry enough that the pains in my belly overrode everything else. "I'll take the chicken, please."

"Who cares about Nora's boss?" Miranda said, giving up her battle to remain neutral in the face of Nora's temper. "He's not even here."

"He's your boss too," Nora snapped, squinting hard as she tried to read the food pouch Miranda handed over.

That reminded me that she'd lost her glasses. Man, how much worse would this be if everything were blurry?

Miranda shifted unhappily and tore open the pouch containing the veal patty. She turned her back to Nora as she addressed me. "The van has to be close, doesn't it?"

"I hope so." I sighed, rubbing a hand over my face and feeling bug bites that weren't there a few hours ago. Even my bites had bites.

"Are we lost?" Miranda asked earnestly, her eyes glued to mine.

When we knew where the van fell into the trees it had seemed so easy to find. Now we were *hopelessly* lost. I drew in a deep breath. "Yes."

She swallowed hard and glanced away. "I'm going up to that spot." She pointed to a high spot about twenty yards away. "Maybe I can see the van from there."

"Stay where we can see you." Nora's eyes blazed with intensity. "I mean it," she barked.

"Fine." Miranda jumped up and stormed away, muttering what sounded very much like, "blow me," under her breath. Oops. She might have picked that one up from me.

Guiltily, Nora looked down at her hands and sighed. Her brow was damp with perspiration, despite the fact that the temperature was quite pleasant and we'd been walking slowly. Her jaw clenched and unclenched as quiet seconds rolled by.

"It's time for more medicine," I said gently, not waiting for her to comment before I went in search of the bottle she'd put back in the pack. "And more water too."

When she looked up at me with bloodshot eyes, her face started to crumple. "I'm sorry I'm being such a asshole. I don't mean to be. I just—"

"Oh, God, please don't cry," I said, a little panicky. "We can live with Bitchzilla for a while longer. Honest. Just don't cry."

She closed her eyes tight, trying to hold back the tears, but couldn't stop her strained burst of laughter. "Bitchzilla?"

"Today it suits. Is it your hand or leg?" I would do anything to erase that look on her face.

Lips thin from pain, she let out a shaky, "Hand."

The wraps on her hand were dirty and coming unraveled. She pulled it back to her chest.

"Okay," I said soothingly, opening the medicine bottle. "Take another pill and I'll rewrap it."

Awkwardly, she pushed my hand away. "You guys have only had one pill each. This will make my third."

"So?"

"So we only have *one* bottle."

"We're banged up, Nora. You're broken. You need them the most…" I shook the bottle.

"And there must be thirty in here." I leaned over and pressed my forehead to hers. "We'll be fine, okay? We'll be fine."

Relief flooded her face. "Thank you," she said softly.

I handed her a pill and she popped it into her mouth.

"And water," I reminded her. "Lots of it."

She took several chugs of warm canteen water and wiped her lips with the back of her hand. "I read how to use the tablets for water on our drive up the mountain. If we find a river or lake or something, we'll be fine."

I opened her food pouch and handed her a metal fork from Lucas's pack. "Should we do that before or after we find the van? We have one more full canteen left."

"How long will that last?"

"It shouldn't last past today. But we could stretch it till tomorrow night or a little longer if we have to."

"One day to find the van and then we go without?"

I cringed. We were all already thirsty all the time. "Right."

Absently, she took a bite of beans and franks. "I don't think we have a choice. Water first."

"We can stretch the food to nearly a week, if we have to." My anxiety spiked. "But if we don't get to the van, no one will know where to look for us after they find it. There's another pack there with more food and water."

"One more canteen only prolongs what we have to do anyway. Without water we'll die, Rachel."

We'll die... The words sunk in like poison. The thought had obviously crossed my mind a dozen times before. But somehow her saying it made it sickeningly real.

"It's four o'clock," I said. "We still have hours till dark. We can't get caught another night without a way for us all to sleep. We need to build something off the ground for one of us. How about we keep heading down hill for another hour or so and then we make a camp? Water runs downhill, right?"

"It does in Denver."

I grabbed a stick from the ground and pushed up a bit of bark with my thumbnail. It was soft, but not sodden. "It didn't rain last night. We might even be able to get a fire going."

She patted my leg. "Deal."

We both looked out at Miranda. She had one hand shielding her eyes as she surveyed the wilderness before her. Then she backed up a few steps and made a dramatic kicking motion as though she was shooting a game winning soccer goal with an imaginary ball. She raised her arms in a cheer.

"So long as Miranda goes for the plan too," I reminded her, doing my best to give her her due as a young woman and not a kid.

"I'll apologize to her when she gets back. You know," Nora paused for a moment while she took another bite. "She's been pretty brave about all this."

I dug into my food pouch. The stuff actually tasted pretty good, and my stomach growled with pleasure. "She thinks she's indestructible."

"Why not?" Nora said a little wistfully. "She's only seventeen."

I felt a tug on one of my heartstrings. How hard must it be for a former athlete like Nora to still be so young and yet so irreversibly past her prime?

"Miranda's in love. She's going to be a star. She can be just who she wants to be."

A vague sense of unease made my skin prickle.

"She's got her whole life stretched out ahead of her."

"So do we, Nora."

She set down her food pouch and took my hand. She squeezed it tenderly then pressed it against her lips in a ridiculously sweet gesture. "You're right. Let's keep it that way."

I looked up to the sky plaintively and wanted to scream. "It's too short."

"How can it be too short?" Nora took the branch from my hand and held it against the other sticks to check the length. "We checked it before we cut it."

I kicked at a rock that sat near my foot. "I don't know what happened."

We were building a bed the size of a small cot and using Lucas's huge knife as an axe to cut thin branches. We laid sticks as big as broomsticks across a makeshift platform that was held together by a length of rope from one of the packs and an extra set of Lucas's boot strings.

We'd been working for more than two hours and we still couldn't get it right. This was our third attempt at something that the breeze wouldn't knock over.

I looked critically at the bed, and then adjusted one stick. "Hang on...try it here."

Nora's face was flushed and she was panting even though

we'd stopped the really aerobic work a while ago. Shocked, she blinked a few times. "It fits."

"Just barely, but yeah. Now we see if it'll hold," I said, distracted with worry over Nora's condition. She'd taken another pill not too long ago, but something else was wrong. I could tell by the look on her face. She'd lost so much blood yesterday and today we'd walked for hours. Maybe we should have stayed right where we were until she felt stronger. What if we'd already done everything in the wrong order?

Clearly exhausted, she murmured. "I'll try lying on it this time."

"Hold on." I pushed on the sticks to test their strength. I'd already ended up flat on my back twice, but this time the platform felt surprisingly strong. Not that it would hold my big butt, but at last there was a real chance it would hold Miranda or Nora.

Miranda piped up from on her knees near the center of our camp where she was industriously trying to start a fire. "Can I take the bed? The hammock hurts the cut on my back and I can't sleep."

It was either a crazy or terribly considerate offer.

Nora gave her a skeptical look and I wondered if she was thinking of the teen's deep snores this morning. "You're sure?"

Miranda nodded without ever looking up from her kindling.

Nora began rooting through Lucas's pack, and Miranda glanced in my direction.

I mouthed a silent, "Thank you." And she smiled quickly.

I gathered the big pile of large flat leaves Miranda had collected earlier and began laying them across the sticks to make the bed's surface more even. Then I retrieved a thin sleeping pad made from foam from the backpack and started to carefully unroll it on the leaves. I surveyed the final product with a mixture of hope, chagrin and pride. "Holy shit, this might actually work."

Miranda mumbled something in Spanish and crossed herself, then went back to stacking wood.

Nora grabbed one of the mosquito nets and gave it a weak

toss, trying to get it over a branch above the bed. The first throw was close, but not close enough. The net fell straight down on top of her head. She cursed a few times as she untangled herself, then took a deep breath for another throw.

On her second attempt, the net hit me square in the face. She blinked slowly at me as though she couldn't believe what she'd done. "I'm so sorry."

I glared at her from behind the net, but let my grumpy retort die on my lips. Her eyes were glassy and unfocused. I peeled the net from my face and handed it back, blowing an unruly, reddish curl from my forehead. "Are you—"

"I'm going to rest now, on the ground. I hope the ants won't eat me. I don't feel…" There was a long pause, then the net fell loosely from Nora's hand and she swayed a little on her feet. "I don't feel right."

"Miranda!" I yelled as I rushed to Nora's side, intent on keeping her upright. Miranda bookended Nora's other side and we leaned into her as her legs started to give way. Instinctively, I pressed my hand against Nora's slick forehead and shock tore through me. "You're burning up!"

She frowned. "Aren't you?"

"No," I puffed, doing my best to keep her from falling. "I'm warm but I'm not hot."

The skin around Nora's eyes bunched when she considered what I'd just said. She looked confused. "Bu…It-It's hot."

Darkness was rapidly approaching and with the steady breeze, the temperature was actually quite comfortable, though it was getting hotter and more humid the farther down the mountain we went. I finally got a good grip on her as I wrapped my arm around her waist to steady her. "You have a fever."

"Maybe she'll feel better if she rests." Fear made Miranda's speech rapid and her accent thicker.

"Do you need to use the bathroom, Nora?" It had only taken me one night to figure out that once you were in your hammock, it was easier to stay there until morning.

Nora stiffened. "My mom's dead, Rachel, and I *don't* need another one."

It was a lot like getting cuffed in the face. I froze, not knowing whether to apologize or snap back.

Miranda's expression turned to stone. I could tell she was on the verge of lashing out at Nora on my behalf, and so I warned her off with a quick look and a softly uttered, "It's okay."

The harsh words were barely out of Nora's mouth when her entire demeanor changed into something more vulnerable. Her eyes conveyed true regret and her chin began to quiver. "I'm sorry again. I-I-I don't know what's wrong with me. I bike. I ski," she explained dejectedly. "I'm in good shape. I shouldn't be this weak after only one day. I just shouldn't."

I held Nora closer, the heat pouring from her making my shirt stick to my skin. "You're sick. Maybe your cut's infected or you caught some sort of bug out here."

Nora looked disgusted with herself and lifted her hand only to let it fall weakly by her side. "Why aren't you tired? I feel like I could drop right here."

I smiled weakly. "I'm *dead* tired. And hungry and thirsty and achy. And I'm pretty sure I stink. But I'm not sick. Your energy will get better when you've had a chance to recover." *She won't get better at all if you don't find water soon*, my mind taunted.

Miranda and I tugged Nora toward the log we'd dragged to camp that served as our bench. The very second she was steady in her seat, a terribly uncomfortable looking Miranda went back to work. I wasn't sure what was up with her, but we could talk later. *Please don't let her be getting sick too.* I wasn't sure I could handle one of them being ill, let alone both.

I crouched down in front of Nora and tossed whatever remaining modesty or propriety I had out the window. "When was the last time you peed?"

Distractedly, Nora pulled a damp tendril of hair off her cheek. "I dunno."

I schooled myself in patience and tried to capture her attention with my gaze. "Think, Nora. When was the last time?"

"This morning, maybe? It was still dark."

Miranda was already digging out our last canteen. It was half full. "Drink more," we both said at the same time.

Nora made a grouchy face. "Double teaming is no fair."

"We both want you to be okay," I corrected. "Time to eat, drink and rest."

Thunder boomed in the distance and I cringed immediately. Then I realized this could be our chance to collect water.

Nora blanched as a flash of light lit the far-off sky. "Rest, yes. But I'm not hungry. And I don't want to waste the food. I'm not sure I can keep it down, Rache. You eat." She bent a little at the waist. "I'm upset at my stomach."

"Maybe you could try just a little?" With more of my attention on Nora than what I was doing, I reached into Miranda's pack and grabbed out a random meal pouch and spoon. I passed it over and couldn't stop myself from petting her cheek. I was about to remove my hand when, quite on its own, it changed direction and I felt her forehead in a motion that reminded me so strongly of my own mother it took my breath away.

As adults, my mom and I had drifted apart. It wasn't that we didn't care for each other. We did. It was more that we had separate lives that no matter how we tried, didn't seem to want to mesh. Blood held us together, but love should have been the stronger bond.

When I was a kid, however, Mom was always great when I was sick. Even now when I don't feel well, I have the urge to call her so she can come over and read to me, make me soup and tuck me into bed with a kiss on my forehead and a promise that by tomorrow I'd feel much better.

Nora was so hot it was scary. I left my hand there a little longer than necessary, fear coursing through me. Apparently too sick to be afraid, she leaned into my touch and let her eyes slide closed.

God, she looked miserable. "The medicine is probably making you nauseous. But food should help that."

When Nora capitulated, I praised her by bending over and pressing my lips to her cheek. Her hair was sweaty but still held just the faintest hint of her shampoo, and the humidity had added a slight wave to it that I hadn't noticed before. Maybe she straightened it back home. Even grungy, she was beautiful. "Good girl."

"Yes. Yes!" Miranda crowed, her pretty face lit up like the

sky on the Fourth of July.

I turned to see the campfire spark to life...and stay that way.

Nora smiled her first real smile of the day. "Awesome, Miranda."

"Beyond awesome," I repeated, hope sparking within me just like that tiny flame. I would gladly cling to every small success. I *had* to.

For a little while, at least, we had a way to keep the monsters at bay. But even if they did come, it was what was going on inside Nora that really had me worried.

Chapter 10

Over the next dozen hours Nora's condition worsened and she began to shiver violently. With my heart in my throat, I'd reluctantly peeled back the filthy bandages on her leg, expecting to see something out of a horror movie. Instead, what I found was that amazingly, and despite the grunge and grime, the cut didn't look infected. The skin hadn't knit back together yet, but even normal cuts took days to heal. And this one was a doozy.

It was the fever that worried me now. With only a few weak aspirin tablets from the first-aid kit to try to stave it off, it was determined to run its full course. And it was taking Nora on one hell of a ride. I'd never seen someone have such a dreadful night. Chills, hallucinations, nightmares, confusion... Eventually, though, Nora settled into a fitful sleep, too exhausted to do anything else.

The source of her fever remained a mystery, and during the few minutes that I wasn't worrying to death, I wondered if it would claim Miranda or me as victims as well.

Rain pounded all around us and puddles formed at the edges of our camp. We'd accidentally chosen high ground and so, for now, it didn't appear as though we'd be washed away in the night. We'd left everything we could think of out in the rain in the hopes of capturing some drinking water. Canteens, cups, even our thin microfiber towels and clean cotton T-shirts that we could wring out in the morning. With our junk spread out and clothes hanging haphazardly across the bushes, our camp looked like trailer trash heaven.

Nora and I remained dry as we lay safely beneath one of the rainflies in side-by-side hammocks. Alongside us were two big piles of dry sticks and a few sizeable pieces of wood that would serve as tomorrow's firewood.

We might be lame campers, but we were learning fast.

The other rainfly had been fashioned into a giant bucket to collect the rain. And even after I'd nagged Miranda like an old woman to take her place under the rainfly with me and Nora, the stupid-ass teenager had her own ideas.

She had insisted that she couldn't stand how filthy she was and that she wanted whatever shower the rain could provide. So for half the night she'd slept gingerly on her back on the platform bed with only a mosquito net for protection and a poncho draped over the back of her head to keep the rain from going up her nose and in her mouth.

How was I going to explain to her parents that their daughter had survived a horrendous auto accident that really should have killed us all, only to suffocate, or maybe drown, while camping? I couldn't. Thankfully, Miranda had spared me that trial by finally deciding she was clean enough. She dragged her makeshift bed to rest on the other side of Nora, which made us as close as three peas in a pod.

The rain had doused our campfire hours ago and once again we were enveloped in darkness, with only the occasional flash of lightning illuminating our tiny camp.

"Say something," Nora said out of the blue, her voice a soft burr that was barely audible above the sharp rapping of rain on leaves, branches and the rain tarp.

I turned my head. Our hammocks were only a few inches apart, but in the darkness she seemed miles away. "I thought you were asleep."

"Ugh." She shivered. "I'm tired of trying."

"You should rest." She hadn't slept for more than twenty consecutive minutes all night. Of course, that was twenty minutes more than I'd gotten.

She let loose a weak chuckle. "You're not going to carp at me the way you did Miranda until she came in out of the rain, are you?"

My brow wrinkled when I thought of Nora's earlier comment about her mother. Once bitten, twice shy. "No," I answered quietly. "I'm not."

I heard her sigh. "I'm sorry about what I said earlier, Rachel." Her teeth chattered a few times. "I'm just cranky because I don't f-feel well."

It was on the tip of my tongue to ask her if she wanted me to dig out more clothes for her to layer on, but I bit my lip to stop myself.

A lot of what Reece complained about during our marriage was bullshit. I know that and so does he. I was a good wife, though I'll cop to being a better friend. One thing, however, that he'd moaned about that was undeniably true was my nearly compulsive need to help, even when that help was unwelcome. At least that's the way I like to think of it. He used the words "control freak" more than once.

"Please talk to me," Nora said. "Give me something to think about besides feeling like shit. Tell me something about yourself."

I gave the tree next to me a tiny push, and the force sent our two hammocks swinging gently in unison. "What do you want to know?"

"Your f-family. Tell me about them."

"Huh." I stretched a little. Hammocks are hell on your spine. "I didn't think you'd say that. I thought you'd ask about my work."

She shook her head. "Nuh-uh. I already know a little about that. I've seen your resume and I listen to your show every morning."

My eyes widened. "You've heard *The Rachel & Reece Morning Show*?"

"I drive to work too, you know." She rubbed her arms, trying to warm up though it was probably at least seventy degrees out. "And I have a radio. Why wouldn't I have heard it?"

I squirmed a little. "It's not that…It's just—"

"What?"

"Even after all these years it's a little weird. I talk about my life on the show all the time. So if you listen, then you know about me, but I don't really know anything about you. It gives you an unfair advantage."

"And just what do you think I'm going to do with this unfair advantage?"

"I have no idea. But it's there."

"Oh." Nora thought for a moment. "If it bothers you, why talk about your actual life while you're on the air? You could make things up and no one would know, right?" She scratched her elbow violently. The bugs were even worse at night.

"It doesn't bother me to think that there's this group of strangers who know things about me. I don't care about them because I don't know them. It's just a little uncomfortable when the person isn't an outsider anymore."

"We're friends, aren't we?" She sounded a little unsure of herself.

I smiled. "For sure."

"So let's get to know each other better."

"You must understand what I mean about people knowing things about your life. If you were good enough to be an Olympian, then you must have been known in at least the world of women's soccer, right?"

Nora snorted softly. "For about ten minutes and to about ten people. It's a small world after all," she sang in that same annoying voice used on the Disney ride, causing me to chuckle.

"Let's even the playing field a little," I said, wincing as a wicked crack of thunder interrupted our conversation. "You tell me what you know about me and then you share that same information about yourself." I wanted to know about her and Jacob. But I was unsure about how to bring up the boning your boss topic.

"I thought you were going to tell me about your f-family." Nora's voice caught as she shifted in her hammock and she groaned in pain.

Hang in there. I squinted at the glowing hands of my watch. *Only one more hour till you can have another pill.* "You thought wrong. Speak, please. What do you know about me?"

"Fine. Fine. Let's stick to family since that's what I asked you about. All I know is that you split up with Reece, who, by the way, seems like a douche bag and a tool."

"Hey!" I covered my mouth to keep from laughing so loudly it woke Miranda. "He is not a douche bag."

"What about a tool?"

I tilted my hand back and forth. "He's sort of a tool, but he's generally a good guy. What you've heard on the radio is mostly a character for the show. He's not that bad in real life." Once again I was reminded about how much I hated being with someone who had to pretend. Everyone expected Reece to act like his character. And over the years, he'd taken to hiding the more attractive parts of his personality when we were in public.

"But you aren't in character, are you?"

"Not really. I try not to do that. I'm more of a what-you-see-is-what-you-get sort of woman. How about you?"

There was a long pause and then a note of self-discovery in her voice. "I guess I'm more like Reece." She sounded truly anguished. "Oh, no. I'm a tool!"

"You're not a tool," I said gently. "But you are different when you're away from your boss."

"Isn't everybody?"

"A little, I guess." *But not like you.*

"Did Reece like your hair?"

The mental whiplash made me dizzy. "I um...*what*?"

"I love the curls." She sighed wishfully. "They look so soft. I want to touch them."

I felt my face heat even though I knew it was the fever that was talking. "Not really. He thought it was a mess most of the time."

"Like I said...a tool."

I laughed.

"Is that why you dumped him?"

"I didn't... Not really. We dumped each other. It was mutual." I'd been the first to walk out the door, but Reece had checked out emotionally and physically months before. By the time I had the wherewithal to walk out, I really wasn't leaving anything behind. "We sort of loved the wrong people."

"One of you cheated?"

I shook my head. "No way. Neither of us are the type."

My words were greeted with utter silence.

Okay, that wasn't nice. Jacob was the married one, not Nora.

"Oh," she mumbled. "But I thought you said—"

"You're asking hard questions about my least favorite topic, you know that?"

"How am I supposed to get to know you better if we only talk about easy things? Besides, you only have to say what you w-want."

I took a deep breath and considered how far I wanted to go. "Okay." To my surprise, it felt good to consider opening up a little with someone who wasn't so close to the situation. Joanie had always been there for me, but she also had very strong opinions about what I should do. Nora mostly just listened and asked questions as though she was interested and really cared, which was...nice. "I think the biggest problem is that we loved people who didn't really exist by the end of our marriage. I loved the guy I thought Reece could be, and he loved the young woman I was when we got married. In the end, we were both a disappointment."

The rain slowed but didn't stop, and I listened to it for a long time, sure Nora had fallen asleep.

"That story was sad," she finally said.

I blinked. "Did you expect a happy tale? We got divorced."

"Do you wish you hadn't?"

"No," I said, surprising myself at how painless the answer was. "It was the right thing to do, even if it felt like going through a meat grinder at the time." I let out a deep breath, having successfully run the gauntlet.

"Did he know about your relationship with a woman?"

I stiffened. "That was over before I even met him. It wasn't that important, and I wouldn't call it a relationship. It was more of a summer romance."

This time it was Nora who pushed off from the nearest tree, sending us into gentle motion again. "You and Reece were together a long time, right?"

"I suppose."

"So why didn't you tell him?"

I thought about that, a little embarrassed that I couldn't come up with a compelling reason. "I…I'm not sure."

"Would he have been angry?"

"Nah. He's not that sort of guy. We each dated other people before we were married. That was no big deal. The fact that it was a woman would have been…hard to explain. But he wouldn't have been mad." I squinted as though I was actually looking back through the pages of my past. "If you want the truth, the experience was mine, and I didn't want to share it with anyone, not even him. And I think…I think I didn't want him to be insecure or jealous."

"But, Rachel, why would he be jealous or insecure over an unimportant summer romance?"

"I-I-I…" I felt cornered. Why was she making such a big deal out of nothing? "I didn't want him to misunderstand, is all. That's the sort of thing someone could misunderstand, don't you think? I mean—"

"Don't worry about it," Nora said lightly, shivering again. "I was just curious."

"Your t-turn," I stuttered, out of sorts. I hadn't expected the conversation to go there. "Let's talk about Jacob Dane."

"What about him?"

I snorted, glad the spotlight was off me. "It's obvious that you're…close. I'm curious about that relationship."

"He's my boss."

"And?" I held my breath, unsure of why this was so vitally important to me. But it was. Two other things hit me with cold certainty in that moment. I was angry on her behalf. She was smart and driven and didn't need to crawl into his bed to get ahead. I was also miserably envious…of him.

"I know what you're th-thinking."

My eyebrows jumped. "You do?"

"You're thinking that I got my position with the Dragonflies because of my relationship with Jacob. Well, that's not true," she said loudly. "I earned this goddamn job. And I worked for years and years to get it...and not on my back!"

I sat up, or at least sat up as best I could in the narrow hammock. "Take it easy. Take it easy." Feeling guilty as sin, I was glad of the dark to hide my face. "I um...I didn't say that."

"You didn't have to say it. But even thinking it doesn't give me any credit for what I've put into this team. For the *sacrifices* I've made."

Oh, shit. She was really upset. "I'm sorry, Nora."

"No, you aren't. Not really." Angry, she wiped at her eyes.

How had things gone from zero to sixty in a matter of seconds? Then I remembered the fever that was making her over-emotional. It wasn't fair to even be having this conversation now. "I *am* sorry."

"You don't know anything about the situation or circumstances, and yet you still think I'm some sort of gold-digging whore."

When she said it that way, I really did sound like an asshole. "If you tell me you didn't, you didn't. I believe you...one hundred percent."

She turned to face me. I couldn't see them, and yet I was certain that those pretty green eyes were blazing. "Promise?"

"Promise."

She sighed and I could hear the strings of her hammock whine as she settled back into place and relaxed.

Maybe she really loved Jacob. But then why had she so brazenly propositioned me? Even injured and ill she sometimes looked at me with what even the densest person could see was open interest. Nothing made any sense.

For a few minutes we settled into a safe discussion about the Dragonflies, and Nora calmed back down.

"That didn't go very well, did it?" she asked regretfully.

I smiled weakly. "Not really."

"I'm not thinking straight. Tomorrow will be better," she said in a thin, sleepy voice. She reached out and took my hand. Her skin was warm and damp, and I willed her body to heal.

I looked up at the sky. We couldn't just exist. We had to start working to survive.

"How much longer until a pill?"

"Fifty-one minutes, thirty seconds."

"Do you hate this motherfucking hellhole as much as I do?"

I smiled coldly. "More. So much more."

"Are we ready?" Miranda asked, her olive skin noticeably darker than it was only a few days before. Nora could barely walk, so despite the cut down her back, Miranda was wearing her own pack and a pair of dark sunglasses that had somehow survived the crash unscathed.

When I looked at her, all fresh and clean from last night's rain shower, I felt twice as grungy as I did yesterday. My fingernails and hair were filthy and my T-shirt had been damp with sweat, and then dried, and then damp again, so many times over that I was certain it could stand up on its own. I tried to make myself feel better by remembering that the second I got clean I'd just have to slather myself in bug repellent and sunscreen anyway. But it didn't help.

"Just about ready," I answered, sloshing through the damp grass to pick up a lighter that was still sitting around the edge of our fire ring. "Don't wanna forget this." I stuffed it in my pocket, being careful not to lose the load on my shoulders.

It had taken us so long to build our bed made from sticks that we dismantled it and decided to take it with us. We bound the sticks together in a big bundle and tied it to the top of Lucas's pack, which rested heavily on my back. I jumped up and down a couple of times to settle it. "Nora?" I said over my shoulder. "You ready?"

I glanced over at her and winced. Dark circles ringed her eyes and her face was flushed. Her picture deserved to be next to the word "misery" in the dictionary.

One look in her glassy eyes and I knew her fever was still burning hot. And despite our efforts we'd only collected a half of a canteen of water that had to be shared among us all today.

Nora was too sick to travel, but we were doing it anyway.

I adjusted Lucas's pack on my back and ignored my rumbling stomach. It didn't approve of our new food-rationing plan: one meal per day. And when that ran out, who knew?

I tightened the belt on my shorts. Normally, loose clothing would be a cause to celebrate, but in this instance I couldn't muster the will to be happy. *What a screw. The only time in my life I have a real chance at being skin and bones, and I might* literally *end up as nothing but skin and bones.*

"So," Nora said weakly. "I have an idea."

I cocked my head to the side and listened. She'd been eerily silent all morning and just hearing her voice, raspy as it was, was a relief.

"Why not head that way?" She pointed to her left, which happened to be nearly the opposite way we'd been walking the day before. "We've been looking for the most level land because it's easier to hike down the mountain. But maybe that's our problem. Wouldn't a stream or river come out of the steepest rocks as it tries to find its way to lower ground?"

Miranda smiled and nodded her approval. "Smart. It is a good idea. But walking there will be hard."

"And dangerous," I added.

A stark expression on her face, Nora turned to me. "That's why I should stay here. We're already near the bottom of the mountain, but I don't think I can hike the steeper sections. I'll only slow you down."

"The hell!" I spluttered, startled.

"I'm not making some noble sacrifice. You can come back for me after you find water. I'll probably feel better in a day or two, and we can keep going from there. Maybe someone will even notice we're not where we're supposed to be by then."

Instantly outraged at that retarded idea, my mouth flew open, but Miranda beat me to the punch.

"No. We will *not* leave you."

Nora and I both turned, and I blinked at the ferocity in Miranda's voice.

"Miranda," Nora began gently, "it's not fair—"

"Nothing about this is fair," she snapped. "We have only one choice. We'll go as far as we can go together, and then we'll stop."

I winked at Miranda to let her know I was on her side.

Nora's eyes flashed and I prepared myself for World War

III, which was about to erupt in our camp.

But Miranda didn't even flinch. "What were you telling me about the Dragonflies? That the team was special? That it would stick together through anything and would never quit, no matter what. Well, *we* are a team now. Me, you and Rachel."

No one liked having her own words tossed back at her. Nora was no exception. "I know what I said," she ground out.

Miranda lifted her chin. "So act like it. Unless you were lying before, we all go as one now."

Then, like two cowboys on Main Street at high noon, Miranda and Nora stared stonily at each other for what had to be a full minute.

A sane person could point out that Nora had been talking about soccer. And that soccer was just a game like bowling or tiddlywinks, even if kids and adults played it. And what we were dealing with in this jungle was a matter of life and death, clearly not a game. But these women weren't sane. They were soccer *fiends*. It was no game to those who would bleed for the cause and their comrades and who attacked the field with the single-minded determination of a hungry infant in a topless bar.

In short, Miranda's words had been nothing short of perfect.

"Okay." Nora sighed, and a tired but determined smile edged its way across her lips. "Here we go."

And with that we started to slowly walk toward steeper ground, and God willing, water.

By that evening we were even out of the additional rainwater we'd collected the night before. We were also all the way down the mountain into an area that was more lush and humid than where we'd spent the previous couple of days.

Miranda was collecting firewood nearby and giving Nora and me a rare moment of privacy. Lord knows we didn't need a fire for the heat, but the light would be nice, and we all prayed the flames would scare the crap out of any animals, particularly the jaguars that were native to this region, and keep them from visiting us in the night. And if there was a God, someone would see smoke where there shouldn't be smoke and investigate.

A warm trickle of sweat snaked between my breasts and I fanned my face with one hand while tugging my bra away from my body with the other.

"If it's bothering you, you should take it off." Despite her fever, which had all but disappeared in the last hour, Nora gave me a surprisingly saucy wink.

With a stiff arm to her chest, I backed her up until her heels were hitting a backpack. Not that it took much force. She was weak as a kitten. "Sorry, sugar, but the bra stays. Gravity is not my friend."

With a start, I realized what I'd called her and waited for some sort of reaction. Thankfully, she didn't seem to notice.

Nora pouted adorably and I laughed, feeling ten years younger. A little levity after a day of hiking down the rugged mountainside and fruitlessly searching for water was more than welcome. Of course, the fact that Nora had crunched down a pain tablet only fifteen minutes ago made it possible.

"You would deny a dying woman her final wish?" she said. "Tsk. Tsk."

I playfully narrowed my eyes. "I've *never* heard of a more pathetic dying wish than wanting to see me braless."

"I don't get why you underestimate your charms, Rachel," she said seriously. "Do you really think your radio station would put a billboard of you up in the middle of Denver if you weren't attractive?"

True, my self-esteem had taken a beating over the last couple of years, but that wasn't the point. "My tits aren't on the billboard."

"Trust me, that's because they had to waste all that room on Reece."

Our eyes met and we both laughed. "Lucky for you, you're not dying," I told her. "But if you start, I promise to lose the bra for the duration. Deal?"

Her eyes glazed over and I could only imagine what she was thinking of. "Deal."

A wave of affection snuck up on me, and I reached out and ruffled her hair. I suddenly wished that we'd had all this time together under any other circumstance. "Now sit, okay? We can set things up for the night."

Dutifully, she plopped down on the rainfly that I liked to think of as our incredibly uncomfortable couch, and rested her elbows on bent knees.

Beams of weak sunlight filtered through the trees and painted her with odd golden stripes that showed off the highlights in her hair and her newly acquired suntan. It was a picture that made me stop and take notice and wish I had a camera.

Nora was so beat her eyelids were drooping, but she was doing her best to hold it together. *If we were in Denver, I'd tuck you into my bed and take care of you until you didn't hurt anymore.* And I had the strongest urge to tell her so, but then I thought of Jacob. He'd probably hire some illegal alien he could underpay to feed her chicken soup while he spent time with this wife. Yuck.

Forcing any thoughts of him out of my head, I checked my watch.

We decided to stop traveling a couple of hours before sunset so we'd have time to make camp and assemble our homemade stick bed, which made me long for the days when I sat on my living room carpet, bitching about the impossibly cryptic instructions that came with IKEA furniture.

I began looking around for a flat spot under some trees where we could hang the hammocks as I laid out the sticks.

"How's your headache?" Nora asked.

I glanced up from my task but didn't stop working. "How do you know I have a headache?" I asked. "I haven't said a word." I rearranged two sticks. Then put them back in their original spots. Then I moved them again.

"Your lips get thinner and you squint more."

"Those are pretty impressive observations for someone as blind as a bat without her glasses."

She nodded. "I guess I'm adapting, Miranda." Her eyes bugged out. "Or is it Rachel?"

"Ha. Ha."

"So?" she prodded. "Your head?"

I sighed. "It hurts. But I've been trying to convince myself that if I ignore it, it will go away."

"I've been doing that with my hand. But the pills are more convincing."

There was no denying that. But I'd stopped taking them today.

"How about a shoulder rub?"

I froze as a thrill shot through me at the very thought. My neck and shoulders were throbbing and had been ever since the crash. And then there was the thought of getting just a little closer to what I'd already labeled as forbidden fruit, the kind you want ten times more when you know you shouldn't have it.

She lifted a hand and waggled her fingers invitingly. "I still have one good hand."

I peered down at the mass of wood that wasn't even close to looking like a bed yet. "Maybe after—"

"C'mon," she coaxed softly, her voice warm and inviting. "We have plenty of time before dark." She patted a spot on the rainfly right in front of her. "You can sit here."

Feeling guilty, I glanced around for Miranda. I couldn't see her, but I could hear her tugging and cursing at the branches of some nearby bush or tree. She was working hard and I'd been sitting on my butt. Then again, I was no saint.

"Okay," I relented. "But just for a minute." I sat down between her legs and leaned back just a little. She was hot and sticky and so was I, and I felt my temperature rise for reasons that had nothing to do with the heat outside.

She lifted my crazy ponytail out of the way, then gave it a little tug and asked, "Can you do this up a little higher?"

I nodded and fixed myself a ponytail so high it nearly sprouted from the top of my head. I looked like *I Dream of Jeannie*. "Better?"

She began to knead my neck, and a low groan escaped my throat unbidden. "Oh, Je-e-e-sus."

She chuckled. "Much better. Damn...you're so tight." Her thumb found a particularly sore spot and she dug in with determination.

"I know," I said, grimacing. "I think I twisted it going down the mountain, or falling on my head as I was trying to get out of van. One of the two."

She increased the pressure just enough to send me into heaven and get my muscles to start to relax.

"Rachel?" she purred right into one of my ears.

"Yes?" I said dreamily, completely under the spell of those magic fingers and sexy voice. If she'd only been smart enough to offer this in exchange for my bra, my breasts would never see cotton again.

"I'm starving." On cue, her stomach rumbled.

Then mine rumbled in return. We hadn't had anything to eat all day and our water, even the newly collected rainwater, had run out mid-afternoon. "Me too," I said. "Dinner when Miranda gets back?" At least we still had a cache of meals. We'd been looking for fruit as we walked, but the only thing we'd found so far was monkey poop. I liked living as much as the next gal, but even at Death's dinner table, turd would never be on my menu.

I bit my lip and whimpered in delight as she dug into the sore muscles that ran down the side of my neck and shoulder.

Nora turned her head to the side, "Miranda," she called, "I'm about to eat your dinner."

I smacked at her good leg. But not too hard. I didn't want her to stop rubbing me. "Why do you keep messing with her?"

"She's a big girl." I could hear the smile in her voice. "She can take it."

"Then I will kill and eat you instead," Miranda called from the woods. "Too bad you're getting so skinny."

I felt rather than heard Nora's snort and decided that she was right. Miranda could take care of herself. Then I thought of their conversation and frowned. If it ever came down to who was the best candidate to be eaten, I was in deep trouble.

Miranda marched into camp with an armful of sticks and Lucas's sword-sized knife tucked into her belt. Every inch of her glistened with sweat, and she'd freed her thick hair from her ponytail to hang wildly around her shoulders. She was wearing a tight, army green, muscle-tee and looked like a female porn version of Rambo.

Miranda glanced at us from the corner of her eye then dropped the wood and began to collect rocks to make a fire ring. "Aww…" she cooed. "Mama and Papa have stopped fighting."

I scowled but couldn't hold the pose because my eyes rolled back in their sockets and I moaned. When I came back to my senses I said to Miranda, "I had better be Mama. Ouch! It's not nice to pinch."

"First it was mud wrestling, and now they are having," Miranda paused and scratched her chin. "What do you call it? You know, before sex?"

I blinked.

"Foreplay," Nora said delightedly.

"Yes. That's it." The girl nodded thoughtfully as though she was cataloging the word in her mind. "Foreplay."

My mouth dropped open and I scooted away from Nora. Certainly, once upon a time, if Reece had been touching me that way there was a good chance it would have ended in sex. As he'd once so poignantly put it, *If you don't want to fuck, you shouldn't let me touch you.* But this was a completely different situation. "That was *not* foreplay."

Miranda gave me a doubtful look. "I guess you didn't hear your own moaning or see the look on your face. I don't like women that way, and *I* am almost coming."

Nora laughed. "Don't be a spoilsport, Rache. You might not be into me, but foreplay with me has to be better than thinking of being stuck in the jungle every second."

"It was not foreplay." I pouted. But she did have a point. Focusing on one's impending demise from thirst or starvation was a real downer. Finally, I gave up my mind to what it really wanted. If it came down to it, I had just settled on *my* dying wish.

Nora awkwardly turned around and tugged out three random food pouches. The procedure we'd all agreed upon so we had an equal chance at getting the coveted beef stew. She tossed one to each of us and then started rooting for silverware. We'd put our own spoons in specific spots in the pack so we could tell them apart. It wasn't like we'd been able to wash them after eating.

I looked down at my pouch. Chicken and vegetables in gravy. Not bad. I could drink gravy by the bucket right now.

"Christ on the cross!" Nora wailed as she passed out the

silverware. "Beans and franks again."

Miranda sniggered and tore open her own pouch. "Mmm. Beef stew."

Bitch, I thought.

"Bitch!" Nora exclaimed.

I rolled my eyes and traded my pouch with Nora's. I nearly called her a big crybaby but remembered that she had, somehow, gotten the same meal for the past three days in a row. I doubted she would ever take a crap again.

"I think I love you, Rachel," Nora said as she tucked in, gravy pooling at the corners of her mouth.

"You just love me for my roughage."

"Whatever," she mumbled around a big bite. "If you can love Miranda for her toilet paper, I can love you even more for roughage."

Miranda stretched out next to Nora. "Do you want to hear what Paulo loves about me?" Her dark eyes sparked with mischief. "And it is not vegetables or toilet paper."

Nora and I traded looks and then shrugged. "Yes," we said in unison.

Hey, it was like Nora had said—my eyes were suddenly drawn to the large toucan who flew down and took up residence in the beginnings of our fire pit—we really needed to think about something other than being trapped in the jungle.

Chapter 11

Three more days crawled by, and still there was no sign of a river or lake. Three days of fighting the insects, heat and sun. Three days of traveling miles deeper into the unknown. A heavy rain the day before, and our desperate collection attempts, which included drinking mud strained through a clean T-shirt, had provided us with a little water, but it simply wasn't enough.

Our cheeks were hollow and our spirits were so low the bug repellent looked like a potential cocktail. Sure, it would kill us, but we'd go out with moist tongues instead of lingering in this state of perpetual dry misery.

On the upside, Nora said that my black eyes had faded away. On the downside…everything else. We were so dry that it was hard to swallow our food. We'd given up the random meal approach and already polished off anything with a sauce or gravy as we desperately sought out every drop of moisture. Now we were left with perfectly edible food that we could barely choke down.

Miranda and Nora looked as though they'd dropped a good ten pounds each. Something neither of them could really afford.

But today was important for something other than a reminder of all our failures. This is the day we were supposed to start a different leg of our adventure in Hell. We should have arrived in another town with Lucas last night. Finally, the day that someone might notice that we were missing was here.

It also happened to be Miranda's eighteenth birthday. I prayed it wouldn't be her last.

It was only three in the afternoon, but we'd stopped for the day, no one having the energy to go any farther. I sat down crossed-legged near our fire, having just come back empty-handed from a hunt for fruit. I'd found what I thought was a mango tree, but the damn thing didn't have any fruit. If it wasn't crystal clear before, today I truly understood the words, *If it weren't for bad luck, I'd have no luck at all...*

Nora was back to normal. Well, as normal as a severely dehydrated person with a broken hand, and slowly healing ten-inch gash on her leg could be. But her wicked fever had come and gone and she'd survived. The tiny cuts on her face had healed. Even though her hand had to still be killing her, she'd tapered down to only the occasional pain pill.

Miranda had lost the bounce in her step, but her bruises were no longer visible and she hadn't mentioned the cut down her back for a couple of days.

I still had a staggering headache, but I suspected it was from dehydration and not the accident. In short, we were all healing. What we weren't doing was finding a way out of the jungle. Soon we wouldn't be able to move at all.

Nora tossed another batch of leaves on our fire, intentionally causing as much smoke as possible.

"Do—" Nora coughed a couple of times, fanning the air in front of her to clear it. "Do you think we should head toward—"

A piercing scream interrupted her. *Miranda!*

We were both on our feet in a flash. It's amazing how pure terror can make you forget how hurt and bone tired you are.

"Miranda," Nora cried. "Where are you?"

"She was over there a few minutes ago." I pointed down a slight hill and into the woods. I looked in another direction. "Or was it that way? Shit, oh, shit." Bored with our adult presence, she'd taken to wandering off a bit once we made camp for the day. Dammit, I knew I should have tied her to a tree the way Joanie does when she takes her kids to the park.

But we didn't have to wonder for long as another yell, this time louder, told us where we could find her. Nora grabbed Lucas's knife and began loping forward, a crazy, kill-or-be-killed expression on her face.

I picked up a large stick as we ran, ready to club the hell out of whatever was eating our friend. "Miranda? Hang on."

Then we rounded a thick stand of bushes with enormous dark leaves and saw her twisting and rolling like she was on fire. We both stopped and gaped, our brains taking their time to interpret the scene in front of us.

The first thing I noticed was that Miranda's hair and clothes were soaking wet. Then I took in her beaming smile. Sweet mother of God, she was sitting right in the middle of a fast moving stream that was about as wide as a twin bed and deep as a bathtub. Water cascaded over her, and Miranda joyously splashed like a toddler on her first trip to the beach.

"Holy—" Nora started to mutter before diving headfirst toward the water and sticking her face directly in the flow. Considering her current physical state, flopping on her belly had to hurt, but she didn't seem to mind.

In a flash, I was alongside her, nearly crowing with delight as the cool liquid slid down my throat. I didn't know whether to cry like a baby or laugh like a madwoman. So I just drank and drank and drank until I thought I would be sick, swearing then and there never to take something so precious for granted again. Gone were the days where I would run the water as I brushed my teeth. Gone were the nights I would toss out a tray of ice just because it was more than a few days old. I had learned my lesson in spades.

"Water," Miranda gushed as we all lay on the grass next to the stream, looking like fat ticks after our liquid feast, "is the best birthday gift in the world!"

"Amen, sister. And it's not even my birthday," I said. I reached into my pocket and pulled out the bracelet I'd made from woven strips of leaves. "Happy birthday, kiddo."

"I thought we were waiting until tonight," Nora complained good-naturedly as she removed a small, damp stone from her pocket. It was an eerie, unusual green color, and I wondered if it was raw jade. "When we get to Denver, I'll have it made into a necklace or earrings for you."

Miranda squealed with delight and thanked us both in two languages, insisting that we tie the bracelet around her wrist that instant.

Then a thought struck me, along with a bout of queasiness. Maybe drinking until I couldn't hold another drop wasn't such a good idea. What had Lucas said on our long drive? Something about microbes? "Hey, guys, should we have used the purifying tablets from the pack?"

"Probably," Miranda allowed, her eyes closed and her face glistening with water droplets. "But it's too late now."

Nora turned her head in my direction, the color of her eyes perfectly matching the soft grass she was resting on. They were tired and oh so soulful, and for just a second, she took my breath away.

"Maybe we won't get raging cases of the trots," she said, yanking me out of my romantic moment. "Maybe for once the fates won't be cruel."

Then I rolled to my knees and promptly threw up.

Nora patted my back gently as I heaved. "Then again…"

All right, maybe it had been a bad idea to drink a gallon of water all at once. What can I say? I suck at moderation and I lost my head.

"How are you feeling?" Miranda asked as she ate her veal cutlet and green beans from a pouch. We'd even figured out how to warm the food without melting the bags by putting a few rocks in the fire until they were hot, and then burying them with along with the pouches, a thin layer of dirt separating them. It was a like a mini oven and it made the food taste and smell a million times better.

"Not as bad as before," I said, embarrassed that I'd chugged the water as though I were a college freshman with his first beer bong. Of course, Miranda and Nora could tell what I was thinking. Miranda smiled affectionately at me from across our small fire and Nora, who was sitting next to me, gently bumped shoulders with me.

"We understand," Miranda said.

"Right," Nora added sincerely.

"All right, all right," I muttered with faux gruffness. "You don't have to try to make me feel better for being an idiot." But I loved it and I was sure they could tell that too.

"So," Miranda said. "Who gets to take a bath first?" She was already digging out a bar of biodegradable soap from her pack.

"How about the birthday girl gets to use the spot closest to camp, and Rachel and I can go up or downstream a little ways to give you some privacy?"

Miranda squealed with delight and sprang to her feet with a renewed sense of energy that had more to do with spirit than good health. She gave us a little wave as she disappeared into the woods.

Amused, I waved back. "Wow, I think she liked that idea."

Nora laughed. "How could you tell?"

I pulled out a soft, extra thin towel from Lucas's pack along with a thick bar of unscented soap. "Okay, which do you want? Upstream or downstream of Miranda?"

"Whichever you want. If we're going farther away from camp, I think we should stick together so we don't get lost."

"I think you just want to see me naked." Then I was struck not only by how vain that sounded, but how ridiculous. A nubile Latina goddess was only a few dozen yards away. Anyone with a lick of sense would be heading in her direction and leaving me in the dust.

Her laughing eyes met mine. "Der-r-r-r."

I smiled. God, how could she make me feel good with one stupid word that I hadn't heard since I was a kid. But deep down inside, I knew exactly how. I was crushing on her. It was ridiculous and dangerous, and here I was doing it anyway.

With one hand, Nora dug out a pile of stinky, filthy clothes that we kept in a cloth sack in the pack. For a guy, Lucas had been neat as a pin and beyond organized. I spared a moment of grief for his family who would surely be devastated by his loss.

Then I turned my thoughts elsewhere. There would be time to dwell on what had happened after we were rescued. For now, it was more important to focus on the future. "So," I said lightly, "you're getting pretty good with just one hand."

Nora nodded. "Hopefully, I won't have to make that a permanent adjustment."

Just the thought of that made me a little sick. "You won't."

We headed toward the stream with Nora using the King-of-All-Knives to chop a very clear path. *Getting lost now...* I cringed at the thought.

When we could hear Miranda singing happily as though she was in a spa at Club Med instead of a rocky stream, we veered off to the north. Well, I'm calling it north. It was upstream and so that was my best guess.

"How about here?" Nora suggested after we'd followed the stream's winding path for a few minutes. The water flow was a little quicker here and the banks were covered in a blanket of thick, tall grass.

I whimpered a little, thinking of the joy to come. "Looks great."

Nora was wearing a T-shirt today, one that Miranda had helped her put on, and she struggled to remove it with one hand.

I reached over and grabbed the hem. "Let me."

She raised her arms over her head and I tugged it off and tossed it on the ground next to the sack of dirty clothes. I kept my hands raised, unsure of whether to offer to help with more. Nora must have seen my indecision, because, with effort, she pulled down her shorts, underwear, and kicked off her shoes and socks, leaving her wearing one last thing.

She paused.

Careful to keep my eyes on the ground, I swallowed hard and asked, "Bra?" The word came out like a croak and my cheeks heated.

"Please," Nora said softly, a concerned look on her face. "The clasp is kind of hard to unhook. If I'd known I was only going to have one hand, I would have planned better."

Nodding, I moved around behind her and licked my lips, which were salty with sweat. Even when we'd been annoyed with each other, it was Miranda who always helped her dress and undress. This was my first time. I tried not to look at all that nakedness before me, but I couldn't help it. All lean muscle and curves in just the right places, she was simply *fine*. But best of all, her skin felt like warm satin beneath my fingers.

"Rachel?"

My hands froze as a stab of guilt hit home as any latent lesbo thoughts that had been sleeping while we were hurt and desperate came roaring back to life. It was so wrong to be enjoying this, but it felt so damn right it was scary. "Yeah?"

"You don't have to be embarrassed. I can see how uncomfortable you are. Jesus, I can practically *feel* it." Her voice was soft, but passionate. "I'm not going to hit on you while you're helping me."

I made quick work of the bra and took a big step backward. How could I explain to her that the problem wasn't that I felt uncomfortable. It was that I felt too comfortable. Not to mention aroused. "Don't worry about it," I said quickly as I grabbed the soap. "You first."

She hesitated for just a second, her brow furrowed, before bending to unwrap her leg. It looked horrible, but I was thrilled to see the skin on her cut had completely closed. She left her broken hand bound.

"Here goes." She gingerly stepped into the water, then dropped down to let the water envelop her. When she moaned at the feeling, the sound rippled through me like a shockwave. "Oh, *God*, it's nice and cool."

My knees nearly turned to jelly on the spot.

"Aren't you coming in?" She reached out and I handed her the soap with trembling fingers.

I nodded, not trusting myself to speak.

Nora smiled, then turned her back to me and dunked her head under water. When she emerged, her back still to me, she began running the bar of soap over her hair. "So, I think we should stay here for a while."

She was intentionally giving me some privacy and I liked her more in that single moment than I had in any since we'd met. What...a million years ago?

"Here...as in right here?" I tossed my socks on the clothes pile. "We'll turn to prunes if the mosquitoes don't eat us alive first." The one bad thing about having a water source nearby was that the bugs were even thicker than usual. And that was saying something. But, at least for the moment, a moderate breeze kept them at bay.

"No, here as in our camp. We've finally got water. We've got food that will last a while and the deeper we go into the jungle, the farther away we move from the crash site. We could keep walking, but I think our best chance to be found is to stay put."

"From your lips to God's ears. Having a place as a home base where we can hunt for fruit has to be easier than it was to look up the entire time we walked down that damned mountain. And I'm sure not anxious to climb the next one."

The rest of my clothes, Lucas's clothes, actually, hit the pile and I stepped into the water only a couple of feet from Nora. My mouth dropped open. Drinking it was not the same as dropping down into it. "Sweet Jesus on Sunday, it's fantastic."

Nora laughed, waited a beat, and then turned around to see me submerged to just above my breasts. I wasn't shy, but I appreciated her giving me a little privacy. Then my gaze dropped from her face and my heart started to pound. We were almost the same height, but the water hit her just below the nipple line. How could God be so kind and yet so cruel in the very same moment?

She was, I mentally noted without wanting to, on the big end of a B-cup, and her nipples were large, and the lightest, most delicate pink color I'd ever seen. Like baby roses.

Nora passed me the soap and started to scrub her hair, obviously having trouble getting the suds everywhere with just one hand.

"You want help?" I asked. I'm nothing if not a glutton for punishment. And to be honest, ever since she'd given me that shoulder rub, I'd been itching to touch her in return.

Relief swept over her face. "I would love it. Thank you. My arm gets really tired by the end of the day."

I frowned. I'd never thought about that. Ever since she'd beat her fever, and despite how much blood she'd lost, she'd been determined to pull a load equal to Miranda and me. Well, sometimes equal isn't fair. And I resolved to do more to help her whether she liked it or not. "Then get ready for the best hair washing you've ever had."

Her delighted smile got my heart tripping even faster. Being around Nora was a great substitute for aerobics.

I dug my fingers into her hair and worked the suds from her scalp to the tips of every strand. I took my time about it, massaging her scalp, chatting aimlessly, and willing her to just feel good. Something that was completely foreign in this jungle.

My fingers were actually getting tired by the time I said, "Time to rinse."

She dunked her head several times, letting nearly a week's worth of grime and sweat be swept away with the current. When she finally came up for air, even wet, her hair looked several shades lighter and her gaze had taken on a happy twinkle.

"Marry me," she exclaimed. Water streamed down her face as she gazed at me with such devotion that I couldn't help but laugh. I hadn't seen adoring puppy dog eyes like that since I was a freshman in high school and let my boyfriend get to second base.

I nodded indulgently. "Right. I'll keep your offer in mind."

"Good. Your turn?"

I actually started to salivate. "I thought your hand was tired."

She shrugged amiably and I smiled at her extreme farmer's tan. "It was. But since you did all that work, it's had a chance to rest." She made a spinning motion with her index finger. "Turn please."

I did and she proceeded to wash my hair with every bit as much loving attention as I'd paid hers. She was careful to avoid the cut in the front of my hairline, but it had never been a bad one and had long since scabbed over. "This is nice," I sighed. It was more than nice. It was heaven. "I *adore* having my hair washed."

She scrubbed behind my ears. "Reece must be an expert after all these years."

"Not really." I let my head loll to one side to give her better access. "He'd always do it if I asked him, but when he did, he was quick and efficient. And I prefer sl-o-o-o-w and steady."

She clucked her tongue. "A premature...shampooer?"

I rolled my eyes, but chuckled anyway.

"Pity."

When I was finished rinsing my hair, we soaped our own bodies from face to toe. The clothes were a bit harder to deal with, but if those chicks from *Little House on the Prairie* could do it, so could we. We spread each garment, along with the now clean bandages, out on the warm grass to dry, then, laughing like a couple of teenagers, jumped back into the water. Our chores were done and we reveled in our ability to just sit there, side-by-side, talking, and feeling safe for the first time in forever, and watching a gorgeous orange sun start to sink over the tree line.

I've had my share of wonderful moments, but only a few so precious, so magical, that time stood still and I completely lost myself in happiness. They were moments that I wanted to sink into and never leave. Moments that made me believe in pure perfection and consider all over again that there was too much natural beauty on this earth for it to all be accidental. Moments where every ounce of pain I've ever felt paled in comparison to the sweet joy I was experiencing simply because they had no choice.

I know it sounds crazy, especially since we were here, stranded in this cruel, beautiful place, but *this* was one of those moments.

Then Nora said something funny and stuck her tongue out at me, and the bottom of my world dropped out from beneath me and I understood something to the very core of my being. My perfect moment wasn't because of the breeze, or water, or fading sunshine. It was *her*. It was her easy laugh and good company. It was her elusive dimples and that damned, lopsided grin that almost always took me right along with it to whatever crazy place it lived.

It was how we fit together. It was *us*.

Everything seemed so clear to me in that second that I closed my eyes so I wouldn't see it. I just had to wait for the moment to slip away. Then everything would be normal again and my crush wouldn't be slipping into something deeper and far more dangerous.

Waiting... Still waiting...

"Penny for your thoughts?"

Shake it off. "I-I…"

"You're not still sick to your stomach, are you?" The warm concern in her voice only made her more compelling. *Damn her.*

"I… Maybe a little." It wasn't a complete lie. I did feel queasy.

"Our canteens will be full from now on so we won't have to drink too much at once."

My throat closed, so I just nodded and wondered what I was going to do.

After a long time, Nora groaned. "I hate to say this, but I think we should head back to camp before it gets dark. By now, Miranda probably thinks we've been eaten by piranhas."

My eyes widened. "Are there piranhas in here?" Cautiously, I peered into the water without moving a muscle. I'd seen a horror movie about piranhas when I was a kid. In the low-budget flick, a hapless cow wandered into infested waters and the evil fish stripped the poor beast of every ounce of flesh in mere seconds.

"They haven't eaten you yet, have they?"

Then something sharp brushed up against my foot. I screamed and generally started to freak out. "Piranhas."

"Rachel—"

"Piranhas!" I shot to my feet. "Run!"

"Rachel!" Nora took my hand and tugged me back down. I began to splash and splutter and try to stand, but she held me firm. "That was my toenail, not a killer fish. I accidentally touched you. Sorry."

I narrowed my eyes and took a calming breath so I wouldn't have a stroke on the spot. "Accidentally?"

"I'm sorry." She glanced up at the sky. "Hey, maybe we could stay another five minutes, huh?"

I knew a peace offering when one was tossed my way. "No, no." Every bone in my body wanted to protest, but she was right. And I could always come back tomorrow during the heat of the day when it would feel the best. *Yeah*.

I sucked in a deep breath scented with bruised, wet grass and the delicate aroma of flowers. Some things about Venezuela were definitely better than others. "It's time to head back."

We dried quickly and couldn't get a layer of bug repellent on fast enough. I slapped at my thigh as I finished dressing and wriggled into my boots. "Damn mosquitoes." I began wildly slapping them. "Die, muthafuckers!"

Just then, a blast of rapid-fire Spanish echoing through the trees nearly caused me to jump out of my skin.

Nora looked to the sky as if talking to God. "*Now* what?"

Predictably, God didn't answer. So we took off running toward camp.

Nora's leg was still slowing her down, so it was me who first burst through the bushes to find our camp in utter devastation and Miranda yelling her head off. It looked like a tornado had torn through the place. The packs had been ripped open and the gear was strewn over every conceivable surface.

"What the—" The bag of clothes and soap fell limply from my hands.

Two howler monkeys, vicious looking little demons with their lips skinned back from their razor teeth, were digging through our stuff and discarding what they didn't want like trash. A third monkey with fur almost my exact hair color—yuck—had his head all the way inside one of the used food pouches as he licked up whatever juice remained.

His bony body twitched as though the mere taste was orgasmic.

Just how stupid were we? In our haste to take baths we'd forgotten to do something we did every single day to keep the predators away. Bury the food bags.

Wet hair flying wildly around her shoulders, Nora came to a stumbling stop by my side. Her eyes were huge as she took in the mayhem. "Little monsters."

My thoughts exactly.

Miranda, who was wet and as naked as the day she was born, chased one of the screeching beasts around the camp in circle after circle. It would have been comical if, oh hell, it *was* comical. "Stop them," she cried. "They're stealing our food!"

Okay, it wasn't so funny anymore.

The blood drained from Nora's face quicker than I would have believed possible, and she joined the chase, going after a particularly loud monkey whose hairy arms overflowed with our food pouches.

I picked up a rock and whaled it at the little devil, missing it by inches. "Dammit." For the first time in my life I was sorry that I'd lied to my gym teacher and told her I couldn't participate in sports because I had my period. Every day.

Miranda whirled around to glare at me. "What are you doing?"

"They're stealing our food," I reminded her needlessly as I began rooting around for another rock. I wasn't willing to chase the monkeys like they were. What was I going to do if I caught one? Negotiate? "I'm gonna kill the stinky bastards from afar. That's what I'm gonna do!" I kicked at one who nearly ran over my feet to escape into the jungle, but didn't come close to touching him.

"She had a baby on her back!" Miranda screamed as she dove for one of the packs and threw her lithe body over it to protect it and whatever food remained.

Her wild move scared the remaining marauders back into the trees where they howled and generally went apeshit, or monkeyshit as the case happened to be, until they grew bored and disappeared.

Okay, I hadn't seen the baby. I just thought the nasty thief was a hunchback. Then I tripped over an empty canteen and saw red all over again. "I wouldn't care if Mother Teresa and the Pope were *both* on that damn monkey's back!" I shouted, too furious to give a crap about PETA or Hell at the moment.

Miranda gasped, but quickly gave in to my prompting and moved aside as I dug through the few remaining items in the pack beneath her. "Jesus H. Christ. How did they manage to steal?" Horrified, I turned the pack upside down, "almost *all* the food? They must have made more than one trip. They probably won't even be able to open them!"

Nora let out a frustrated yell that shook the leaves on the trees and put Tarzan to shame.

My eyes closed in fury. Why was this happening to us! I turned to Miranda with my hands on my hips. "Where are your clothes?"

She blew a wet strand of hair from her eyes. "I forgot a towel so I came back to camp to get one."

"You had better go back and get them, unless you want the monkeys to steal those too." I wanted to snap at her, but she couldn't help it if she had the bleeding heart of a teenager.

Miranda blinked slowly and crossed camp, yelping every time she stepped on something sharp. Which was every single step. Then she disappeared.

My emotions were still as scattered as our camping gear and I wanted to sit down and cry. So I did.

Nora dropped down next me.

After a good long sob, one that had been building since the crash, I sniffed a few times. "Aren't you going to tell me not to cry?" She was being suspiciously quiet. "That everything will be all right?"

Looking a little dazed at the recent turn of events, she shook her head. "Nope. We're…We're in big trouble."

I wiped at the tears that clung to my lashes. "What are we going to do, Nora?"

She sighed and rubbed her temples as she thought. "What do monkeys eat?"

What kind of stupid question was that? "*Now* they eat chicken chow mein or salmon and couscous!"

She ignored my sarcasm. "I think they eat fruit. That means there are fruit trees nearby. There has to be." She turned and gazed into my eyes as she took my hand in hers. "And we'll find them."

I nodded, feeling a little better. We had no other choice but to find food, so we would make it happen. "I can finally take a crack at that fishing gear too. God knows we have enough bugs around here to bait the hook."

Nora leaned to the side and rested her head against mine, mingling our damp hair. I could feel her chuckle tiredly.

"What?"

"Did you see that red monkey who looked just like you?"

I peeled my skin back from my teeth and let out a screech of my own.

Chapter 12

Three days and three painfully shrunken stomachs later, Nora was proven right. We found a mango tree about ten minutes from our camp, and then only hours later, a banana tree even closer. Both were laden with ripe fruit.

Letting the sticky, sweet juice drip off our chins, we gorged ourselves and celebrated cheating death one more time. Our luck would surely run out. But it wouldn't be today.

Back at camp Miranda and I filled one of the packs with fruit while Nora went to top off the canteens. Earlier in the day my hands had trembled from gnawing hunger the likes of which I'd never known.

Now, after several pieces of juicy, sweet fruit that only remotely resembled the tasteless stuff in my local supermarket, they were shaking again. God only knew what the unexpected sugar rush was doing to my body.

Each one of Miranda's ribs and Nora's collarbone was starkly showing, and for once, I wasn't jealous.

"Rachel?"

Surprised, I looked up from my work. Miranda had taken to calling me and Nora Mama and Papa as some sort of weird running joke that only she and Nora really understood. She hadn't called me Rachel in days.

"Yeah?" I replied, trying to hide my worry. Something in her face chilled me to the bone.

"No one's coming for us, are they?"

I refocused on the pack, making sure I tied the top shut with a knot even a sailor would have trouble undoing. I was determined to thwart our monkey enemies, should they decide to attack again. I also tried to remember how to breathe. Miranda was the chipper, optimistic one of the group. If *she* started to doubt things…

"Of course they are," I said a little gruffly. "They just haven't found us yet."

"It's been nine days."

"I know."

"Someone should have missed us by now."

I exhaled deeply, not knowing what to say. She was right. "That's good. That means they're looking."

"That's not what that means." Her eyes filled with tears. "We have fire every day it doesn't pour rain. They should be able to see us. Something is wrong."

"C'mon, hon." I stood, my hand moving to the small of my aching back, and motioned for her to sit down on our well-used log. When she was comfortable, I straddled the log to face her. I petted her midnight black hair, unsure of how it happened, but I loved this pain-in-the-ass like my own kid sister. "It's going to be okay."

"But—"

"It is."

Her hands shaped fists. "No one is going to rescue us!"

As quiet as a ghost, Nora came up behind her and captured my gaze over Miranda's head. "I hate to say it, but I think she's right, Rache."

I suddenly felt like an elephant had plopped down square in the center of my chest.

Nora's words seemed to be the last straw, because Miranda stopped trying to hold back her tears and just let them fall.

Nora took a step closer and laid a comforting hand on Miranda's shoulder, giving it an affectionate squeeze. My eyes were drawn to Nora's long fingers and I recalled the manicure I'd admired when we first met. Now, several of her nails were torn and ragged and they were all filthy from her recent trip to cut and collect firewood with Miranda. I promised myself I would help her clean them before bed.

Nora drew in a deep breath. "The first thing we have to do is eat enough to get some energy back, which means we have to stay here for a few more days."

She bent and kissed the top of Miranda's head, all the while her eyes drilling into mine. "And then—"

I could feel our joined wills mingle and determination built within me like lava in a volcano looking for a place to blow. "And then…" I smiled resolutely. "We're going to rescue *ourselves*."

"We can't abandon the stream," I argued. "It took us forever to find and with only two canteens we can't risk going days before we find another one." It had been three days since the monkeys had stolen all but our last two meals, twelve days since the accident left us marooned.

But our bellies were full of fresh fruit and clean water, and our wounds, all except for Nora's hand, which needed a real doctor in any case, had healed. We felt better than we had since before the crash.

If we were going to make a move, tomorrow was the day.

Our fire crackled contently, sending the occasional spark into the night sky. No rain today and the stars above hinted there wouldn't be any tonight.

Nora carefully added a heavy armload of thick sticks to the fire so it would burn until dawn. "The stream will eventually lead to a river, and rivers mean towns."

"But if we do that, we'll stay between the mountains, in the lower lands." Miranda used her hands when she spoke and her eyes looked like black mirrors as they reflected the orange flames. "It could be days or weeks before we come to a town. This is almost an empty part of my country. If we climb another mountain we will be able to see for miles and maybe see a small village or road."

"Miranda," I began, dread lifting the hair on the back of my neck. Her plan was *so* dangerous and it flew in the face of everything we'd tried so far. Then again, everything we'd tried so far had failed with flying colors. "Okay, let's say we climb up one of these mountains, which will suck, by the way, and at some point we're high enough to see a road or village, how do we get to it? What's to stop us from getting lost along the way? The van was only a few hundred feet away from where we were and we never made it there."

Miranda scrubbed her face. "I...I don't know. But the land is more open up there. No one will ever see us down here under all these trees."

"How about we sleep on it and vote in the morning?" Nora suggested, a yawn interrupting her. "We're not going anyplace tonight."

Miranda looked shocked. "*I* get a vote?"

I smiled wryly as I lifted up one of the mosquito nets and scrambled underneath. "You've always had a vote."

Miranda looked at Nora in question and she nodded while I smacked at a bug that snuck in under the net with me. "We were just afraid to tell you about it," I added.

Chapter 13

Another seven, torturously hard days passed, but we refused to deviate from the plan we'd agreed upon. My plan. Follow the water until we find civilization. The going was slower than slow, and at points, the underbrush alongside the stream was so thick we had to walk directly in the water. But even then, our trek was often so winding that there were days we were left to wonder if we'd made any real progress at all.

The good news was that we spotted fruit trees along our route almost every day. So we were able to replenish our food supply as we went. The bad news was, and there was a lot of it, we hadn't caught a single fish, a particularly virulent rainstorm had ruined our remaining toilet paper, and the land we traveled, just between the mountains, was so humid and the breeze so stagnant, it was as though we were hiking through a steam room.

Somehow, even living on fruit alone, Nora didn't seem to decline at the same startling pace Miranda and I had, which told me in yet another way just how hurt she'd been immediately following the accident. She'd clearly lost too much weight, but her eyes were now consistently bright and had the same interested alertness they had back in Caracas.

My energy was seriously flagging, but I no longer felt like I was going to have a stroke and a heart attack after a long day of slogging through the jungle. I was down to having just one of those now.

Miranda, however, had problems of her own. Nora and I constantly pestered her to eat, but she seemed to have the metabolism of three men and the weight fell from her the way snow melted off the roof on the first warm day of spring.

And while blisters peppered all our feet, the skin on Miranda's was peeling off in small sheets. They reminded me of an old film I saw in junior high school that showed soldiers in Vietnam on a combat mission. Trench foot had set in.

Miranda sat down next to our small fire. Thunder boomed in the distance and all three of us booed and hissed at it as though it was a dastardly villain gracing an old-time movie screen.

Nora didn't have any popcorn to throw, so she tossed her banana peel at the sky instead. Then she pointed at Miranda's feet. "You'd better dry those out."

Miranda made a face, but didn't complain as she shucked her shoes, then socks, and propped her feet up closer to the flames. I couldn't think of anything much worse than roasting your feet on an already sticky evening, and I gave her a sympathetic look as I adjusted the mosquito netting around us.

We should have been back at Miranda's house days ago. We *knew* someone was looking for us by now. To make us feel even worse, we'd heard a helicopter the afternoon before, but hadn't made camp, so we'd had no fire to use as a signal. We screamed our fool heads off until our throats were raw. And we jumped around like idiots, waving anything we could get our hands on, but the chopper just flew away. After that, we'd seriously considered trying to burn the entire jungle down as a way to get someone's attention, but the recent rains had everything too wet. Even getting enough wood for a fire today had been close to impossible.

"Time for dinner?" I said in a cheerful voice that was entirely forced.

"I'm not hungry," Miranda grumbled, sticking her hand outside the mosquito net, picking up a rock, and tossing it into the gurgling stream about twenty feet away. The stone disappeared into the darkness but I could hear the dull *ker-plunk* as it landed.

"Me neither," Nora added.

Sometimes they were two rotten peas in a pod.

"Fine. I'll bet you can't guess what I'll be dining on tonight." I nudged Miranda with my shoulder. "Try. Go on. Go on. I dare you."

She gave me a suspicious look. "Bananas and mangos?" she finally said, knowing full well it was the only thing we'd had for days and days.

"Ha. Shows what you know." I smiled triumphantly. "I'm having mangos and bananas."

She rolled her eyes but smiled, just a tiny bit, anyway.

We ate in silence and I was happy to see Nora and Miranda at least share a mango. When we were finished I rinsed my hands and face. "Nora, how about I braid your hair for the night?" I'd done Miranda's earlier and it still looked pretty darn good, if I do say so myself.

Even with just the firelight, I could see her expression brighten. "Sure."

"My comb is in the side pocket of my pack," Miranda said absently as she moved under the second mosquito net, which was on the other side of the fire, her book in her hand. She'd finished the darn thing after the second day in the jungle, but it wasn't as though there was anything else to do.

I motioned for Nora to sit on the ground in front of me and I leaned my back against the tree that held one of the hammocks. We'd taken to piling large leaves on the ground of our campsite. They weren't much padding for the hard ground, but they kept our bottoms from getting soaked on the wet grass and dirt.

Wordlessly, Nora passed me the comb over her shoulder. She'd washed her hair the night before and it still felt silky soft. I combed it out gently, making sure to work out any snarls with the utmost care.

"So," Nora said under her breath. "Her feet are bad."

"I know," I whispered back. "I'm worried they're going to get infected."

She nodded. "Ours are probably next. Nobody can walk in the mud and water all day and not have something happen. It's only a matter of time."

I began plaiting her hair, taking a moment to think. What was the old Irish saying? *When God made time, he made plenty of it.* Well, time was our enemy now. It was only a matter of time before we couldn't find food. A matter of time before one of us got sick, or hurt, or completely consumed by insects. A matter of time before the searchers gave us up for dead. Time was the only thing we had too much of, but still couldn't afford.

My hands stopped and I moved my lips close to her ear. I still believed that it was foolish to abandon the stream, but even I wasn't stubborn enough to stick to a plan until it got us all killed. "Should we split up and try Miranda's plan?" I offered hesitantly. "I could head up the mountain to see what I can see."

My heart started to pound at the possibility she'd take me up on my offer. I had the worst feeling that if I said goodbye to Nora in this jungle I'd never see her again. But how could I insist we stay together when it was my bad plan that had us wandering in circles for the past week?

"We go together. That hasn't changed," she whispered quickly. "But I do think it's time we tried Miranda's idea. We mark our way as we go in case we're forced to come back. That way we won't lose the water. We can draw a map or something."

My insides were still and quivered with relief over her answer. "Why don't we stay here tomorrow, drink a ton of water, and keep Miranda off her feet?" The thought of pulling up stakes once again was more than I wanted to deal with at the moment. "We can have a fire all day in case the helicopter comes back. And if it doesn't, we can head out day after tomorrow before her feet get any worse."

It was common for Nora to take her time to answer. So I waited patiently, squinting as I tried to see off into the distance. But there was only darkness.

"Good plan," she said after a moment. "I was so smart to hire you."

I finished off the braid, enjoying the feeling of her hair against my fingers. "You didn't hire me. I'm pretty sure I would have remembered you."

"Then our HR department is smart. But I own a lot of private stock. That should count for something."

I gave her braid a tug and she yelped.

My gaze turned to Miranda. Her book was in her lap and she was looking right at us, an engrossed, slightly guarded expression on her face. She knew we were hatching something. But I had to give her credit for sitting there and waiting until we filled her in. I wouldn't have been as patient.

"Hey, Miranda?"

She cocked her head to the side as Nora spoke. "We were thinking of heading up one of these mountains day after tomorrow. How does that sound to you?"

"We're staying here tomorrow night too?"

"Yup."

She glanced at her bare feet and nearly swooned with relief. "*Bueno.*" Then she relaxed against a small outcropping of rocks and started to read.

"That was easy," I said to Nora in a hushed voice. Miranda had been especially moody the last couple of days and I was relieved to finally be doing something that made her happy.

"It should be easy. We need a day of rest in the worst way, Rachel. This being lost seven days a week is hard work."

"Tell me about it."

"Can I—" Slowly, she started to lean back against me again, giving me the opportunity to push her away. I grinned.

"Sure," I said, letting her back rest against my chest while trying to wrestle the smile from my voice.

"Just for a minute," she said quickly. "My back is sore and—"

"Shh. You're fine." It was too hot and sticky to be this close, and she could have easily used another tree for her backrest, but she felt so nice against me, I couldn't muster the will to deny her. Tentatively, I wrapped one arm around her slender waist and gave her a hug. I felt her stop breathing, but then she patted my arm and let out a long, satisfied breath as her entire body relaxed against mine.

I wanted to purr like a contented kitty. Oh, wait, I *was* purring like a kitty. But no one seemed to mind.

Miranda glanced up from her book and took in our intimate

position. But the look she gave us was one of fond indulgence instead of wariness or disgust. My, how nearly three little weeks of harrowing, death-defying experience can change things.

Nora and I were quiet for a long time, soaking in each other's company and the sounds of the night, as I mentally formulated my plan of attack for tomorrow.

First, gather fruit. Screw wasting all day trying to fish. That is never going to happen for us. Next, get enough wood to signal Cleveland. Oooh, her skin is so soft. Third, look for natural markers we can put on a map. Third-and-a-half, admit to Nora and Miranda that I know nothing about maps, and hope one of them does. She fits so nicely against me, I could stay like this forever. Last, convince Nora to take a ridiculously long bath with me so I can ogle every inch of her.

My lustful feelings for her were like a boulder rolling downhill. Slow and ominous at first, but unstoppable once they really got going.

"Tell me more about your family?" Nora said, breaking me out of my trance. "You haven't mentioned any of them since you tried to convince me Reece wasn't a douche bag."

"And that conversation was so riveting that you want more?" I chuckled. "I find that hard to believe."

"Don't. I'm easily amused. So tell me about parents, sibs, pets." She turned around and stared at me. "Oh, my God. You don't have any children do you? I should have asked. I—"

"No, no kids."

She let out a weak laugh and mopped some sweat from her brow. "Whew."

My eyebrows spiked.

"Not that kids are bad or anything," she added hastily. "But that would make this mess even harder, right?"

I frowned. "Yeah, I guess they would." Then it struck me. Maybe she asked me because...but she never mentioned... "Do *you* have any kids?"

She looked appalled. "I would have mentioned them by *now*, Rachel. What kind of shitty mother do you think I am? Jeeze."

"Well, I would have mentioned mine too!"

"I do want them someday," she said almost wistfully. "Kids, I mean. Someday it could happen."

She said it as though her chances of having a family of her own were about the same as hitting the Powerball. For the millionth time I thought of Jacob Dane and the cost of her being the *other* woman. Then, for the millionth-and-one time, I pushed the obnoxious wanker out of my mind and off an imaginary cliff.

I liked that she was talking about the future though. About a time when we'd be away from this godforsaken jungle forever. "Me too, I think," I ventured cautiously. I'd never even told Joanie this. "I wasn't sure when I was with Reece. But I think that was the situation more than anything else. With the right person…yeah. If I don't get too old first, that is."

"You're a long way from that."

"True. I'm thirty-four, so I still have time, but aging ovaries wait for no woman."

She snickered with the smugness of someone a few years younger.

"For now," I continued, "my baby is a five-year-old, fat black cat named P-Diddy Kitty. Joanie is watching her for me."

"Joanie?"

"My sister." A sliver of pain shot through my heart. *Oh, Joanie.* "She probably thinks I'm dead. She's probably going through all the stuff in my townhouse, right this very second. And my mother is helping." A dreadful thought lodged unhappily in my brain. "Please don't let them look in the nightstand next to my bed."

Nora's grin lit up the darkness and she waggled her eyebrows. Her voice dropped to a scandalously sexy register. "What's in your nightstand, you naughty minx?"

"Never you mind. Goddammit, I'm going to go home to an empty shell and no, no… relaxation apparatus," I whispered harshly. "Stop laughing. It's not funny!"

"She wouldn't sell off your stuff yet. Christ, we haven't been gone *that* long."

"You don't know Joanie. She's insanely organized and a neat freak too. Either all my stuff will be gone when I get back or she'll have cleaned and I won't be able to find anything ever again anyway. The result will be exactly the same."

"I take it you're not a neatnik like your sister?"

I snorted at the preposterous idea. "My place is clean, but lived in. Unfortunately, operating rooms are messy compared to Joanie's house. She's worn out three Dyson vacuums. Those are supposed to last forever. How she manages that with her kids, I'll never know."

"Does she look like you?"

"Not even close." I waved a dismissive hand. "She's all fresh and cute."

"And what are you?" She full turned to catch glimpses of my face by the firelight.

"Umm…" I tapped my temple as if I was thinking hard. "Covered in bug bites, patches of sunburn and blisters?"

Nora drew in a heated breath, but must have changed her mind about what she was going to say because she calmly asked, "Is your sister a redhead?"

"Nope. Curiously, I'm the only one in my family."

"It's not that curious. Did you have a redheaded mailman? Was your dad ever out of town for business…say…nine months before you were born?"

A small smile appeared. "He never seemed uncertain about my parentage, but knowing my mom, maybe he should have been." My smile melted away quickly. "He's…he died last year."

For a few seconds she stopped breathing. "I'm sorry, Rache."

Uncomfortable, I turned the tables. "What about you?"

"No redheads in the bunch."

Oh, I was close to pinching her hard. "That's not what I meant."

"Okay, you asked for it. I have eleven brothers and three sisters. We're devout Mormons."

My eyes popped wide open. "No shit?"

"Please," she scoffed. "I'm an only child. But I was born in Utah and I can name exactly…errr…two of the Osmonds."

"Smartass," I grumbled.

Her voice gentled. "Tell me about your dad?"

"Look…" I sighed. "He's just dead, okay?" Thinking about what had happened still hurt, and talking about it was worse.

Even with Joanie. His death had been completely unexpected, a heart attack while he was washing his stupid car.

I'd watched each of the seasons come and go since his death and it still felt as though it had happened yesterday. I didn't cry about it every day anymore, though, but only because I ruthlessly forced it from my mind.

"My mom died from skin cancer when I was eight," Nora said, her voice a little remote. "I don't really remember much about her though." She smiled sadly. "So it doesn't hurt too much."

I somehow doubted that last part and I ached on her behalf. At least I'd had my dad until I was an adult.

"But I'm sure it's not like that with your dad," she continued. "I didn't mean to be matter-of-fact about it. I just want to get to know you. Maybe you could tell me about your best memory of him?"

"I don't... Nora..." I rubbed my eyes, apprehension surging through me. "I don't know."

She gazed at me with soulful eyes that all but erased my will to say no. Reece and my mother had badgered me to talk about my feelings. You'd think people who knew me for as long as they had would know better. *Bleck.* Joanie, God bless her, was in even bigger denial than me and pretended that we'd been hatched and that Dad was just on a really long vacation.

But this was something different altogether. Gentle persistence. Who knew it was so devastatingly effective against me?

And for the first time since he exited my world so abruptly, I found myself talking about my dad's life instead of fixating on his death. It was hard at first. But soon I lost myself in my own words and it didn't take long for it to begin to feel...normal. Maybe even cathartic.

The story was a lengthy one of when I was a girl and just my dad and I had gone to buy our Christmas tree. The simplest errand had turned into an adventure filled with mishaps and laughter and ended with a shared cup of hot cocoa bought at a gas station that, if I closed my eyes and remembered, was still sweet on my tongue. Nora's interested comments dragged the tale out even further, and soon our conversation mingled with the predictable sound of Miranda's snores from across the fire.

By the time we were through, my cheeks felt a little stiff and I realized with a start that I'd been smiling the entire time.

Nora laughed softly. "He sounds like he was crazier than you. What a great story."

I'd been so mad at him for dying that I'd forgotten so many more important things. "He was great."

I guess I was stunned by my newest revelation—I never said I wasn't a little slow when it came to self-realization. Impulsively, I threw my arms around Nora and wrapped her in a hug so tight a beam of light couldn't have fit between us. Then I noisily bussed her cheek, doing my best not to tear up. "Thank you."

She sank into the embrace with no resistance, but I could tell that she was confused. "What for?"

For asking the right question and really listening to the answer. For caring. For being my friend. "For giving me my dad back."

Chapter 14

The next morning dawned gray and gloomy. But as always, rain or shine, I awoke starving.

The term "gathering" fruit made it sound a helluva lot easier than it really was. To keep from eating a mouthful of crawling bugs, we needed it to be fresh, which meant we had to get it out of the trees. We threw rotten fruit, sticks or rocks from the jungle floor in the hope of knocking loose what was edible. We'd tried climbing the trees early on, but after several nasty falls that hurt like hell, and one especially bad one that scared the life out of me and Nora, and left Miranda limping for two days, we all agreed we were less likely to die if we stuck to throwing.

I had my eye on a particular fat, ripe mango and was on my hundredth attempt to knock it down, when Miranda joined me.

I cinched Lucas's belt a notch tighter around my waist and glared at the offending piece of fruit. "I thought you were supposed to be resting your feet," I said absently as I circled my prey, my eyes never leaving my target.

"I've been doing that all morning. If I sit there any longer, I'll go mad." She picked up a mango to throw, then realized it was half squashed and crawling with ants, and dropped it like a hot potato. "Ugh."

I took aim. "Where's Papa?"

"Trying to catch fish."

"Ahh…" Now the occasional cursing from the stream made sense. "*Are* there fish in Venezuela?"

"Three weeks ago, I would have said yes."

I launched my mango and, miraculously, hit the right branch, shaking the prized fruit free. "Yes!"

Miranda scuttled sideways, and caught it as it fell. She held it out to me, but I shook my head. "I've already eaten. You take it."

She glanced away. "I'm not hungry."

Worried, I studied her carefully. We were always hungry and her most of all. "Hon, are you sick?" I stepped over to her and ran my hands down her slender arms. She was actually shaking. "You haven't been yourself for the last couple of days." It had been a bit longer than that, but sending her on a guilt trip wasn't my intention.

Her chin quivered. "Maybe something is wrong with me."

When she didn't elaborate I prompted her. "Can you, um… be more specific?"

Looking bereft, she whispered, "I think I'm sick or… pregnant."

Somewhere Nora's ears were bleeding.

"What?" I screeched, scaring the birds in Colombia from their roosts. "Why do you think that?" Then I cleared my throat and lowered my voice to something resembling normal. "Why do you think that?" I repeated. Hadn't we had this conversation back at the hotel?

"I haven't…" She mumbled something in Spanish and then pointed at her crotch. "You know…not since we have been stuck here."

Aghast, I gawked. "You haven't had sex since you've been out here? I should hope not!"

She gave me an annoyed look. "No, I haven't…" Her next gesture made it look like she was having a baby. But I got the idea anyway.

"You mean you haven't had your menstrual cycle?" I hated calling it that. Clinical terms always sound so nasty to me. But I wasn't sure she'd know what I meant if said "a dreaded visit from Aunt Flo."

"That's it." She sighed, clearly pleased I'd finally caught on. "Yes. I mean, no. I haven't had that."

My eyes drilled into hers. "And that's the only reason you think you're pregnant?"

"Isn't it the biggest sign?"

She had me there. "I haven't had my cycle since I've been here either. And you don't want to know how long my dry spell has lasted. I *know* I'm not pregnant."

A glimmer of hope entered her eyes.

"I don't know for sure, but I'd bet Nora's answer will be the same as mine. Our bodies have been through a lot, Miranda. It's not unusual to miss your period under conditions like this, especially when you're not eating enough. It doesn't mean that you're ill or pregnant."

"No?"

I smiled gently. "No, sweetie. Were you and Paulo careful when you...?" Now, I had a great hand gesture for this that nobody could mistake, one that got my mouth washed out with soap when I was twelve-years-old, even though I hadn't said a word.

She nodded decisively. "Yes. Always." Her full lips curled into a wry grin. "Well, except for this time when we were rudely interrupted in the barn before anything could really happen."

A little light-headed with relief, I let out a shaky, but thankful breath. "Don't remind me." The fact that I'd been aroused by watching them now disgusted me as much as if I'd accidentally walked in on Joanie and her husband. I shivered inwardly. "Then I'm sure it's nothing to worry about."

"You really think so?" She was begging for reassurance and I was happy to give it. Now I understood the source of her bad mood over the past few days. Not that I could blame her.

I'd had a similar scare in my late teens, and did what any red-blooded girl does. I cried until my eyes were sore, considered jumping off the roof of my parents' house, made myself nauseous from worry, and generally twisted myself into more knots than a pretzel before I got brave enough to take a pregnancy test. But the Fates weren't done messing with me for evilly fooling around with my boyfriend in his parents' Ford Escort. I started my cycle while standing in the check-out line of Walgreens just as I bought a dozen expensive pregnancy tests that I was too embarrassed to return.

"Really," I said. "Besides, it's a blessing. Who wants to have her period out here? We'd have to sit in the river for days or something. It'd be torture and we'd prune."

I watched as the color slowly returned to her cheeks.

"Now, for God's sake, go eat," I ordered as I pointed toward camp. "I can practically see through you."

She hugged the mango to her and eyed me. "You too."

I snorted. "Yeah, right. Go on. I have more fruit to murder."

Miranda bounded back to camp, looking happier than I'd seen her in days. Poor thing, I wished she'd come to Nora or me sooner, but I was still pleased she'd come to one of us at all.

If my boss at the radio station knew what a bonding catalyst near-starvation was, he'd ban lunch hours and donuts in the conference room forever.

I picked up a rock this time, and tossed it up and down a few times in my hand as I craned my neck to hunt for a new victim.

Nora, who had come running the second I'd raised my voice, but had kept her distance in the bushes while I'd talked with Miranda, strolled over once I was alone. "That was pretty good, Mama." She said that last word in an uncanny imitation of Miranda's light accent.

"Don't you start with that, too. I already feel like Methuselah next to her."

"Well, you don't look it." She held up a pretty white blossom I hadn't seen during our travels, and then neatly threaded it behind my ear. "To replace the one you lost in the accident."

"Th-thanks," I stammered and blushed like a besotted teenager. I'm such a girl sometimes.

She held my gaze for a long second before her face broke into a radiant smile. "My pleasure." Then, whistling to herself, she walked back toward the stream. No, I mentally corrected myself, it wasn't a walk. It was more like a strut. Damn her for being able to pull it off.

I removed the flower from my hair and sniffed its delicate fragrance, feeling hopelessly, and irretrievably smitten as I watched her go. "Rachel Michaels," I murmured to myself, "what have you gotten yourself into?"

That night it rained. And I'm not talking spring showers. I'm talking time-to-build-an-ark-and-find-an-animal-mate kind of rain. Because things weren't awful enough, sometime just before dawn, the stream rose at an alarming rate and sent our little camp into a state of utter chaos. From the corner of my eye, I saw one of our packs begin to float.

Already soaked to the bone because our rainflies were no match for the downpour, we all began to chase the pack, but it was no use. It, along with anything else we couldn't grab in our mad dash, disappeared into inky water and darkness in the blink of an eye.

Lightning flashed, illuminating our panicky faces and suddenly I wasn't afraid anymore. I was *pissed*.

"Fine, God. I can take a hint. Let's fucking go!" I yelled over the deluge, pushing a shock of drenched hair from my face. "Let's start up the mountain right this *goddamned minute*."

There really was no reason to wait. The mountains were tall in some spots, but this particular ridgeline looked manageable and wasn't nearly as steep as the cliff we'd tumbled down. It would be slow going, like every single dismal step we'd taken since the crash, but by the time morning rolled around and we could see more than a foot in front of our faces, we could be well up the face. Or lost even worse than we were now. One of the two.

We didn't even have a map to worry about because we'd drawn the one to use tomorrow inside the cover of Miranda's book, which had been in the pack that just washed downstream.

So this was a good idea. Right?

Lips pressed together tight in misery and frustration, Nora was muddy up to her waist. "Let's do it." And she began the arduous task of trying to untie the wet rope that held up our hammocks while Miranda filled our last canteen.

Then both of them unceremoniously stuck their faces into

the muddy water that was now more like a river and drank their fill.

We walked for hour after hour. The higher we went, the more the rain began to taper off. By the time we could feel a noticeable drop in temperature, dawn had broken, and the storm had blown over. Bright sunshine lit up the vivid green forest around us, making the water droplets on the leaves sparkle like millions of tiny diamonds. It even smelled different up here, as new, but equally impenetrable plants surrounded us.

I took a good look at my companions and my heart twisted. Two sets of sunken, red-rimmed eyes gazed back at me. Each head of hair was stringy and matted and their bones stood out in vivid relief against their tanned, filthy skin.

For the first time, I truly wondered whether we'd have been better off perishing in the crash. I knew I should be shocked by what I was thinking, but I was just too depressed to care. This slow, cruel disintegration of our bodies and minds was more than I could bear.

Nora glanced around. "We need to find a place where the trees aren't so thick," she said tiredly. "I can only see ten feet away." She rubbed her eyes with one palm. "And not very well at that."

Hands on slim hips, Miranda considered one of the very tall, heavily branched trees in front of her and I could practically see the gears turning in her mind.

"Miranda?" I said warily.

"Hmm?"

I waggled my finger at her. "Don't even think about it."

"Oh, God," Nora groaned. "Not this again."

"Wha-a-a-t?" Miranda said innocently, batting her eyes.

"No. No. No," I said firmly. "Last time you tried to climb you almost ended up with a broken tailbone."

Nora nodded grimly. "It's too dangerous. Let's find a more open spot."

"We've been trying to find an open spot for days," Miranda reminded us as she circled the tree like a dog trying to find a good spot to pee. "If there are more open spots, we can't find them. This isn't a mango tree. I can climb this one. I grew up with these trees in my backyard."

Miserable from my hot, damp clothes that clung to me like a saggy second skin and made me itch, I shrugged out of our remaining backpack with a loud groan. It hit the damp ground with a dull splat. "No."

Miranda lifted an eyebrow at me. "It's the best answer. Why climb higher if I can see something from here?" We'd had this argument many times, but this time Miranda had a stubborn set to her jaw that I hadn't seen in days and always meant trouble. *Oh, boy.*

Nora opened her mouth to stop her, but I gently grabbed her arm. "Don't bother. We can't stop her."

The muscles in her jaw stood out. "The hell we can't. I can break her skinny neck. That's what I can do!"

"You could *try*," Miranda growled back.

I shook my head. If they weren't getting along like BFFs from grade school, they hated each other. "Nora—"

"I umm…I need a hand," Miranda muttered, clearly unhappy about having to ask. She dried her moist hands on her T-shirt. "Just to the first branch."

"No," Nora said. But I could see that it was because she was worried. She was also exhausted and her nerves were frayed. All our nerves were frayed, and a big part of that was my fault.

In my spat of childish rage, I'd been too hasty to leave the flooded lowlands. And now we were all paying the price. *I am a flippin' idiot.* "So now we're supposed to help you get killed?" I asked. But there was no real sting in my words.

"You don't have to help me," Miranda said calmly. "But it will only take longer if I have to build a ladder."

She smiled at me, full of affection, trust and pleading and I began to cave. This was why P-Diddy Kitty needed to lose five pounds.

Nora looked to the sky in silent appeal, then shook her head. "Here." She got on her knees in front of the tree. "You can step on my back." She repositioned herself. "*Carefully*."

Using Nora's body as a stepping stool, Miranda scaled the tree slowly, working her way higher and higher, and weaving between the branches and thick leaves in surprisingly monkey-like fashion. Soon, she was nearly out of sight.

Worry brewed in my belly like stale coffee.

Nora looked up and sighed, then focused on her tattered bandages. We'd taken off the sticks that held her fingers straight days ago, but kept them bound together as best we could. Two of the digits, including her thumb, looked fine. But the other two either hadn't healed at all or hadn't healed correctly. They were still twisted at gruesome angles. And short of re-breaking them and snapping them straight, something I wouldn't do for a million dollars, we just had to wait and hope a doctor could repair the damage.

She gently cleared her throat to capture my attention. "Can you help me rewrap my hand?"

I swallowed back the bit of bile that always stung my tongue when I considered her poor fingers for too long. "Sure." I began to unwind the cloth by rote.

"Are you okay, Rachel?"

I took a breath to lie, then decided not to bother. "I'm not even close."

Nora frowned. "But I've been marking our way with the knife. I think we can make it back to the stream when our water runs out." She held up our well-used knife, its blade dulled from almost nonstop use. "Trade you for the pack?"

Even with the pack sitting on the ground, my shoulders ached. Then again, Nora's good hand had to be even more tired. She'd become our default weed-whacker. "Of course. You should have said something sooner." I knew she'd waited until she was in pain to ask.

Miranda's voice suddenly boomed from overhead. "I see something."

My head snapped up and my heart leapt into my throat.

"Never mind. Just more monkeys."

I made a face and willed my thundering heartbeat to slow. "More of those fuckin' flea-bitten monkeys. Whoopee."

"You know, I used to think those things were cute. When I saw them in the zoo, that is. Now I hate the furry little bastards."

I'd learned the hard way that they were called howler monkeys for a reason. They carried on endlessly and the cacophony of sounds was enough to drive an insane person crazy. A few of them lived in the trees near the camp we'd had the longest, and we'd named them. Regis Philbin was the most annoying of the bunch and never shut up. Then there was a skinny, mean one we called Victoria "Posh Spice" Beckham out of pure female jealousy and spite.

Resigned, I took a cigarette from Lucas's pack and slid it between my lips. Thus far I'd resisted their demon lure. But this morning, no matter how hard I tried, I couldn't convince myself that I should be denied this small pleasure. What were they going to do? Give me bad breath? Been there, done that. Kill me? Maybe. But not before the jungle did. So, ha.

"Me too?"

"Sure," I muttered, my voice high with surprise. I didn't particularly like this unexpected turn of events. Smoking was a nasty habit, after all. "Since when do you smoke?"

Fatigue lines were etched into Nora's dirt-caked forehead. "I'm starting today." She gave me a small, lopsided grin that told me she felt just as down. And that caused something inside me to snap.

My lower lip began to tremble, and suddenly there wasn't enough air.

Hold it together, Rachel. Just for one more day. Okay, one more hour. One more minute, even. Fake that you're not falling apart. Fail. Repeat as necessary.

Nora's concerned, almost desperate gaze drew me in. "Don't give up now. Just don't. If you go to pieces, I'm going to follow you, Rachel."

We had tried and tried, but nothing we did worked. *Nothing.* We weren't going to make it and I couldn't do this any more. "But—"

"Don't!" she said so fiercely that my mouth snapped shut. "I won't give up on you and you won't give up on me. That was our deal. You promised!"

"I did?"

"Right after the crash."

Bewildered, I squinted as I tried to remember. That day seemed like ages ago. "I promised?"

Her chest heaved and she looked like she was going to lose it. "You stared me right in the eye and promised."

Look at her. Is she crying? I must have promised. "Okay, okay." On the very edge of being distraught, I began digging for a lighter, throwing anything else out of my way with unsuppressed rage. "I keep my promises."

"Smoke?" Miranda yelled down.

"The answer is the same as before," I shouted up. "No." A quick flick of the lighter and I was inhaling a deep, beautiful breath of poison. I felt like I was going to puke and my heart began to race. *God, how I've missed you.* "You can't have one, Miranda."

Nora yelped and darted away. "Look out!"

A small branch came hurtling down from the sky and hit me in the head. Either the howler monkeys were in full revolt or it was Miranda who had just beaned me. Rubbing the sore spot, I craned my neck. "What the hell? Now I'm going to let Nora break your neck!"

"I don't *want* to smoke. I *see* smoke!" Miranda crowed, an excited smile transforming her face into the picture of youthful beauty. In fact, her entire body was suddenly so filled with energy, it was quaking. She pointed and screamed in delight. "And a few houses."

My mouth opened and closed a few times in astonishment. "F-f-for real, kiddo?"

"For real!"

Thank you, God! I put my hand against a tree trunk to help keep me upright, careful not to shake it. The last time I'd accidently done that, an enormous snake had dropped from a branch and nearly landed on top of me. I have no doubt that I'm now sterile from the fright.

Nora closed her eyes before wrapping me in the strongest one-armed hug known to man. Or woman. Then she snatched the cigarette from my lips and viciously stomped it out. "We're gonna be okay, Rache," she said softly, her words brimming with emotion.

Tears stung my eyes and a feeling so alien it felt exotic rushed over me, leaving me spent. Hope. I blinked a few times and rubbed my eyes with the back of my hand.

Nora pecked my cheek before she stepped back and cupped her hand around her mouth to shout up to Miranda. "How far?"

"I can't tell. But not too far." She began to climb down far too quickly for my comfort and ended up sending a shower of warm water droplets down on us so fierce that it felt like it was raining again. Not that I could blame her excitement.

We finally had a chance and we were all eager to grab hold of it and hold on for dear life. Literally.

Far is a relative term, especially when there is a nearly impassable wall of bushes, trees, rocks and vines between you and your target. And so it took us until late afternoon to hack our way to a place where we finally caught sight of several thin tendrils of smoke snaking through the trees.

Another hour and several more trips into the trees to make certain we were still heading in the right direction, and we were there. Wherever "there" was. Calling it a town, or even a village, would be a grand exaggeration.

Cautiously, we peered through a stand of lush palms with leaves that were taller then we were.

"Those aren't houses," I told Miranda, wiping the dripping sweat from my forehead with a worn blue bandana. When I was finished, I stuffed the cloth into my back pocket. "They're huts."

About six huts were clustered in the center of a small meadow that held a few fruit and shade trees. Several donkeys munched on tall grass in a large, crudely fenced pen, and three mangy dogs dashed between the huts in an apparent game of chase. Rusty farming equipment was piled up next to a rickety shed, but I couldn't see a vegetable garden or crop of any kind.

There were no wires, satellite dishes, or even wells in sight. This was primitive living, though I did see what I hoped were two outhouses about fifty feet behind the huts. Funny how luxurious even those seemed after weeks of taking care of business in bushes filled with insects the size of playing cards and plants that, if I brushed against them just right, caused my butt to break out in hives. If these folks had toilet paper, I was positively going to die.

"Who cares what their houses look like?" Nora murmured. "These people are our ticket home. They didn't make those farming tools. They bought those someplace, and that means civilization."

Miranda hunkered down so close to me that our shoulders were touching. Eyes bright with terror flicked my way. "I think they're Indians. But they could be drug farmers." The blood drained from her face. "If they are, we should turn around right now." She backed up a step. "Mama warned me about these men."

"Are you crazy? We're not leaving," I said, shaken by her sudden paleness. I didn't care whose hideout this was. "Here. Sit down before you pass out."

"Rachel," she answered gravely. "I do not think you understand. Drug farmers will not help us. They will either shoot us on sight, or rape us and then shoot us."

My mouth went dry. But who did she think she was talking to? I watched the news. Hell, I'd grown up on *Miami Vice*. I knew how bad bad guys could be. And during any other time in my life, the mere chance of running into one of them would have been more than enough incentive to send me bolting in the opposite direction.

But not freakin' today!

"I'll go check them out," I announced, my chest puffed out, my voice full of stupid bravado. I gripped the knife until my knuckles were white. If Nora could face the unknown with her head held high—and more importantly, without soiling herself—so could I.

"Wait." Nora grabbed me by the collar of my shirt before I could leave. "Look." She pointed. "Over there."

A heavyset woman with skin several shades darker than Miranda's exited one of the huts carrying a large woven basket full of laundry. The scent of something cooking wafted out the door with her and I nearly screamed in rapture.

The woman wore flat sandals that made a soft clacking sound with her every step, a brown headscarf over her silver-streaked hair, and a red, many-times-patched, rough-hewn skirt. If these were drug lords, they sucked at their job.

A handful of small, barefoot children clustered around the woman like happy puppies before laughing and darting off in several different directions, all out of sight. After a few seconds, another woman, much younger, a daughter maybe, joined the bigger woman and they began walking to a clothesline strung between two trees, chattering away in rapid Spanish as they moved.

Nora visibly relaxed. "It's just a family doing laundry, not a band of marauding killers."

The color returned to Miranda's cheeks and she stuck out her palm and spoke quietly. "Give me all your money and anything else of value. I'll talk to them and get one of them to take us to the nearest town or call for help."

I didn't have a dime on me, but Nora had a money clip in her pocket when we'd crashed and Lucas had a wallet in his pack that held a small wad of cash. I began to fish them out, already thinking of who to call first. Both Joanie and Reece would have, no doubt, sent the cavalry looking for me. "I'll come too."

"I think I should be the one to go in first." Nora said, a steely look on her face. "Just in case."

Great. When it was time to hunt for fruit everyone was all "I did it last time" or "I'm going fishing instead." But now ev-v-v-erybody wanted to be a hero?

Miranda rolled her eyes. "When did you learn to speak Spanish, Nora?"

Nora scowled. "Still, I could—"

"You can both stay hidden here and come rescue me with our big knife if I'm not back in five minutes," Miranda said impatiently. "Do you still have those earrings?"

Nora looked my way and raised her eyebrows in question. But I could only shrug. It wasn't a bad plan.

"The earrings are in the pack." Before the words were all the way out of Nora's mouth, Miranda spun into action.

Nora turned around so I could fish out the diamond studs, a

compass and a small pocketknife from the side pocket of Lucas's pack.

Chewing her lip, Miranda sorted through our money and goods, looking disappointed with our meager booty.

I mentally snapped my fingers. "Wait." I grabbed the cigarettes and lighters, hating to lose them, but knowing there was no better cause. "These too?"

"Yes," Miranda breathed, much more pleased.

"Oh, just take it all." Nora slipped the pack off her back and fitted it to Miranda's back, tugging the straps tighter on her broad shoulders. "Either we're saved or we're screwed. I don't think there's much in between at this point. If they want more, promise them more."

"Promise them anything," I added hastily. "Unless they're intent on selling you as a love slave, say yes to what they want. As a matter of fact, say yes to that too. We can figure out a way to get you rescued later."

"But try to avoid offering up your body, okay?" Nora said, glaring at me for giving Mirada the idea in the first place. "Jacob Dane owes me anything these people want. He owes us all."

I pointed to the huts with Lucas's knife and reminded Miranda that she had five minutes and not one second longer before we charged in and started cutting off people's body parts.

Nora looked at her watch. We weren't kidding.

Christ on a crutch, this really *was* an episode of *Miami Vice*.

Miranda nodded, excitement pouring off her like sparks from a dragging tailpipe. The instant the pack was fully in place, she took off in a quick jog.

"Shit," Nora hissed, stepping out from behind the trees to drag Miranda back, but quickly thinking better of it and returning to our hiding spot. She threw her hands in the air. "I wanted to talk more about our plan."

"We don't have a plan. So quit complaining, Tubbs," I murmured as I watched Miranda make a beeline for the women who were hanging clothes on a line to dry. "You'd have done the same exact thing."

Nora's body practically thrummed with anticipation and she

crouched down, ready to pounce at the first sign of trouble. She frowned. "Who said you get to be Crockett?"

I smiled tightly, my eyes never leaving Miranda as I held up our huge knife, the blade glinting in the waning sun. I chuckled wickedly. "The star always gets the weapon."

The Indian women—or drug lordesses, depending on our luck—seemed startled to see Miranda, but after a few seconds, they all three heartily embraced.

I blew out a thankful breath and tried to remember how to make my feet work. Barely daring to believe, I said, "I think this could actually almost be over."

The expression on Nora's face was indecipherable, and I wondered what was swimming around in that sharp mind of hers. Thankfully, I didn't have to wonder for long.

"Rachel," she began slowly, the look of longing on her face so compelling my heart nearly stopped. "Has it been a million goddamned ye—"

"Yes!" I wound my fingers in her shirt and pulled her into a blistering, electric kiss that made my insides curl. It was sure, and steady, and felt oh-so-right. And when her hot tongue caressed mine, my knees began to melt and I thought I might die from sheer pleasure.

"Rachel. Nora. Come on!"

From the corner of my mind, I heard Miranda yelling for us, but I didn't want the kiss to end…ever. And Nora didn't as much as slow down her welcomed assault on my mouth.

Her lips were baby soft and they fit perfectly against mine. When she moaned into my mouth, I lost my mind. I deepened the kiss further, pressing our sweaty bodies together in an explosion of delicious sensation.

"Nora. Rachel. It's safe. You can come out."

In the distance I heard pounding footsteps and knew it was Miranda coming to get us, but it was Nora who somehow found the fortitude to break our kiss. We separated, wide-eyed and panting.

Nora's cheeks were flushed and her lips were plump with arousal. "I-I-I" she stammered, helplessly. Then she touched her lips as though she couldn't believe they were hers.

Was that thundering sound my heart? "Mine still tingle, too." Actually, I had to admit to myself that a helluva lot more than my lips were tingling. I smiled tentatively and prayed that she thought the kiss was as amazing as I did.

Nora's face broke into a gorgeous, full smile. The kind that stretched her cheeks and forced those adorable dimples into a command appearance. "Wow."

"Hey." Miranda came sliding to a halt in front of us. "The women are going to help us."

She grabbed my hand and began to tug me out into the clearing. "What's wrong with both of you? They have food. Food! And their husbands will be back from fishing in the morning. They can take us to a town after that."

Allowing Miranda to drag me, I stumbled forward, but Nora remained rooted in place. I glanced back at her from over my shoulder, dazed, thrilled and snared like a rabbit in a trap. "Aren't you coming?"

It took a second for her to come out of what looked like a thoughtful stupor, but when she did, she smiled again, though I couldn't help but notice this time it didn't quite reach her eyes. "Right behind you."

We bathed, one after the other, in a large empty barrel that leaked and had some small splinters, but was continuously refilled with clean water by two preteen girls who stared at us as though we were circus oddities. I don't think they'd ever seen someone who was still alive and as pale as me. The thought made me laugh.

I was as tanned as I'd ever been, which was about the rose-tinted complexion a normal person might achieve after a short afternoon in the sun. To these girls, I must have looked like something from another planet. I could tell they wanted to touch my skin, but were too shy to ask. But, before I could offer, the smallest girl did touch Nora's now clean, naturally sandy-blond hair that had been further bleached by the sun into a nearly golden blond.

I couldn't blame her. It shined like spun gold.

I soaped myself until I was squeaky clean, paying special

attention to the grime in my ears, nails, hair, belly button and anyplace else hidden. Then I dressed in a borrowed shirt and thin cotton skirt.

It turned out the village had eight women in all and almost two dozen children. I skipped putting my sweat-stained bra back on, but wasn't worried I'd scandalize anyone, as the locals seemed to believe in going *au naturale*.

A woman named Inez gestured to me, and I interpreted that to mean she wanted to know what to do with my filthy clothes. I pointed to the fire pit. Burning those nasty things would be a kind fate for them at this point.

I was the last to bathe, and when I finished I joined my friends, barely able to look Nora in the eye. God only knew what she thought of me now. Tease? Crazy? Waffler? All those words seemed to apply. I'd rejected her advances at every turn and then I'd gone and kissed the hell out of her. Reckless. Yes, I should add that word too.

Not that the kiss wasn't worth every ounce of my current embarrassment—my heart sped up just remembering it—but this had been building for days and it was something we needed to talk about. Soon.

Dry and clean, the three of us wiggled onto a wooden bench to wait for our dinner at a slightly rickety communal table under a large tree. Apparently, Miranda had promised the Indian women enough payment for us to be treated like queens for the evening. Which was fine by me.

As we settled in, the women and children scurried away to take care of business.

We all shared nervous smiles and did our best to ignore how ridiculous we must look in long rough-hewn skirts and odd-fitting shirts. We kept utterly silent about our impending rescue, as though if we dared mention it, somehow it would all just go away.

Just then, a tall, floppy-eared white dog trotted over to us and sniffed my outstretched hand. When he leaned into my touch and let me scratch him behind the ears, I tried not to think it. I really did. But I couldn't help but wonder what he'd taste like barbecued. I was *starving*. And for the first time in my life, I really meant it.

Shooing the dog out of the way, a small girl with a beaming smile and a shaggy-haired little brother in tow, approached us carrying a heavy bowl. My stomach growled loudly in anticipation.

"Yes, oh, yes," I heard Nora mumble. "Walk faster. I'll give you my car if you walk faster."

The girl set the bowl down in front of us, rattling off a string of Spanish to Miranda. Then she took the toddler by the hand and left. The only word I understood in the entire exchange was "Mama."

I wondered not for the first time, whether it was a bad thing that my high school allowed me to substitute ceramics for a foreign language. I thought about that for a second. Nah. It wasn't like I didn't get a lot of use out of the ceramic blob I'd made. Besides, I didn't really care what the cute kid said, so long as it meant I was only seconds away from being full for the first time in weeks. Bread? Meat? Vegetables? Sweets? *Yes, please.*

My hands shook as I pulled the bowl closer and we all peered inside, drool pooling in our mouths, just before our jaws sagged in disbelief.

Bleakly, Miranda wrapped her arms around her middle and burst into tears, looking a lot like a girl who, on Christmas morning, found out Santa was a fraud.

Nora let her forehead fall to the table with a loud thwack. "You've got to be kidding me," she cried softly, her shoulders shaking. "Mangos and bananas? Come *on.*"

I looked upward toward the heavens and released a heavy breath. "Very funny."

Despite the rough beginning, we ended the evening pleasantly stuffed, not from mangos and bananas, which I would never voluntarily eat again, but from the bowls of spicy rice filled with chunks of fish that turned out to be a much appreciated second course. Because all of us had eyes bigger than our bellies, we ate regretfully small portions, but still ended up full and happy. No, not happy. We were darn near giddy.

When we'd finished our meal, a couple of the older Indian

women motioned Miranda over to a small group of females so they could chat in private. After a moment, one of the women pointed at our table, then Miranda repeated the action.

"I wonder what's up?" Nora said, tilting her head in my direction and scooting closer to me as she warily eyed our hosts.

"It…" The scent of clean cotton and the soap she'd used on her hair momentarily distracted me. Inwardly, I rolled my eyes at myself. *Focus, Rachel.* "It can't be too bad, Miranda's smiling. Then again, Miranda said that Indians were superstitious. Maybe they've decided your green eyes are the sign of the devil and that our arrival foretells a curse that will be a blight on their families for a dozen generations to come, and they're going to sacrifice us at dawn to a cloud of mosquitoes."

Nora could only stare me. "What *is* wrong with you, Rachel?"

"Nothing." I smiled. "I just have a very fertile imagination."

"Ya think? Maybe they're planning what we're going to do tomorrow." The breeze tousled her hair and she tucked a strand behind her ear, slightly mesmerizing me. I hadn't seen her wear it down for more than a few minutes this entire trip. It was beautiful.

Nora frowned. "Earth to Rachel? Are you in there somewhere?"

Miranda's return saved me from answering. "So, Miranda, do they want to sell you into slavery after all?" I asked dryly. "I'm sure you'd fetch an excellent price."

"Umm…not exactly." Smiling, she began to fidget with the hem of her shirt. "But it's time for bed. Now."

Nora blinked. "It's not even dark."

She nodded. "I know, but the village women have decided for us. And they've given us our own hut for the night." Miranda extended a finger. "It's the last one way over there."

"They're banishing us to the edge of camp?" I asked, ready to be insulted.

Miranda rocked back on her heels. "They all got together and decided that just in case their men come back early, they want the 'pretty one' already tucked away and sound asleep until morning."

"The pretty one?" Delighted, I laughed and my gaze flicked to each of them. "Who's the lucky girl, huh?" Not that you could go wrong with either choice. Even the ravaging effects of our time in the jungle couldn't erase the beauty these two had going for them.

"Let's see…" I tapped my forehead with one finger. "Did they pick the one who has a smile with enough wattage to light up Las Vegas and a body that belongs in a fitness magazine? She has the husky, sultry voice of an old-time blues singer, looks as American as a slice of apple pie, and is only made more hot by the alpha female confidence she exudes with every determined step."

Nora narrowed her eyes playfully, making it clear she didn't buy my description.

To my surprise, Miranda shook her head no.

"No?" I turned my grin toward the other excellent candidate. I should have known. Never bet against the home team. "Then it's the tantalizingly young one."

Miranda's cheeks tinted, and I knew I was right.

"She's exotic, and has a wicked gleam in her eyes that matches a body built to be far more naughty than nice." I shook my head with exaggerated sadness. "She's the sort of trouble that tempts men to risk everything."

"You are *loco*, you know that? They were talking about you," Miranda cheerfully informed me. "Apparently, they see you as a potential threat to the happiness of their homes and the peaceful structure of their village. But I say that's a good thing. At least we get our own place to sleep, and it's not outside. And they'll want to get rid of us first thing tomorrow."

Nora flashed me an enormous smile and nudged me with her hip. "Don't look so surprised, Rache."

"I-I-I…what?" I exclaimed, dumbfounded. "There has to be some mistake." Someone picked me over them? Was there actually a culture that revered pale, curly-haired, chubby, redheads? If so, why didn't I know about this when I was looking for spring break locations as a student?

"No mistake," Miranda said matter-of-factly. "They

described you very clearly." She made a wavy motion with her hands that universally meant a curvaceous woman.

Still shocked, I didn't know what to say.

Looking smug, Nora whispered in my ear. "I agree with the wise village women." Then she eased away, but took my hand as she went. She gave me a gentle pull. "Let's go see this hut they have for us. I wouldn't want you out in the open when the men arrive." She actually sounded half serious. "I can't chance the Dragonflies newest color commentator falling in love with someone while she's in Venezuela."

When she squeezed my hand, I couldn't stop my heart's whisper. *Too late.*

Our hut had a wood frame and straw walls and roof. It consisted of a large room that was halved by a hanging piece of cloth that extended from ceiling to floor. The living area held a few chairs, and an upside down washbasin serving as a table. Two trunks made from thick woven leaves were tucked neatly against one wall, and the colorful thatched rugs were soft under our feet. A stained, small homemade mattress sat in one corner directly on the floor and toys were scattered all around it.

The Transformer action figure sitting near the modest bed made me feel a little better. We were obviously deep in the wilds of this remote land, but civilization *was* out there, lurking almost within our grasp.

Miranda claimed the straw-filled mattress by flopping down on it and screaming, "I saw it first. It's mine." She cracked up laughing at the stunned looks on our faces. "It's hard to be old and slow, yes?"

Nora and I exchanged looks, then both dove onto the tiny mattress, effectively smothering Miranda as we all squealed and laughed and wrestled for position like a trio of hyper six year olds. The carbs from the rice must have gone directly into our bloodstreams.

Normally, Nora, with her lanky strength, would have probably bested us both, but only having one hand put her at a serious disadvantage. One that Miranda and I happily took complete advantage of.

"You can't make me move," Miranda cried triumphantly, when no amount of tickling or pinching torture seemed to work. The girl was glued to that mattress like rust on a Volkswagen.

Breathing hard, I rolled off of her and onto the floor. "Ouch. Fine," I panted as I faced the ceiling and blew a strand of hair from my eyes. "You can have it. But there had better be some place for us to sleep in the other half of this place or you're going to have two visitors on this bed."

With a groan, it was Nora who was up first, but not before she gave one cruel pinch to Miranda's bottom.

"Yeowch." Miranda covered the offended area with one hand and glowered. "That was mean, Papa!" Then her eyes took on a mischievous twinkle. "Wait until I do it to you."

"Oh, boy," I muttered. "Hello, World War III."

Not looking worried in the least, Nora merely snickered and offered me a hand up, doing her best to keep me from getting tangled in my own long skirt. By the time I turned back around, Miranda's eyelids were already drooping and I could tell by the reddish-golden light streaming in from around the door that the sun had started to set.

"Bedtime for hapless travelers?" I asked, watching affectionately as my words set off a chorus of yawns. "I guess that answers my question."

"Good night, Miranda." Nora made up for her evil pinch by bending and dropping a sloppy kiss on the top of Miranda's head, which she clearly loved. "If you have to leave the hut tonight for any reason, come get one of us, okay? I don't think we should be walking around this village alone. Who knows when these mysterious husbands might show up."

For once, Miranda agreed easily and she let her eyes start to slide closed, her thick lashes fluttering fitfully until she fully relaxed. "And in the morning we will go home."

A lump formed in my throat at the thought. "Amen to that."

We pulled aside the canvas draping to discover that the second half of the hut had been made into a bedroom. The room smelled strongly of wood smoke and, unpredictably, honey. My gaze flitted around the room for the source, finally landing on a

large, drippy candle. I padded over and gave it a sniff. Mmm…
beeswax.

The room held another trunk, several baskets and short
stacks of what looked to be his and hers clothing. I especially
liked the yellow "Vote for Pedro" T-shirt and wondered idly
whether it was the husband's or wife's.

The bed consisted of another straw mattress, but this one
was perched about a foot off the ground by a bamboo frame
held together with rope lashings. It was roughly the size of a
large twin mattress back home, and I winced as I considered
whether it would hold us both.

"Not a bad place," Nora murmured as she milled around,
looking a little nervous. She grazed one of the baskets with
her fingertips. "Makes me feel like such a glutton. I have more
clothing in one closet than this entire family."

I nodded. "Me too."

"I think maybe I'll go through my stuff back home and make
a big donation to the Salvation Army, you know? Give it to folks
who need it more than I do and get rid of excess baggage."

I smiled warmly. "I think that's a great idea. I'll do the
same. There's a women's shelter near my townhouse that would
probably appreciate it."

Finally finding something to do with herself, she sat on the
edge of the bed and began to struggle out of her shoes.

The kiss. We have to talk about the kiss. I recalled the glorious
sensation of her lips against mine and felt myself go damp. *Or
maybe we could just shut up and repeat it?*

My brows knit when I noticed that she was struggling.

"No, thanks."

"No thanks, what?"

"You were going to offer to do this for me." She gave her
laces a sharp tug. "No, thanks."

So stubborn. I also hated the fact that she was right. "Well,
I'm doing it anyway."

I dropped to my knees and focused on her feet as I spoke,
ignoring her long-suffering sigh as she submitted to my
assistance. "I hope the couple that uses this bed doesn't fight a
lot. If I'd had to crawl into something that size when I was mad

at Reece, which was often, well, let's just say we'd be shopping for stain removers that worked really well on blood."

I set one shoe on the floor and gave her foot an affectionate pat.

There was a brief pause before Nora asked, "And how do you feel about crawling in here with me? And not to just sleep."

Her second shoe tumbled from my hands and I glanced up, startled by her directness. "I-I-"

"Because I really want that." She laid her hand on my cheek. It was warm and slightly rough from our days of cutting our own path through the jungle. "I've been attracted to you since the moment I saw you. I felt something that I couldn't ignore. Interest. Attraction." Helplessly, she shook her head. "I'm not sure what. But it's been building since the beginning."

Interest? Okay, I'd pretty much already figured out that she wasn't madly in love with me. But I was *interested* in the Sunday crossword puzzle and my neighbor's flower garden. "Is that all?" I asked quietly, unsure of what the right answer even was.

"That's not all. I...I care about you so much, Rachel." Whisper soft, she ran her fingers down my throat. "I'd like to show you how much. I want to be as close to you as possible." Her gaze dropped from mine, breaking the sizzling connection between our eyes. "If you've changed your mind about things being too complicated, that is."

There was something different in her voice. Something that wasn't there when she'd so boldly propositioned me back in Caracas. A flash of vulnerability chased its way across her face and then was gone.

When I didn't answer, she started to remove her hand, but I grabbed it and held it firm. "Wait."

She froze.

"I don't want you to stop touching me."

"But—" I gazed back over my shoulder at the thin canvas that separated us from Miranda. I could already hear her characteristic snores.

"Quietly." Solemnly, she drew her fingers through my hair and gave me a lopsided grin that caused my heart to skip a beat. "We'll be very, very..." She pressed a finger against my lips and her voice dropped to a devastating sexy whisper. "Quiet."

"You're not going to yell 'Go Dragonflies' during sex, are you?"

"I haven't ever thought of doing that." She grinned rakishly. "But now that you've given me the idea, you'll have to wait and wonder."

A few seconds ticked by, but neither of us moved. Suddenly, I felt like something I'd never been, a nervous virgin on her wedding night. My face heated with embarrassment even as my mouth went bone dry at the thought of getting sweaty with her. God, the things she could do to me without even touching me. I wasn't sure I could survive actually having sex with her.

Nora scooted up the bed and lay down on her side, beckoning me to join her with crooked fingers. Her eyes were dilated with desire and I felt a surge of moisture pool between my legs at the sight as my body responded in kind.

She watched me like a hawk as I moved around the other side of the bed to climb in. "There's nothing to be nervous about," she said gently.

Damn my inability to hide any emotion.

"It's not like you haven't done this before."

I kicked off my shoes and fought the competing urges to flee the hut and pounce on her. "Ages ago, Nora. I did this ages ago."

Her eyes were kind and just a tiny bit teasing. "Don't tell me you've forgotten what it feels like to be with a woman."

I was sure she wasn't trying to seduce me, but, somehow, she was still doing a fine job of it. An involuntary, and altogether wistful, sigh escaped me. And Nora's knowing grin told me she already knew the answer. "Still, it's been more than ten years."

"I get it. Back when dinosaurs ruled the earth." She winked at me and I couldn't help but chuckle. "I'm sure you'll find everything in the same place as it was back then. But if females have undergone some evolutionary changes since the last time you went exploring, and you can't locate the really fun body parts without a map, be sure to let me know."

I lay down next to her, sinking into the straw mattress as I lightly slapped her arm. "You're making fun of me."

Her expression softened into something that looked suspiciously like devotion, and my heart clenched. "Only a little." She took my hand and laced our fingers together, then kissed it. "Only so you won't be scared."

Emboldened by her tenderness, I voiced a little of my fear. "Do you think this is a mistake, Nora?" With every passing day I'd grown more and more attached to her. And indulging in that attraction was so not going to help when we had to say goodbye.

She scooted closer and lightly brushed her lips against mine, setting my body on fire as easily as if it were dry tinder. "Maybe," she admitted honestly as she pressed her forehead to mine, putting us so close together we were breathing the same air and our brows were touching. "But I don't want to let that stop me. I want you too much for that."

The current between us crackled with anticipation and she waited for me to say no. Little did she know, my inner slut would no longer be denied. Instead of speaking, I lifted my chin just enough to draw my tongue slowly along her lower lip, daring her to take my mouth with hers. When I rested the flat of my palm just below her neck, I felt her heart pounding wildly.

Jesus, she's as excited as I am.

With a soft growl, she kissed me again, this time deeper than before and without restraint, unleashing a torrent of passion that crashed over me like a tidal wave, and robbed me of any semblance of reason. The gloves were off.

And I was lost.

When I finally came up for air I breathed, "I don't want *anything* to stop us." It was the truth and I wasn't stupid enough to deny it for another second. With that, I stopped thinking all together and just trusted what I was feeling.

And I'd never felt so alive, as though every sensation was magnified a hundredfold. Nora's lips, brimming with kisses, supple and wet. The fresh scent of her skin and hair. The slippery tongue that dueled playfully, yet passionately with mine, and ratcheted up my excitement with every passing second. The warm, comforting weight of her body, pressed against mine. But what I felt most, was that maddening hand that started to travel up and down my torso, administering feather-light touches that ignited a firestorm across my skin and was more than enough to make me want to scream in pleasure and demand *more*.

I waited to feel self-conscious, the way I'd been the first time with my other lovers, but it never happened. Maybe it was because we'd seen each other naked again and again and that now meant nothing would be a surprise or a disappointment. Or maybe it was because even though I'd had generous partners in the past—I'd even been married to one—none had accomplished what Nora had already achieved. None had made me feel beautiful even before we'd hit the sheets. And with her every movement, sigh and look, she told me that what I had was *exactly* what she wanted.

It was liberating and it was sexy as hell.

I expected her to dive right for my breasts, something everyone I'd ever been with had done. But to my shock and delight, she focused her first attentions elsewhere, undressing me slowly as she let kisses flutter down on each newly exposed piece of skin like tiny snowflakes.

Soon I was naked and writhing beneath her, a fine sheen of perspiration coating my overheated body. She was relentless in her attentions, and I loved it. "You too." I let out a soft whimper, reveling in the way her fingers skimmed across my skin. "I-I-I want you naked too."

"You feel so damn good, Rachel," she whispered hotly, dragging her tongue down my throat and kissing a path to the well between my breasts. "I don't want to stop what I'm doing."

I buried my fingers in her silky hair, and in a stunning act of willpower, pulled her away from me just enough to look deeply into eyes gleaming with passion. I gasped as I almost came on the spot. "You said you wanted to be close to me?"

Her breathing was labored and she nodded impatiently. "Yes."

"I want the same thing."

A tiny pucker formed between her eyes. "You don't have—"

I silenced her with a searing kiss and realized I could kiss her all night and never grow tired of it. But I still wasn't sure my point had hit home, so I gently pulled her head away again. "I know I don't. But my hands, and mouth and tongue are itching to be all over you. To be *in* you." I paused to let my words soak in, and then watched in satisfaction when her nostrils flared and her eyes narrowed. "You'll let me do that, right?"

My question was still hanging in the air when she flipped onto her back and we both began tearing off her clothes. I hoped that the Indian women weren't too attached to them because they were going to be rags by the time we were through.

Not showing a smidgen of the restraint that she had, the second her breasts were free, I caressed them with the back of my hand, drinking them in with my eyes and catching just a hint of the bluish cast of veins just below the skin. "God." I swallowed thickly, my eyes darting up to meet hers. "Your skin feels like silk."

There was so much to love about a man's body, but I'd never been a hairy chest fan. This sensory experience was different in a smooth, delicate, spectacular way.

She smiled. "So does yours." She sat up a little and twisted as I helped her finish yanking her skirt off. Then I unveiled *the* most perfect bottom I had ever seen. And I told her so in a soft murmur as I kissed the body part in question before moving up alongside her to let our naked bodies come together in an explosion of raw sensation.

I swooned.

Maybe I *had* forgotten what it was like with a woman, but more likely what I was feeling had more to do with who I was with right now. I'd *never* been so aroused. My center was needy, swollen and hot and already pulsing right along with the beat of my heart. My breasts, the ones she'd so cruelly ignored up until this point, were on fire, and every part of me ached for her touch.

When she shifted her body and her firm nipples scraped against mine, I jerked at the exquisite sensation and sucked in a sharp breath through my teeth. Unable to wait another second, I reached down and grabbed her hand and fitted it over my breast. "Squeeze."

Mesmerized by her own hand, she did exactly what I asked.

Eyes hooded, I arched into her touch and panted, "Harder, baby."

She squeezed again, this time with more authority as she planted a scorching kiss on my mouth, robbing me of my senses and breath. In that second I knew she could have me begging if she only asked.

Her mouth joined her hand, open-mouth kissing, nibbling and finally sucking my painfully hard nipples with gusto. "Jesus," I moaned, doing my best to be quiet and not wriggle off the bed, but not being very successful. I tried to listen for Miranda's snores, but it was hard to hear anything other than the sound of my hammering heart as my body blossomed beneath Nora's touch.

Not wanting to be left out, I slipped one hand between us and began to gently stroke her, sliding my fingers in her warm wetness. Her body instantly went stock-still and I froze, worried I'd done something wrong. Then she released a low, sexy moan that went right to my head and made me want to devour her alive.

"Yes," she whispered raggedly as if undergoing some sort of luscious torture. "Just... *yes*... Just like that."

The alluring scent of her passion wafted around us and seeped into my blood until she filled my senses completely. Like a greedy child, I was determined to devour everything before me.

Thrilled, I kept up my attentions even when it was all I could do not to force her head between my legs. I was so ready, I was near to exploding and spontaneous combustion was becoming a real threat. I swirled my fingers again and again, slipping one, then two fingers inside her. I pumped them with long, fluid strokes, grazing her sensitive clit with my thumb whenever I could. The sounds she was making were more satisfying than the food we'd had at dinner, and for a brief moment, I was certain I could survive on them alone.

In far too short a time, her entire body began to tremble.

Nora buried her face in my neck. "Like that. Don't stop," she said against my skin. "Oh, God. I'm go-going to—" She thrust against my hand and inhaled sharply as she shuddered against me, a rush of wetness coating my fingers before she collapsed on top of me, breathing as though she'd just sprinted a mile.

I did that, I thought joyfully. Slowly, I removed my hand and hugged her close, suddenly wanting to cry at the deep intimacy we'd shared. I don't know what I whispered in her ear, it was just a babbling free flow of how much she meant to me and how grateful I was that despite everything, we were going to make it through our ordeal intact and together.

I stroked her back as she caught her breath and I could feel her ribs beneath my fingers. I frowned at her thinness. The jungle had been merciless.

It took a moment for Nora to come back to earth, but when she did, she peppered my face with soft kisses. She chuckled as though she was a little embarrassed. "You were supposed to get to come first, but I couldn't help myself!"

I grinned wholeheartedly, my pride swelling.

Then her mouth found my ear and she nibbled gently, bringing her own hand down to my center where she began to tease. "Now it's your turn," she said softly, spiking my adrenaline.

I sighed as she stroked me, then began to kiss her way down my body, paying loving attention to each breast along the way. Every pull on my nipples with that hot mouth sent a pulse of sensation between my legs. This was heaven. She was heaven. When her tongue finally found my lower lips, then dipped inside me, I wanted to scream, but settled for a whimper as I tried to keep from waking up the entire village.

She moaned her pleasure against my slick folds, sending shock waves through me. I willed the experience to go on and on, but my climax was rushing toward me like a meteor hurtling through space. *Yes. Yes. Yes*, my mind chanted, unwilling to wait another second for what I craved so badly it hurt. *Let it come.*

Chest heaving, I planted my feet on the soft straw mattress and buried my fingers into her hair, pulling her against me as I came furiously against her mouth, unable to stop the deep groan that was torn from my chest as I saw stars. I jerked my hands from her hair so I wouldn't hurt her and grabbed onto the soft mattress cover, winding my fingers in it until my knuckles were white. A volcano erupted inside me, shaking me to the core, and sending molten lava singing through my veins.

Even through the heart of my orgasm, Nora's tongue slowed, but never stopped. And only seconds after the first climax was over, my eyes flew open wide as my center contracted again and again in ecstasy. I threw my head back and rode the feeling, holding on tight so I wouldn't implode completely as a wave of ecstasy swept me away.

Finally spent, I had to coax Nora away from what she was doing. She didn't show any signs of tiring, and I didn't think I could live through a climax as strong as the first two, so I tugged her higher up my body to snuggle, despite the jungle heat.

She kissed, then nibbled the underside of one of my breasts and I groaned throatily, my body coming alive again with shocking speed. "Are we finished?" she asked, grinning so wickedly that I knew that we weren't.

Delighted, I half gasped, half laughed, then thought of all the things I wanted to do to her, but hadn't gotten the chance. Oh, well. I could catch up on sleep when I was dead. "Only for a little while so I can catch my breath," I vowed.

"Good." As happy and bouncy as a new puppy, she settled against me. Then she laid her cheek against my chest and hugged me so tenderly that if I'd ever doubted that I was madly in love with her, my doubts would have evaporated right then. "You're beautiful," she whispered, and I curled up enough to press my lips against her damp temple.

Overwhelmed with emotion, I really didn't have any words for what we'd experienced and so I didn't even try to speak. I heard her swallow hard and she hugged me again, holding me so tightly it bordered on painful. We lay there together, wound around each other like the tangled roots of a tree.

I looked forward to tomorrow with both hope and worry.

I had a new problem. Something was standing between me and what I desperately wanted. A month ago that something might have been my self-appointed label of heterosexual. But after everything I'd been through, what was really important came into such sharp focus I felt as though I'd been blind before. The decision to keep the labels inside my clothing where they belonged, and well away from my heart, was surprisingly easy. Nora was right. It was time to get rid of excess baggage.

What *was* a problem was Nora's relationship with Jacob Dane.

And as the moon rose over the jungle, I considered what to do about it.

Chapter 15

The next day's events were a whirlwind of activity. The village men did come home, and after some further negotiation with Miranda, they agreed to take us to the nearest village. The trek was treacherous, hot and horrible, and by early evening we were in a small town that had more donkeys than cars. But it also had phones.

We were saved. And it was nothing like I'd expected. I'd pictured a tearful reunion with our families and copious apologies from local law enforcement for not being able to find us sooner. Maybe even a few television cameras would document the momentous event. After all, Miranda was a quasi-celebrity in the world of women's soccer.

Instead, we were immediately separated, placed into tiny, hot interrogation rooms in the local police station, and questioned by the Venezuelan National Guard, who, over protests from American Embassy and our families, had declared us dead and abandoned the search several days ago, strongly hinting that the fact we hadn't been found at the crash site meant we'd been up to something nefarious in the jungle in the first place.

Now the government was going to be embarrassed, and was looking to save face any way they could, preferably by showing we were part of some ridiculous drug cartel.

It was close to midnight by the time we were released onto the deserted street in front of the police station with no possessions and no money. Hardly believing what had happened, we all three looked at each other, dazed.

"Are you okay?" Nora asked us both, her jaw set in anger.

Miranda nodded, then turned and screamed something horrible in Spanish at the police station.

"Oh shit," Nora mumbled, and we each grabbed one of her arms and began to drag her in the opposite direction. "Do you want to get us arrested?"

"We will sue them," Miranda seethed.

"But not tonight," Nora said. "C'mon. One of the guards told me there was a hotel down the street."

Nora turned to me and lowered her voice. "Once we're alone, we need to talk, okay?"

I nodded, a feeling of foreboding settling over me like a rain cloud. "What about?"

"Later," was all Nora would say.

"How are we going to pay for the hotel?" I asked, trying to appear like I wasn't freaking out inside. This wasn't how it was supposed to be. I hadn't done anything wrong. She was going to dump me and we weren't even together yet.

"I'm not going to pay right now," Nora continued, her voice tight. "I'm going to beg them to let us use their phone and get a room until I can get some money wired in."

Miranda cleared her throat and we glanced in her direction as we walked down the deserted streets. "Umm... You might want to get a lot of money."

Nora's eyebrows lifted. "Why?"

Miranda tried to pull away from our little group, but Nora held her firm. "You didn't bribe them into releasing us, did you?"

If she did, I owed her a big kiss.

"No," Miranda said, clearly affronted.

"Good girl," Nora murmured.

"But in order to get the village Indian men to take us to town, I had to promise they could come to America for a visit."

"Okay," Nora said, shrugging a little. "That's not too bad. A few plane tickets is no big deal."

"Tickets for the entire village."

Nora stopped walking.

"And I told them that you live in a mansion like Britney Spears and that they could stay with you for two weeks."

Nora's eyes bugged out. "What?"

"I had to invite the *entire* village. That's twenty-five people and one dog." She winced at Nora's withering glare. "What? One woman wouldn't leave her dog. You said to promise them anything."

Even though there was a knot of anxious worry in my gut, the horrified look on Nora's face made me laugh.

"Goddammit, Miranda, I don't live in a mansion. I live in a condo."

I wrapped an arm around each woman's shoulders and we started moving again as one. The hotel's flashing sign was only a few buildings away. "So put them in a nice ski lodge and give them soccer tickets," I said. "It could have been worse, they could have asked for a ton of money too."

Miranda cringed and looked away, causing me to laugh even louder. This time Nora shook her head and joined in. Jacob Dane was going to die and it couldn't have happened to a more deserving person.

Suddenly, a careening van plowed down the street, splashing mud everywhere and causing us to jump out of its way. The van skidded to a halt in front of the hotel. We were all about to scream something nasty at it, when its sliding door opened and Jacob Dane climbed out, holding his lower back in obvious discomfort.

"Jacob!" Nora cried, bolting for him.

My heart sank as she jumped into his waiting arms and he spun her in a circle. I knew I should be glad to see him, but I'd hoped the Dragonflies would send anyone but him. If he cared about Nora enough to come down here personally, it made it that much harder to hate the man.

They hugged forever, then Jacob began fussing over her injured hand as though that was the worst thing we'd faced. Nora, however, soaked up the attention like a dry sponge. But before I could formulate a plan for his immediate assassination,

William Dane climbed out of the van, along with Joanie, Reece and Miranda's father.

As soon as she caught sight of me, Joanie dropped her bag, screamed my name, and ran toward me in a scene eerily reminiscent of my daydreams of what our rescue *would* be like. It was nice to have one thing in my life that was reliable. And for a moment, I lost track of Nora and Miranda.

Weeping like I hadn't seen her do since my dad's funeral, Joanie hugged and kissed me again and again, acting like I would disappear if she let go. "They said you were d-dead," she cried brokenly, instantly bringing tears to my own eyes. "But we wouldn't stop looking. I was ready to move to this damn country! Oh, Jesus, I have to call Mom. I didn't tell her when the National Guard called us this afternoon. They weren't sure they'd found the right people."

The hell? "They found us because we walked into their police station and told them who we were and what happened."

"I don't care who found you," she said seriously. "I only care that you're alive and okay. You are okay, right?" She hugged me again.

"I am. And I'm sorry you had to come all the way here," I whispered, patting her back as she sniffled.

In typical Joanie fashion, her weepiness only lasted a few seconds. Then she smacked my arm. "Jesus, Rachel, I'd go to the moon to haul your ass back home. You know that."

I nodded, my throat tight.

"I love you." She drew in a shaky breath. "Even though you left me with that horrible cat! What is *wrong* with you? By the way, I cleaned up your townhouse. You're a pig and a pervert, you know that?"

We laughed even though we both knew she was dead serious. *I am so lucky to have her.* "Come on now, sis, don't cry," I murmured. "I don't have any tissues and we'll have to use leaves to wipe your face. Hey, can I borrow money for the hotel tonight?"

Exasperated, she nodded, and only then stepped aside to give Reece a chance to say something.

The man looked like he'd been on a three-day bender. We

stared at each other for a few long seconds. It was so great to see him. I rubbed his stubbly cheeks affectionately. "Too lazy to shave, huh?"

He snorted and hugged me hard. It was a tiny bit awkward, but at the same time, achingly familiar. "I knew you were too stubborn to die before you bothered to take me off your life insurance," he said.

Were those tears in his voice? This was a little like getting to witness your own funeral without having to be dead.

I'd actually taken him off my insurance policy about a week after we separated, but he didn't need to know that now. I smiled gamely. "When you're right, you're right, Reece."

"My God," Joanie exclaimed, having already lost patience with him. She pulled me under the neon hotel light. "What happened to the rest of you?"

I looked down at myself. Okay, I was still filthy from tromping through the jungle to get to town, and I probably smelled. I couldn't tell anymore. "Trust me, I can't wait to take a real shower and brush my teeth. Hey, can I borrow a toothbrush? And comb? And…everything?"

"You can have anything you want, you goof." She looked me over with wide eyes. "You're skinny!"

"The no food diet is surprisingly effective."

"And tan," Reece added, sounding like he was saying I'd sprouted horns. "Or green. I can't tell in this light. And what's with the *Vote for Pedro* shirt?"

I looked past Reece to see what was happening with Nora. At that same moment, she walked over to me with Jacob and William in tow.

"Ms. Michaels…" Jacob stuck out his hand. "I can't tell you how thrilled I am that you're okay."

I grudgingly shook it. "I'm pretty thrilled myself."

"Nora has been filling us in on how instrumental you were in everyone's survival," William chimed in, his arm around Nora's waist in a possessive fashion I didn't appreciate.

"Ms. Butler's fiancé has been so helpful here, Rachel," Joanie gushed. "We'd still be in the embassy in Caracas if it weren't for him."

I gawked at Nora, who was suddenly ashen-faced. "Jacob is your fiancé?" *What the hell? I thought he was already married.*

Nora wouldn't meet my eyes. "Rache—" she started.

"Not Jacob, William," Joanie said. "Jeeze, didn't you guys get to know each other at all out there? You had three weeks to talk."

"I thought you knew about William," Nora said with forced brightness. "Jacob practically takes out ads in the newspapers."

I felt as though I'd been kicked in the stomach.

"Me, her fiancé?" Jacob laughed as though the very idea was ludicrous. He bent and pecked Nora on the cheek. "I should be so lucky." He beamed at this son. "But she's all William's and the daughter I never had. Now if I could only get these two to set a date, I could get a few grandchildren out of the mix too. Life would be perfect."

Both William and Nora looked painfully uncomfortable.

I closed my eyes. How stupid was I? Jacob was like a father to her, not a sleazy office affair. And not only had I fallen in love with someone who only wanted a worry-free fuck, but she was engaged too? Was this what she had to tell me? Well, it was a little goddamn late. "I-I don't feel very well," I said haltingly.

Concerned, Nora was instantly at my side. She put her hand on my arm. "What can I—"

I jerked my arm away and stepped aside as though she wasn't even there. "Joanie and Reece, can we get a room and turn in?" I wanted to die in privacy.

"Of course," Reece said, his questioning gaze moving between Nora and me. "I'll—"

"Let me," Jacob boomed, his larger-than-life personality overshadowing everyone and everything else. "I had my secretary call ahead. This is the only hotel in town and it only has rooms with one double bed. Can you believe that?"

Tugging a straw cowboy hat down farther on his head, Miranda's father jogged over to Jacob and Reece. As they entered the hotel, Miranda rubbed her face. She'd been crying, but it didn't look like happy tears. I suspected it had something to do with Paulo's conspicuous absence.

"Hey, kiddo," I said softly, welcoming her to my side.

"Where's…?"

Tears continued to stream down Miranda's cheeks. "He wanted to come, but my father wouldn't bring him. So Paulo told him that we were married. And—"

Aghast, William squeaked, "She's married? Since when?"

"And?" Nora asked Miranda warily, ignoring him.

Miranda wiped at her eyes. "And they fought and Papa fired him. He's gone."

"Oh, boy." Nora rubbed the back of her neck. "Okay, let me talk to your dad. Maybe I can help. It's going to be okay, Miranda. We'll find him and get him back."

Joanie watched with the same single-minded interest she paid her soap opera back home. Come to think of it, this was disgustingly similar.

"Really?" Miranda asked Nora, her eyes glistening with fragile hope.

Nora gave her a reassuring smile. "We'll figure something out." She glanced my way and I could easily read the fear in her eyes. "Just let me talk to Rachel for a minute first. I—"

"I'm going to bed," I said dully. "Go help Miranda if you can."

Nora reached for me. "Please, Rache."

I moved away and held up a hand to forestall her. "Don't touch me."

Hurt, she let her hand drop. "You need to let me explain."

"I don't need to do shit!" I exploded, whirling around to face her. "Go be with your *fiancé*." I pointed an angry finger at William, who looked like he wanted to run in the opposite direction.

Nora glared at me and I couldn't decide whether she was going to hit me or burst into tears. Not picking either, she stormed off into the hotel.

"Fiancé?" Miranda whispered, shocked.

Obviously uncomfortable, William said, "I guess she didn't tell you about me either, huh?" Then he introduced himself to Miranda and blathered on about soccer and the Dragonflies. "I'm so glad to meet you. Your father and I have become fast friends. I've invited him and your mother to stay with Nora and me for your opening game."

Oh. My. God. This was getting better and better. "You and Nora live together? Like in the same house?"

The deer in headlights look didn't suit William. "Yes?"

I put my hands on my hips. "You don't know?"

His face flushing in a combination of embarrassment and frustration, he said, "Well, I'm afraid to answer wrong and get everyone even more upset. Yes, we live together."

Miranda scratched her chin, trying to wrap her mind around what he was saying. "How long have you been together?"

"We've known each other since we both played soccer in college." He smiled happily. "But we've been engaged for five years."

I bit the inside of my cheek. *Fuck. Fuck. Fuck.* "That's great," I said weakly.

"Yeah, great." Miranda was furious and she didn't mind letting it show.

"I'll… um…" William looked around for a quick escape. "I'll go help the folks in the hotel." He nearly ran for the door.

"What in the hell is going on?" Joanie demanded. "I don't get it, and that means I'm missing the juicy parts of this drama."

"The story is too long to even start," I said tiredly.

Joanie felt my forehead for fever. "You really don't look so good, Rachel."

No kidding.

"Some sleep will help," she pronounced firmly. Joanie'd always been good at playing mom. Often, she was better than my real mom, in fact. "And food. And a doctor tomorrow. Yeah, God only knows what sorts of shots you need now. And then a dentist."

I didn't want to go into that hotel. I felt betrayed and fully knew that I was a fool for feeling it. I couldn't even look at Nora. But it was either the hotel or the street, and I'd been without a roof over my head for long enough.

Jacob got all of us our own rooms. Well, all except for Nora and William, whom he took great pleasure in announcing, would want to share. *Thanks for reminding me, asshole.*

With her in a chair and me laid out on the bed like a dead

body, Joanie and I spent the next couple of hours talking in my room, which smelled like dust and stale cigarette smoke.

But I steered the conversation away from my feelings for Nora and the harder things we'd experienced in the jungle, discussing the future instead.

When I couldn't keep my eyes open any longer, she slipped next door to her own room so I could get some rest. My bed was soft and the pillow even softer, but I was too miserable to enjoy either. So I got up and took a hot shower, letting the water cascade down me until it went cold. Then I used the bathroom, barely noticing the toilet paper I'd been waiting for.

Finally, I stared into the small mirror, a crack in the glass distorting half my face.

Who was that woman? I didn't even recognize her. I had lost a shocking amount of weight, changing not just the shape of my body, but also the planes of my face.

I looked younger, but felt as ancient and empty inside as a plundered tomb.

Wearing pajamas that now looked as big on me as they did on Joanie, I clicked off the lights and lay on the bed, dejected. I missed Nora, the filthy lying slut. And I missed Miranda and her unholy snores. My sister, my closest confidant was right next door, but I couldn't explain how my whole life had changed since I'd been here. I couldn't tell her what it was like to fight every day just to stay alive, or how one look from another woman could fill my heart to bursting.

Would she understand? Sure, eventually. She was smart and compassionate. But I simply didn't have the energy to take her on that journey tonight.

I'd never felt more alone. And I let my tears fall unabated.

A soft knock woke me from a fitful sleep and caused me to pad to the door. I must have dozed off for only a few minutes because a quick glance out my window told me it was still hours until dawn. "Who is it?" I asked hoarsely. It wouldn't be Joanie. She had a key.

"It's me."

Brows knit, I opened the door. "What are you still doing

up?" I ushered Miranda inside, my eyes darting around the empty hallway before I closed the door and locked it.

"Can...?" She wrapped her arms around herself and looked longingly at the bed, then back at me.

I was glad it was dark and she couldn't see my tearstained face. She had enough to worry about without pitying me. "You want to stay here with me?"

She nodded, obviously relieved that I invited her before she had to ask. Hell, I was just as relieved.

We crawled into bed and let out twin sighs. A few silent moments passed, but by her quiet breathing, I could tell she wasn't asleep.

"You love her, right?" Miranda asked, her voice barely louder than the ticking clock.

"Yes." She'd been through everything alongside us. She would understand.

"And Nora loves you. You should have seen her when you hugged your ex-husband tonight. She looked like she wanted to tear his throat out."

"She's marrying someone else." Just saying it made my stomach hurt. I clenched my hands into fists. "I was an affair, Miranda. A fling."

"Fling?"

"That means...it means that what happened between us in the jungle doesn't matter now." What happens in Venezuela, stays in Venezuela. My life had become a cheesy marketing slogan.

"Loving each other doesn't matter?" she asked doubtfully.

"Bu-but it's not like that."

"Didn't you see her face when you wouldn't talk to her tonight? It's exactly like that."

"She didn't trust me enough to tell me about William. That's not love." I swallowed hard. "Besides, our deal was fun with no strings attached. We told each other so in Caracas." I paused. "Don't be angry at her for it."

"But you love each other and she is breaking your heart!"

"I—" *I will not cry again.* "Even if she is, it's my own fault, hon. I knew better. I knew I couldn't separate my feelings from what I was doing, but by the time I fell in love with her, I didn't care."

Miranda let out a frustrated groan, unhappy that she didn't have a response to that. "You want a hug?"

I nodded, unable to stop the tears that had been threatening to fall this entire conversation. I didn't just cry. I wept. Finally, I had unlimited access to water and I was going to die from dehydration.

She shifted a little, tucking my head under her chin as she held me. It was a role reversal we hadn't experienced yet, and it added a new facet to our relationship. I needed the comfort so desperately and she gave it so freely that I dissolved into her welcoming arms. And at that moment, I lost sight of the willful girl and came to fully appreciate the kind young woman she was.

After my tears turned to soft hiccups, and then melted away entirely, I turned sideways to face her, my heart on my sleeve. Moonlight spilled through the windows and splashed over our bed, illuminating her face. "Thank you."

"We're still a team, right?"

She was offering a real friendship that went beyond these crazy circumstances, and I was honored to accept. I could know a neighbor or coworker for a million years and not feel for them what I felt for Miranda right now. "A permanent team." The sweet pang in my chest at her smile let me know that even though my heart was broken, it was still there. "And that means we work together to find Paulo. He's probably trying to get here right now."

In a vulnerable voice, she said, "Papa said horrible things to him and threatened to involve the *policia*. What if he doesn't want me anymore?"

"Puhleez. What's not to love? A father-in-law who wants to shoot you is practically an American institution. You'll be fine in the States. And if you need a place to live, and not just until you can find someone on your team who doesn't mind having your stud husband as a roommate, you can stay with me. I have plenty of room." I chuckled softly at her gasp. "And I'm sort of used to having you around and I wouldn't mind keeping it that way. If you're interested… If not, we can—"

"I'm interested." She thanked me a hundred times and ended her chatter with a sincere "I love you" that took my breath away and had me responding in kind.

If friends could say it and mean it, why was it so hard for lovers? I sighed. "Let's go to sleep."

Her breathing was already evening out, but she managed to say what I was thinking. "We've got a lot of things to fix tomorrow."

Some things, I thought darkly, *are easier to fix than others.*

Another gentle knock on my door roused me from slumber, but this time bright sunshine made me squint. I mumbled something about Grand Central Station and reluctantly climbed out of bed.

Miranda sat up with a yawn and we each smiled at the other's bed head. "Who is it?"

There was a pause. "Nora."

I rested my forehead against the door and closed my eyes. "Go fuck yourself."

I heard her sigh. "I need to talk to Miranda. Is she there?" I turned around and headed back to bed. "It's for you."

I threw the covers over my head as Miranda stretched and shuffled to the door. As she opened it, I peeked over the covers, unable to resist.

"Yes?" Miranda said sharply, still angry on my behalf. I'd have to talk to her about that again today.

Without being invited, Nora stepped into the room looking tired and haggard. Her clothes were dirty and her hair was oily and pulled into a haphazard ponytail. Why hadn't she gotten cleaned up last night?

Her pained gaze drifted to me, then moved away, landing on Miranda. "There's someone in the hallway to see you."

"Uh-oh. Papa's probably going to yell. I didn't tell him I was leaving my room last night." Miranda blew out an annoyed breath and stuck her head into the hall. "Paulo!" Then she flew out of the room as though she had wings, but not before soundly kissing Nora on the cheek. "*Gracias!*"

Relieved, Nora rocked back on her heels and grinned softly. "You're welcome."

Miranda's delighted screams were immediately muted by what I could only assume was a mind-blowing kiss from Mr. Wonderful. Good for her.

More than a little impressed, I sat up and cleared my throat. I was mortified that I was still hoarse from crying so much the night before. "How did you find him?"

"By driving Jacob's rental van all night and looking up and down the road. Poor guy was trying to hitchhike his way here. I found him a couple of hundred miles away sitting in the middle of the highway so he wouldn't miss the next car."

In her quest to reunite the young lovers Nora hadn't slept or even had a bath. Christ, no wonder I was in love with her. What on earth was I going to do?

"We need to talk about us."

Okay. Brutal honesty. "I don't think there's an us to talk about."

She spoke from behind clenched teeth. "But there could be if you would stop being so unreasonable."

"I don't want—"

"I don't care what you want." She stalked over to the door, slammed it shut and threw the deadbolt. Then she spun back at me, her face scarlet. "You had your way last night by running and not even giving me a chance to explain. Now it's my turn." Her voice was a low growl that sounded as much animal as it did human.

My eyes widened at her anger and my own resentment flared. "This isn't a game. We aren't children. And there are no turns!"

"Then stop acting like a child."

"Isn't your *fiancé* waiting for you somewhere?" I sneered. "He must be worried by now, so take a hike."

She sat down at the foot of the bed and I kicked at her until she gritted her teeth and grabbed a chair instead. She sat closer than I would have liked, but short of screaming my head off, something I would never do, or physically throwing her out, something I might try if pushed, I had to let her be.

"William knows I'm here," she informed me bluntly. "I told him all about us last night."

My eyes went round. "He knows you and I—" I made my favorite obscene gesture with my hands again. I was getting to use it way more in Venezuela than I did back home.

"Yes, and he doesn't care so long as I'm careful."

"Careful of what?" My anger and embarrassment reached a crescendo as I realized what she meant. "Careful not to bring home any diseases? You bitch. Are you implying—"

Nora jumped out of her chair and clamped her hand over my mouth. "I'm not implying anything like that. All I meant is that Jacob can't find out. William doesn't mind if I see other people. In fact, he was thrilled when I told him about you." Her eyes blazed. "William has other lovers who are not me. Get it? We. Do. Not. Have. Sex."

Utterly confused, a big part of my anger turned to mist, and I relaxed enough that Nora let me gently peel her hand from my mouth. I felt like a cork in the ocean, helplessly tossing and turning. "I don't understand."

"I know." She looked longingly at the space next to me on the bed. "Please scoot over and let me stay. Just while we talk? I promise not to touch you."

I thought of what I'd said about the small bed we shared in the Indian village. I'd meant it. I couldn't stand the thought of lying next to someone who had hurt me the way she had, even if it was mostly my own fault. But she looked so strung out, I found myself agreeing.

I moved ridiculously far over until I was nearly falling off the other side. We both stayed sitting up, our backs resting against the headboard, the space between us feeling as vast as the Continental Divide.

Nora closed her eyes. "I'm going to condense the last twelve years of my life into something really simple."

I had already learned the hard way that nothing about Nora was simple. "Good luck."

She gave me a low-wattage, wry smile. "Touché." She gathered her thoughts for a moment. "Do you know what a beard is?"

One of my eyebrows quirked. "Sure. Reece's mother has a pointy one like the Devil on the tip of her chinny-chin-chin."

"In gay vernacular, Rachel."

"I… Okay, I think it means a fake boyfriend or girlfriend. Where one person is covering for the other, so people don't know you're gay."

She let out a relieved breath. "Exactly. That's what William does for me."

I let that soak in for a moment, afraid to hope that meant we still had a chance. "So you don't love him?"

"No, I *do* love him. Very much." Her gaze softened when she spoke about him and jealousy reached out and slapped me in the face. "But like a brother, not a real fiancé."

My emotions were so scattered I didn't know what to feel anymore. "And you need this…cover?"

"Yes."

"And William needs it because he's gay too?" I ventured, still deeply adrift.

She snorted softly. "Hardly. He's the biggest man-whore alive. A sweetheart, but a woman loving hedonist to the bone."

I felt like we were living on different planets. "You live with him to pretend to be straight and he lives with you so he can be a slut and no one will find out?"

"I know it sounds extreme." She cringed. "And sort of bad. But it works, Rachel." She shook her head a little. "At least it has up until now."

"But there are gay people on television, and in magazines, and…well, everywhere. I see them every single day. Do people in the twenty-first century really still need to live fake lives and pretend to be something they're not?"

Nora nodded sadly. "They do when their father or boss is Jacob Dane."

His name had become a curse to me. "He can kiss my ass."

Nora punched the pillow that was on her lap. "Don't you think I've thought the same thing a million times? But he's not a bad man. He's kind and giving, but he's also very devout in his religious beliefs.

I don't think William or I meant for things to end up this

way," she continued. "We started 'dating' in college to keep our families happy when Jacob began pressuring him to settle down and stop playing the field. And we just kept doing it. By the time we'd made our careers with Jacob's soccer team, the lie had been in place for so long that neither of us wanted to rock the boat."

I gaped. "You're living this elaborate lie just for your *job*?" I pitched a bitch and threatened to quit when my boss wouldn't let me take my lunch when I wanted. This was beyond ridiculous.

"It's not just a job to me." She leaned forward intently, trying to make me understand with the force of her will alone. "It's not what I do, it's who I *am*. It's been my whole life. William and I have worked like dogs for more than a decade to get our own team. The Dragonflies will be it, Rachel." I could hear the excitement and passion in her voice mounting with every word. "We're almost there. We're building it from scratch too, just the way we've always wanted. Jacob will retire someday soon."

Uh. Huh. I thought skeptically. The man looked like he lived and breathed the business. "Someday when?"

Nora's lips tightened. "Five years. Maybe less," she quickly added after getting a good look at my expression.

I flopped back on the bed scarcely able to believe what I was hearing. "And you're going to keep doing this for five years?"

"That doesn't mean we can't see each other. I-I..." Tears filled her eyes.

I cocked my head to the side. "You what?"

"I'm in love with you."

Flabbergasted, I fell silent. How had I missed *that*?

She held up her hands as though to ward off another attack. "I know we said it would be just a vacation romance, but I can't just let things end like that. We could be so great together, Rachel." A tear fell from her eye and glistened in the morning sun. "We should be more than an affair."

I blinked a few times. "You're in love with me? Since when?"

"Haven't you been paying attention?"

I wanted to kiss her tears away, but I felt like my head was going to explode. "I don't... I don't know what to say."

She clasped my hand with hers, breaking her promise not

to touch me. Her hand was cold and clammy and shaking just a little. "Say that you love me too."

My heart thudded unevenly in my chest. "I do," I whispered, unable to hold her gaze. "You know I do."

Optimism filled her eyes and she began to smile.

I bent at the waist, feeling ill again. An ulcer the size of a softball was surely forming in my gut this very second. "But I don't think that's enough." This was worse than when I thought she didn't care. Way worse. "Why didn't you tell me about William?"

"Don't say it's not enough." She held my hand tighter. "I thought you knew about him. Not that we really weren't together, but at least that I was engaged. You acted as though I'd gotten my job for some reason other than talent."

"No matter what you said, I thought you were sleeping with Jacob."

She blanched. "Gee, thanks. Anyway, everyone knows about the engagement. That's the whole point."

"I didn't know."

"I figured that out last night when you looked like you were going to strangle me when Joanie called him my fiancé."

I touched my own naked ring finger. It had taken months to get used to not wearing a wedding band. Even now I sometimes absently felt for it. "You're not wearing a ring."

"I never do when I travel. It's too easy to leave it on some hotel sink and forget about it."

My face hardened. "You lied to me."

She looked truly wounded by my accusation. "I *never* lied."

I could see her pulse pounding in her throat and knew she didn't believe her own words.

She licked her lips. "I was doing what you wanted by keeping things simple. You said you weren't ready for complicated. Everything about my life with William is complicated."

"You could have told me about William from the very start, before I really cared about you. If I had just been a jungle fuck, none of this would have mattered."

Nora's jaw worked angrily, but she looked away.

"Instead, you didn't just *let* me fall in love with you. You *tried* to make me love you. We stopped being about just sex long before we even had sex, and you know it. Every day after that you were just screwing with my heart by keeping your dirty little secret."

She covered her face with her hands. "Fine! I was afraid that if you knew, you'd think my life was a big mess and you'd never let anything happen between us. I'm not proud of how I'm living, Rachel."

"Then stop living that way."

She snorted and stared despondently at the ceiling. "God, it's not that easy. If I come out, and Jacob finds out that my and William's engagement is a sham, both of us will be out of the Dragonflies organization for good."

I narrowed my eyes. "If Jacob is such a Jesus freak, how come he approves of his son living in sin with you?"

"He doesn't. But we've been pretend-dating forever. We had to make *some* progress in the relationship or it wouldn't have looked real. Besides, we're great roommates. We both work all the time and are never home to fight. I drool from afar at the parade of women he brings home, and he's an escort for me when I need to do something public."

Looks like they had the perfect screwed up engagement they'd both dreamed of. Problem was, there was no room for a third person in that equation. "You want us to see each other while you're still living with him?"

A sliver of hope crept into her expression. "More than anything."

"And we're supposed to sneak around to do it?"

"You make it sound impossible. It's not."

I ground my teeth together. Just because she wanted something didn't make it possible. She had to be willing to sacrifice for it. I didn't want her to ruin William's life. But she couldn't trade his happiness for hers and mine. She still wanted to have her cake and eat it too.

"Nora, you don't understand," I said, gesturing with my hands as I spoke. "Our situation wouldn't be like William and some woman he picked up." I shook my head. "Wherever he picks up women. All the publicity the station has done to get our radio show to number one, not to mention that stupid billboard, means I'm recognized all over Denver. At the movies, in restaurants, at gas stations, people come up to me all the time. If you're with me, someone will figure out we're together. I want to hold your hand. I want to kiss you. I don't want to hide."

Nora jumped out of bed, causing the mattress springs to protest loudly. She ran an agitated hand through her hair. "We can be careful and just do those things in private. William's made it work."

"Has he ever had a real *relationship* with any of these women of his?" Her long pause gave me the answer she didn't want to say. "Bringing someone home for sex isn't the same thing as trying to build a life." Then a terrible thought struck me. "Unless that's what you're really proposing here?" My stomach started to drop.

"No!"

"Because if it is—"

Her gaze drilled into mine. "I want more than that. And we can have more. We can find a way to make it work." But she sounded as though she was trying to convince herself as much as she was trying to convince me. Upset, she went right for the jugular, her voice a broken whisper. "You're giving up. We promised never to give up."

I got out of bed too, but I went to the window, turning my back to her and gazing out, not seeing a thing. I wrapped my arms around my middle and ruthlessly ordered myself not to give in and promise that I'd do anything to stay together. With the last bit of my willpower, I steeled myself. "I don't promise that, Nora. I didn't promise to sneak around like I was doing something wrong."

For a handful of heartbeats the only thing I heard was my own breathing. Then…

"You're sure you won't reconsider?"

No! my heart screamed. I wasn't sure of anything. I was two seconds from dropping to my knees and professing my undying love and willingness to tag along after her like a puppy on a string. But as much as I wanted to, I knew deep down that we'd never make it if we lived like that. All we'd be doing was prolonging the inevitable pain of separation. My chest began to heave and I grabbed on to the windowsill and held on tight. There was only one truth in this entire mess that I could think of. "I really do love you, Nora."

Her thick swallow was audible. "I love you, too."

I heard her walk across the room and unlock the door. And when I turned around, she was gone.

Chapter 16

After Nora left, I stayed at the window for a long time, dully watching the constant train of strangers amble or drive down the street. I half expected to see Nora and her entourage among them as they fled the hotel. When that didn't happen, I started to grow restless.

I opened the window and let the scent of fresh-brewed coffee drift into the room from the café downstairs. My stomach growled in response, but it was just one more negative sensation to add to the list of many. I've never been one to wallow in self-pity, but then again, I'd never been this shaken. When my marriage dissolved I was sad, but I'd been leaving something irreparable.

Nora and I weren't broken. We were all raw anticipation and wasted potential. We'd barely started. And somehow, that was even more upsetting.

"Shit," I grunted, just to hear it. But like sex, swearing was always better with a partner.

I stripped carelessly, letting my clothes land where they may as I climbed into another hot shower. The tiny bathroom quickly filled with enough steam to power a freight train. The water pounded against me until I was as raw on the outside as I was on the inside and the towel felt rough against my skin.

Not bothering to do much more than brush my teeth and

run a comb through my curls—never an easy task—I tugged on my sister's T-shirt and shorts, deep in thought about Nora.

On the dresser sat my only real possession. The somewhat pathetic remains of the last flower Nora had given me that had survived being stuffed in several pockets. And now I couldn't even bear to look at it. Doubt reared his ugly snout and sniffed in my direction.

Maybe none of this was real. Maybe I wasn't in love with her at all and I was just a victim of circumstances. Yeah, if this was Circumstances' fault, it wasn't mine. I warmed to that idea even though it made me think of women who stay with men who beat them or young mothers who pitch their unwanted babies into Dumpsters.

Circumstances, not my heart, made me think I loved her. After all, her only competition at the time had been a married teenager whom I loved like a sister, and Regis Philbin, the monkey. I would never go gay for Posh Spice. In a situation like that, anyone could confuse reliance with attraction and friendship with love. Couldn't they?

It was Circumstances that made me ache for her touch and my skin burn from the memory of her kisses. Not that sizzling smile or breasts worthy of being bronzed. They had nothing to do with it. Circumstances tricked me into feeling pain when she was hurting and wondering with a warm sense of fondness what she'd look like when time turned her hair silver and lines formed around eyes the color of new grass in the springtime. When I got home I would remember that women were too complicated and messy and not what I wanted at all.

Circumstances and Doubt were bitches of epic proportion.

So what if my heart hurt with every beat? Now that I knew the source of all these confusing feelings, I could put all of this behind me like nothing more than an extended bad dream. Reece would continue to be one of the joys of my life and banes of my existence. I'd look forward to Joanie's phone calls and visits, and I'd do my best to be a good aunt. She and my mother would set me up on dates that were bound for failure from the very start, and I would wonder if everyone was really this lonely but afraid to talk about it. One reliable but boring day at work would melt seamlessly into the next. And it would all be enough *without her*.

I would wish for more, but settle for less. Just. Like. Before.

Suddenly, I was swept up in a surge of misery and longing so gigantic I could hardly keep from keeling over. No matter what the circumstances, I wasn't the same person who boarded a plane for an exotic land. Deep in my bones I understood in a way that I never had, just how short life was. This was *it*, and if I didn't make my own happiness I wouldn't get another chance. I didn't want to settle for anything anymore. But Nora had left me with no other choice.

The more I thought about that, the angrier I got. How could someone so smart be stupid enough to ignore something so precious? The angrier I got, the more I wanted to take that anger out on someone. And so I resolved to do just that.

The hallway was quiet and empty. I knocked sharply on several doors—our party took up the entire second, and only, floor of rooms—but there was no answer.

Where is everyone? I could understand Joanie wanting to let me sleep in, something I never did because of the crazy hours I kept for work, but it was already mid-morning.

Letting the enticing scent of food be my guide, I navigated a small set of squeaky stairs, my aching feet feeling awkward and tender in Joanie's flip-flops.

My temper wavering on a razor's edge, I entered the café and glanced around the sparsely populated room.

"Hey." Reece smiled and waved me over to the table where he, Joanie, Miranda and Paulo were eating breakfast. The table was nearly overflowing with half empty plates, bottles of sauce and coffee cups. Miranda, her hair still damp from a recent shower, was eating as though she'd been starved, which was apt. Paulo, his manly jaw resting on his hand, watched her every move with undisguised adoration.

I felt a twinge of envy. The person I adored was sitting at a nearby table with her fiancé instead of me. She was wearing clean clothes that must have belonged to William, and she still looked as though she'd been awake for a year. I glared in her direction and then took a seat next to my sister.

Nora not only noticed my glare, but gave me one right back, her hurt and resentment palpable. She felt as awful as I did. Good.

Jacob and Miranda's father were noticeably absent and I hoped Mr. Gutierrez had gone to fetch Miranda's mother. I was surprised she hadn't accompanied her husband in the first place, but maybe their household was old school enough that she'd been left behind while the man handled things. Uck.

"Here." Joanie passed me a piece of soggy wheat toast. "I saved you some. I stopped by your room to get you for breakfast, but you were in a never-ending shower. I yelled for you, but you must have been zoned out or something. I was actually getting a little worried." She stopped talking as she stared at me, and after so many days of smelling blood, sweat, bug spray and lush plants, I noticed for the first time how many competing scents she had going on, all of them good. Shampoo, perfume, soap, coffee. "What happened to your teeth on the side of your mouth?"

Oh. I'd forgotten about that. I must look a sight. I smiled thinly. "I pulled them out because I was bored."

Reece snorted as he sprinkled hot sauce across his food and then scooped up a bite of eggs.

"What do you think happened?" I went on tiredly. "They got knocked out in the accident."

Joanie tried to push more food my way. "Maybe if you eat something you won't be so grouchy."

"I'm not hungry," I said moodily. My appetite had fled the moment I walked into the room. Nora was still giving me the stink-eye and it was pissing me off. What did *she* have to be mad about?

Miranda stopped mid-bite. "How is that possible?"

I dragged my eyes off Nora. "Huh?"

"How is it possible that you're not hungry?"

I shrugged. "I'm just not."

Unhappy, Miranda sighed. "You didn't fix things, did you, Mama?"

"Hardly."

"Mama?" Joanie asked.

"Nickname," I explained absently, wondering if Nora was

going to stare daggers at me all day or actually speak.

Joanie blinked a few times. "Weird. You're the least maternal person I know." She took back her toast and slathered on a thin layer of jam, before prodding me with it again. "By the way, I called our mom."

"That's nice," I murmured.

Giving up, she tossed the toast on Reece's plate the same way you'd drop scraps in the dog's dish. "She wants to come here."

Startled, I turned fully to face her. "No. No. No. That is the last thing I want. I do want to see her, but at least let me catch my breath first."

Joanie patted my hand. "I know. Don't worry. I talked her out of it. But you've been summoned to her house the second we're back in Denver. I mean it, Rachel. She's been scared to death for you. Don't even go home first or my ass is grass, got it?"

Miranda pushed aside her plate and leaned forward on her elbows. She looked me dead in the eye. "Why in the blue fuck are you just sitting here on your butt?" she grated. "Go fix things with her." Meaningfully, she tilted her head toward Nora.

Wow, her English had really improved being around Nora and me.

"Okay," Reece said around Joanie's toast. "What's going on now?"

"Yeah," Joanie chimed in. "What do you have to fix with Ms. Butler? You didn't make her mad, did you, Rachel? Isn't she like your boss or something?" She shook her head woefully and gave me a look. "Oh, man, you were together all those weeks. I *know* you did something stupid."

There was that fish eye from Nora again. My simmering blood finally came to a full boil and I pushed away from the table as I stood, my gaze riveted on Nora. "Miranda, will you please explain everything to my sister and Reece?"

From the corner of my eye, I saw Miranda point her thumb at her own chest. "You want me to tell them everything?"

"Please."

"*Everything*?"

Impatiently, I glanced at Joanie and Reece. "I had sex with Nora in the jungle and now she won't publicly see me when we get back to Denver. I want to have a real relationship with her and she's too chickenshit to risk it."

Reece snorted orange juice through his nose and Paulo jumped up and began slapping him on the back. Miranda's husband hadn't even looked in my direction when I spoke. Then I remembered he didn't speak more than a few words of memorized English, the lucky bastard.

Joanie's mouth dropped open and stayed.

"You can use that as a starting or ending point, hon," I said to Miranda. "I have something else to deal with right now."

"Go get her," Miranda urged softly.

I marched over to Nora, who stood just as I reached her table. She furiously threw her napkin down and clenched her fist, looking like she wanted to sock me in the face.

William's eyes widened. "Thank God, you're here, Ms...I mean Rachel. I'm so sorry about yesterday. I didn't know you and Nora were such...close friends or I would have explained everything."

"It's not your fault Nora never mentioned your engagement. It's hers," I said coldly.

He paled a little. "Please take her back," he blurted before Nora could stop him. "She's been crying all morning. Forgive her for anything stupid—"

"Shut up." Nora snapped, reaching out to choke William, but he deftly moved out of her reach.

He quieted, but not because he looked particularly intimidated. He seemed more concerned when he reached out and gently touched her shoulder. "Nora—"

"Can I have a moment alone with your fiancé?" I asked, trying not to gag on the last word.

Looking at Nora for consent, he nodded reluctantly, then hurried over to Joanie's table, leaving me face-to-face with the object of my desire. And the source of my pain. I blocked out Joanie and Reece's continual, "No, really?" And, "You're shitting me," statements that drifted over from their nearby table.

Miranda was literally holding Joanie back so my sister

wouldn't stalk over and get her answers straight from me right this very second. Corralling her was a little like trying to get your arms around a tornado, and I silently wished Miranda luck.

Then there was Nora, who was even harder to hold than that. "Why are you so mad?" I asked. "You're the one who walked away from me. So stop making stupid faces over your coffee cup." They weren't really stupid, more like seething. But whatever.

"Faces?" The color rose in her sun-darkened cheeks. Nostrils flared, she drew in a sharp breath. "Walked away? I practically begged you to do anything to make this work and you wouldn't bend even an inch." She poked my chest with her index finger, daring me to take things to a more physical level. "Not a millimeter."

Shocked, I clutched my chest. "Ouch!"

"I love you and you suck."

"I love you too." *Stupid move with the finger, blondie!* "And you…" I poked her chest right back, only twice as hard. "Suck more."

"Ouch!" Teeth bared, she reached for my finger, but I'd already snatched it back.

"You're not fast enough to catch a disease." She was actually much quicker than me. I'd just gotten lucky, and I knew it. But that didn't mean I was above rubbing it in.

"I like a good catfight *way* more than the next guy, ladies," William called over. "But not in a country where the National Guard is looking to toss you in jail anyway."

"Shut up," Nora and I barked in unison.

I refocused on Nora. "You're afraid to live your own life."

"And you're a stubborn, unreasonable quitter."

We stared daggers at each other for another few seconds. We were both breathing heavily and adrenaline was singing through my veins, making my hands twitch to do something… anything. Strangulation was looking particularly appealing.

The room had gone completely silent and I knew what Joanie had to be thinking. Now we weren't just like her soaps, we were actually *better*. "I'm glad we got that straightened out," I said, my voice dripping ice.

"So am I. So then why do I feel like I want to cry?" She blinked hard a few times. "For your information, I'm done crying over you."

I crossed my arms over my chest, wanting to throw up. "Likewise."

Angrily, she rubbed at the spot where I'd poked her chest. "So then why haven't you left Venezuela yet?"

"Because we aren't finished and I'm no goddamned quitter!" I roared. "You told me you *loved* me last night and then left me standing there. How could you do that?" Damn my traitorous voice for breaking.

Her demeanor softened instantly and her eyes swirled with emotion. Not the crazy Sean Young sort of swirly eyes, but the soulful, gentle kind that gave me the nearly unstoppable urge to kiss her.

God, I couldn't even fight with her without wanting her. Now that's messed up.

"That's not what happened," she said, wounded. "I told you that I loved you and that I wanted us to be together. You're the one who acted like there was no hope. Like you wouldn't even try. How could *you* do that?"

And that stopped me cold. She was right. How could I do that? "That's not... That's not what I meant." I stepped a little closer. "I do want to try. That's all I want. I just don't want to start off with nothing but lies all around us. I've already had a public life that didn't match my private one and I failed miserably at it. I couldn't reconcile Reece's provocative radio personality with the quiet man at home every night, and it was part of why our marriage went down the drain."

Nora frowned deeply. "I didn't know that."

"That's because I didn't tell you." I drew in a tremulous breath. "But I need to learn from my mistakes. I didn't just live through the shittiest years ever just to repeat them over and over. I can't repeat them and survive."

"I'm not Reece. And I know I was asking a lot, but I didn't deserve an ultimatum."

How had I messed things up so badly? "I didn't mean for it to seem like that. You don't have to come out to your boss.

I understand if that's something you're not ready to risk. But I have to be honest too. I can't be with you while you're engaged to someone else. Even if that engagement isn't real."

I was embarrassed to even have to say this. But every ego, even one as well battered as mine, has its limits. "I can't live with you caring about your job more than me."

She gasped. "Is that what you think?" Then she closed her eyes for a few seconds. "Of course that's what you think. That's what anyone would think." She lifted her head and squared her shoulders. I'd never seen anyone look more intent or sincere. "But it's not true, Rachel. I swear it."

Wasn't it? Maybe it wasn't a matter of who or what she loved more. Maybe it was pure fear that drove her. But whatever it was, she was still firmly in its grasp now.

She chewed her lower lip as though she were debating whether to say something. "Have you ever thought that when we get back home, we might not feel the way we do about each other now? The love part?"

It was a verbal slap that caused me to recoil a half step. I had to take a few breaths so I could speak through my closed throat. "I guess… The thought crossed my mind."

She looked pained. "Mine too. Especially this morning when you seemed happy to let me walk out of your life."

Happy? I was dying inside.

Just then, Jacob Dane, Miranda's father and three uniformed men carrying rifles entered the restaurant. Jacob hurried around the military men and over to our table. "I'm sorry, girls, I'm afraid you both and Miranda need to come to the police station for more questioning. We tried to work this out but…"

What else did these people want from me? What did Nora want? Suddenly it all seemed like too much and, at my wit's end, I snapped. "She needs a doctor." I pointed to Nora's bandaged hand. "And Miranda needs to have a doctor look at her feet. And I need to get the hell out of this place. I'm not going *anywhere* with these guys."

Miranda and her father were instantly at our side and the rest of our group arrived right at their heels. "I am so sorry," Miranda said, looking mortified. I knew she was embarrassed by our treatment. "My papa tried to explain things to the soldiers."

"It's not your fault, Miranda," I said gently, doing my best to smile. She was being treated as shabbily as we foreigners were.

Jacob chafed Nora's hand with his. "Don't worry, I've arranged for a doctor to see you all this afternoon."

"Here?" Nora asked, incredulous. "Can't we at least go back to Caracas first?"

Jacob eyed the National Guardsmen warily. "Unfortunately, I'm not sure we'll be able to leave today. I—"

"I'm calling the embassy again," William announced, his cheeks flushing with anger.

"Me too," Reece added. "This is bullshit."

Both men excused themselves from the café.

Apparently, this was all taking too long, because one of the waiting soldiers roughly grumbled something in Spanish to Miranda and made the mistake of copping a feel as he tried to hurry her along.

Her father exploded.

"Hey," Nora yelled, but the word was barely out of her mouth when Paulo coldcocked the soldier and was promptly, and violently, arrested by the other two men.

In her surliest voice, Nora ordered the soldier who was now holding a screaming and kicking Miranda to back off, promising that we'd all go peacefully, which I actually doubted. But the guardsman did release Miranda, only to grab Nora instead, spin her around, bend her over the nearest table and try to slap a pair of handcuffs on her. Dishes flew everywhere.

Nora howled in agony when he yanked on her injured hand. Tears sprang to her eyes and leaked onto the stained Formica tabletop as her arms were wrenched up her back by her twisted fingers.

Livid, I cursed and shoved the solider away as hard as I could, putting myself between him and Nora, my fists raised in case he came one step closer. Where was our big knife when I really wanted it? "You asshole," I spat. "She was cooperating."

Everyone in the place started shouting a cacophony of angry Spanish and frenzied English.

Teeth bared, the soldier I had pushed slung his rifle over his shoulder and rushed me, but before he could make contact, Joanie administered a full body block that knocked him halfway across the room and sent her sprawling into several chairs. It was a move so spectacular it was a pity we only got to see it once. The crash sounded a little like a bowling ball splintering the pins.

Then, as if I couldn't say this with complete confidence before, all hell broke loose.

It was shaping up to be another lovely day.

Chapter 17

If anyone ever tells you that spending the night in jail in a foreign country sucks, consider his or her frame of reference. Even with the stench of sweat and urine, it was better than the jungle. Though that still made it way worse than just about anyplace else on earth.

The Venezuelan National Guard had finished questioning me after a half dozen long and supremely confusing hours. I couldn't tell how much of what I was saying they understood, and I know I only caught about half of their broken English, but I guess I finally uttered the magic words, because they thanked me, then dumped me in a tiny cell alone, where I'd been since yesterday.

Near as I could tell, I was now being held for assaulting that soldier. If I'd known I was going to have to do time anyway, God only knows what I would have done to the jerk that had hurt Nora. I had heard her hand snap and knew she must be in agony now.

So far, I'd spent the entire time separated from my comrades, and by the time Joanie and Reece picked me up from the station late in the morning on my second day, I was frantic to know what had happened. By the way, that one phone call thingie only applies inside the United States.

"Tell me," I simply said as we walked out the front door and into a blessed breeze. I pulled in a deep breath and tasted my freedom. Okay, maybe the jungle had been a little better.

"Miranda and Nora are both back at the hotel already," Joanie assured me as she gave me a big hug. "You were the last to get out, well, except for poor Paulo."

We started walking. "When can we get him?" I prayed this could be settled without a trial and started to wonder if I was ever going to be able to leave this place.

"Tonight, we think," Reece said. "He broke that soldier's jaw and it's costing Jacob a fortune to bribe all the right people."

"But he's doing it, right? He's not going to leave Paulo in jail?"

"He's doing it. He's at the local bank with the town mayor getting the cash right now. They're pretty blatant about the money thing here."

There was no sidewalk, only a wide dirt road that accommodated people, cars and animals. And I quickly stepped out of the way of an old jeep that rattled by at a ridiculously high speed. "Why didn't he have to bribe someone to get us out then? I pushed one of the soldiers and you should try out for the fuckin' Broncos!" I told Joanie, my admiration showing.

She shrugged as though I shouldn't have expected anything less. And in truth, I didn't. "I couldn't help it, I was worried for you."

I stopped walking and tugged her over to kiss her on the cheek. We weren't normally affectionate in that way, and for the first time I wondered why. "I love you," I whispered, a little choked up. "Thanks for coming to get me...again."

She smiled and I had the oddest memory of pulling her out of a scrape during lunchtime on her very first day of kindergarten. I guess some things never change. "No problem, sis. Just don't make a habit of it, okay?"

I crossed my heart.

"The reason you and I aren't rotting in jail right now is that Jacob Dane was able to convince the local authorities that we were defending Nora when things turned nasty. They weren't happy that she yelled at one of the soldiers, but then that prick rebroke her hand when he tried to cuff her." She winced. "She saw a doctor today. She needs surgery, Rachel."

Oh, shit. My eyes widened and I picked up the pace to the hotel. "And Miranda?"

"Is fine," Reece said. "But worried for Paulo. They gave her some sort of pills big enough to choke a horse for her feet."

I nodded briskly, weaving my way through a few pedestrians and avoiding the mud puddles and occasional dung pile as best I could.

"So, Rachel, you're a lesbian now?" There was no censure in Reece's voice, only honest curiosity and maybe a tinge of hurt.

"Nosy much, Reece?" Joanie said, giving him a sideways glance.

"You said you were going to ask her yourself."

"I'm her sister. I'm allowed to ask nosy questions, you're not."

I swear, Joanie was more bitter about my divorce than I was. I knew they both wanted to talk to me, but now just wasn't the time. "I'm sorry, guys, but the only thing I am right now is in a hurry."

I started to run.

"They're in the café," Joanie called after me. "And don't start any more brawls."

The scene in the café was eerily reminiscent of yesterday morning. Miranda and her father sat at one table and William and Nora sat at another. Jacob was missing again and I knew that Joanie and Reece would follow me inside.

Miranda gave me a little wave, telling me she was all right, and inclined her head toward Nora.

I smiled wryly. She was persistent, I'll give her that.

As soon as I approached the table, both Nora and William stood.

"Are you okay?" William asked, clearly concerned.

Despite myself, I was starting to like him. But only a little. "Yeah, I'll live."

"Good." He nodded briskly. "Then if you'll excuse me, I'm going to go and visit with Miranda and her father."

When he left, an awkward silence bloomed between Nora

and me.

"Are you really okay?" Nora finally asked, her eyes slightly glassy.

I'd have bet a week's paycheck she was on some heavy-duty painkillers at the moment. I eyed her clean bandage and splint. "Never mind about me. What about your hand?"

She shrugged lightly. "I need an operation. Or three. But I'm not doing it here. It'll keep until Denver."

A fist wrapped around my heart. "I'm so sorry you're hurt again."

She smiled affectionately. "You shouldn't have come to my defense like that, Rachel. It's why you spent the night in jail."

I smiled back. "Time well spent."

"Can we finish our discussion from yesterday morning?"

My pulse picked up as I nodded. I didn't want to be there when she lowered the boom. But it had to happen sometime. "You're not too stoned for it, are you?"

She laughed softly. "The drugs are only taking the edge off. Sadly, I still want to scream. So I must be lucid." Then she sobered. "I asked if you ever wondered if when we got back to the States, we'd feel differently about each other, remember?"

"I remember." I held my breath. Her body was ramrod stiff as though she was preparing herself to ward off a physical blow. Worry snaked through me making me feel a little sick.

"I've had a long time to think about that. And I don't think I will. Every day on my way to work when I passed your billboard, I wondered what you'd be like. And right in the airport in Denver, when you looked like you'd rather die than go on the adventure tour or even read the lame company handbook, and especially when you wore those goofy clothes just to be comfortable, I thought to myself…even if this flight is cancelled and we somehow don't end up in Venezuela, I *have* to get to know this woman better. How can I get her to notice me?"

Charmed, I couldn't help the slow smile that stretched my lips.

"The jungle might have made things happen more quickly, Rachel, but it didn't manufacture chemistry or attraction that wasn't there in the first place. At least not for me."

I felt the same rush of surprise, then heat, I'd felt when she first propositioned me so boldly in our hotel in Caracas. I'd been captivated from the very start. "It didn't for me either," I admitted, still unsure it mattered.

Then, our eyes met, and all I could think was that I couldn't lose her. Not now. *I can't leave my heart stranded in this place.* "What if we compromise by dating in a nearby town or something?" I didn't like that option, but I had to be willing to bend. "Someplace where people won't recognize me and we won't have to hide. We can have lots of weekends away. At least then when we're together, we'd really be together. And—"

She held up her hand. "Stop. That's not what I want."

My heart sank.

"I don't want a casual love affair where we sneak away like we're cheating on our spouses. I want to be with you and only you. And I want you to want that too."

My eyes widened. "Why do you think I'm not already walking to the nearest train or bus station to get out of this place? I'm near to grabbing you by the hair and dragging you back to my house in Denver so I can chain you in the basement!" I wanted to shake her so she got this through her thick head. "I'm in a hundred percent."

Her face relaxed in relief. "Then I need to be in a hundred percent too. Probably more. One of the reasons I was so eager to have an affair with you on this trip, besides the fact that I was so hot for you it was embarrassing, was that I was buckling under the pressure of the lies. I needed five minutes where I could just be myself because as soon as the trip was over I knew I was going to turn into a pumpkin all over again."

Nora gnawed a little on her lower lip. "I've worked so hard to get where I am that the thought of my making one wrong move, and then having the rug yanked out from under me..." She shuddered.

She was being slowly tortured. "That's no way to live."

This time her smile was rueful. "I did it to myself."

"I know the feeling."

"And I know I need to make a change."

My stomach tightened in anticipation. "What does that

mean? Exactly."

"It means that I spoke to William this morning and told him it was time to cancel our engagement. It's off, Rache."

Shocked, I flicked my gaze at him. Even if she wasn't in love with him, she loved him. That meant his reaction was more important than I would have liked. And she'd broken their engagement even though she thought I was willing to see her walk out of my life? "What did he say?"

She snorted a little. "He wants you and I to be together, but he also wants everything else to stay the same."

I narrowed my eyes at him. "Selfish prick."

"He has a right to be worried about himself. Besides, he's been doing this as much for me as for himself over the years. I'm the one who's backing out on our deal."

Suddenly, I felt like a heel. She was risking everything and I wasn't anteing up the same investment. I already knew how the people I cared about most would react to us being together.

Joanie would be okay once she got over the shock, which wouldn't take long. Her curiosity would get the best of her, which meant we'd talk about it endlessly, but we'd find our way through this just like we did with everything else. She wouldn't be satisfied with any short version, however. I'd have to start at the beginning and tell her about Lola. A month ago that thought would have filled me with dread. But I'd come to realize that that particular wound had healed long ago. It felt right to talk about it now.

Ultimately, I couldn't decide whether Reece would be more surprised, titillated or hurt. Probably a combination of all three. But he'd deal. Nothing about the way I felt for him while we were married was a lie and I'd make sure he knew it.

My mother would never accept my seeing a woman, but Joanie would work on her enough so that we'd all three manage to be civil and even cordial. I knew I was setting the bar pitifully low, but honestly, it was enough for me.

Now I just had to get the girl.

I took Nora's good hand and placed it over my heart and asked the question that worried me most. "What about your job?"

I expected a wave of anxiety, or maybe even that she'd lash out in her own defense. Instead, she looked mostly at peace. That must have been some discussion she had with William.

She patted my chest. I knew she could feel the furious beat of my heart. "There are other jobs, but only one you."

I went weak in the knees. Those were the words I didn't know I'd been longing to hear. More even than "I love you," which even though it made me feel as though I could take flight, wasn't always enough. "You don't have to do this now, you know. You can deal with your engagement after the soccer season's started or even when it's over."

For once, I was glad that my feelings showed. I wanted her to understand that I wouldn't give up ever. If she was willing to open the door for there to be an "us," I could at least be patient about when we stepped through it. "I love you with all my heart and would wait a million goddamned years for you, Nora."

She flashed me one of those smiles that made me dissolve into a puddle, and I was lost again. But this time she was lost right there alongside me.

"Problem is, I love you with all my heart too. And that means I'm not willing to wait that long, Rachel. Not anymore."

As natural as breathing, I cupped her cheeks with my hands and moved in for a kiss. When our lips met it was bliss and I couldn't stop myself from deepening the kiss to get even closer, willingly drowning in a sublime sensation of passion and belonging that I soaked in like sunshine.

We were going to be so good together that I could hardly wait.

From the edges of my consciousness, I heard a few gasps and I figured I'd shocked the hell out of Miranda's father or some waitress. But when we separated, I saw Nora looking over my shoulder with wide eyes.

Jacob Dane had just walked into the room along with Reece and Joanie. I swear I heard an ominous, "Duum-dum-dum-dum-duuuuuum."

"Nora?" he said, confusion coloring his every feature. He glanced to William, who was suddenly as white as a sheet. "What's going on here?" His voice shifted from questioning to authoritative in the blink of an eye, and I felt a stab of pity for the people who'd endured his censure over the years. It must have been like working for your junior high school principal for your entire life and never quite measuring up.

Nora threw her shoulders back and lifted her chin, making her appear about ten feet tall. She let out a long, relaxed breath. "Well, I guess this makes things even easier."

Oh, *shit*, that was so not true. But it certainly cut to the heart of things whether she was ready for it or not. "I'm *so* sorry," I whispered, horrified at what I'd done.

She squeezed the hand she was holding to let me know it was okay.

"William?" Jacob said, turning to his son for an explanation.

"Oh, my God! She's gay?" William gawked, looking at Nora as though he'd never seen her before. "No wonder she keeps postponing the wedding."

Nora rolled her eyes at the slimy coward and Reece elbowed him hard in the side, causing him to hunch over and a loud "uuff" to explode from him.

Nora's gaze slid sideways to fix on me.

"A hundred percent," I assured her. It was a promise I intended to keep.

"Jacob," Nora said confidently, drawing his attention from his gasping son as she moved around me to confront him. "We need to talk."

Chapter 18

Six months later Nora, Miranda and I sat in the control booth at my radio station, all of us wearing headsets as I interviewed two of my very favorite people.

Nora's hand had only just come out of what I hoped would be her last cast. Some of the damage had turned out to be permanent, and she was dealing with it better than I would have under the same circumstances. The cut on her leg was now just a thin white line and a nasty memory. A few tiny scars from the cuts on her face were the most visible reminder of her ordeal, and they peeked out even more when she got a touch of sun.

Miranda and I had fared better. Her scars didn't show and her soccer performance had never been better. She and Paulo were well on their way to becoming US citizens and were surprisingly good roommates. They could have moved out of my townhouse months ago, but we all liked the arrangement and were determined to keep things the way they were until that changed. Around her neck she wore a necklace with a pendant that contained the stone that Nora had given her in the jungle. She never took it off and I understood exactly why.

Other than a much-slimmed down physique—I'd lost thirty pounds in the jungle—which I loved and worked hard every day to maintain, I had no physical reminders of the accident. Why hadn't someone mentioned how weird it felt not to have your upper thighs rub together when you walk? And my fake teeth, which had cost a small fortune, looked even better than my real ones.

Considering everything that had happened, all of us, except for poor Lucas, had gotten off lucky. And more than that, I'd ended up with something I'd never expected. The love of my life.

My socked feet were propped up on my desk and I chewed the end of a pencil as one of our station breaks came to a close and I was forced to stop mooning over the woman sitting five feet away from me. "Welcome back to *The Reece & Rachel Morning Show*, it's eight seventeen on this gorgeous morning."

Nora grinned at me and lifted an eyebrow at my cheery mood. Sue me. I was in love and in a romance so hot it was a fever. I had a right to be ridiculously, obnoxiously happy.

"For those of you just joining us, Reece is off to Cancun for his honeymoon with his lovely, yet terribly unlucky bride. Have a margarita on me, Tonya."

Miranda covered her mouth to quiet her laughter.

"And I'm here with soccer sensation Miranda Gutierrez and the Denver Dragonflies Assistant General Manager Nora Butler. We've already discussed their great inaugural season. So now it's time for you to call in or text your questions." I repeated the numbers automatically and read the first of the text messages as it appeared on my computer.

"Nora," I said, and she leaned forward paying rapt attention. "Here's an *excellent* text from Ted and the guys at Crawford Plumbing. They want to know how anyone in your office, or on your team for that matter, gets anything done around you because you're SUCH—that's in all caps, folks—a stone cold fox?"

With a wicked gleam in my eyes, I smiled innocently and tapped my desk with my pencil. The text had actually been some lame recruiting question, but this is what those guys *should* have asked. And I should know. Nora had looked so delicious this morning that I could barely keep my hands off her as we were leaving for work. She was the sweetest of tortures.

Nora's eyes widened and she froze as she tried to figure out what she could say. Then her mouth began to work, but no sound emerged.

Jerry The Producer just shook his head at my laughter from behind the glass that separated our booths. I stuck my tongue out at him.

"Is the answer in your team handbooks?" I teased. "I have it on good authority they're excessively large."

Seeing Miranda's confusion, I mouthed a few silent words of my newly acquired Spanish so she would know what a stone cold fox was.

This time she couldn't stop her laughter. So I turned to her. "What can you tell Ted and the guys at Crawford Plumbing, Miranda?"

"Well," she said, her toothy grin evident in her voice. "Ms. Butler uses her powers for good instead of evil. It's true that we can barely function around her because we're under her spell. But because of that, we score goals only to see her smile."

"Miranda!" Nora exclaimed, still flustered. Then she glared at me.

Oh, man, I wished the listeners could see her beet red face.

"That's what I thought," I said, more than satisfied. "Okay, time for another song."

Jerry The Producer rapped on the glass hard and held up a sloppily scrawled sign that read, *No, it isn't!* Ouch. That's gonna leave a mark on his knuckles.

I ignored him and looked at my morning playlist. *Bleck.* "Let's have Miranda pick something."

Jerry The Producer started to freak out and rushed inside the booth to help Miranda because I was already pulling off my headset and moving out of my seat.

"Okay," Miranda said gamely. She jumped into my seat, her interested gaze flicking over my control console. "Do you have anything in Spanish? What? 'Feliz Navidad'?" She made a face. "I don't think so."

Off mic, I laughed as I moved to kiss Nora, who was already rising to meet me, her own headset now in her hands.

Life was good.

Who you're stranded with can be more important than the

fact that you're stranded at all. And on that score, and many others, a girl's been known to do a helluva lot worse than me.

THE END.

Publications from Spinsters Ink
P.O. Box 242
Midway, Florida 32343
Phone: 800-301-6860
www.spinstersink.com

ACROSS TIME by Linda Kay Silva. If you believe in soul mates, if you know you've had a past life, then join Jessie in the first of a series of adventures that takes her *Across Time*.
ISBN 978-1883523-91-6 $14.95

SELECTIVE MEMORY by Jennifer L. Jordan. A Kristin Ashe Mystery. A classical pianist, who is experiencing profound memory loss after a near-fatal accident, hires private investigator Kristin Ashe to reconstruct her life in the months leading up to the crash. ISBN 978-1-883523-88-6 $14.95

HARD TIMES by Blayne Cooper. Together, Kellie and Lorna navigate through an oppressive, hidden world where lines between right and wrong blur, sexual passion is forbidden but explosive, and love is the biggest risk of all.
ISBN 978-1-883523-90-9 $14.95

THE KIND OF GIRL I AM by Julia Watts. Spanning decades, *The Kind of Girl I Am* humorously depicts an extraordinary woman's experiences of triumph, heartbreak, friendship and forbidden love.
ISBN 978-1-883523-89-3 $14.95

PIPER'S SOMEDAY by Ruth Perkinson. It seemed as though life couldn't get any worse for feisty, young Piper Leigh Cliff and her three-legged dog, Someday.
ISBN 978-1-883523-87-9 $14.95

MERMAID by Michelene Esposito. When May unearths a box in her missing sister's closet she is taken on a journey through her mother's past that leads her not only to Kate but to the choices and compromises, emptiness and fullness, the beauty and jagged pain of love that all women must face.
ISBN 978-1-883523-85-5 $14.95

ASSISTED LIVING by Sheila Ortiz-Taylor. Violet March, an eighty-two-year-old resident of Casa de los Sueños, finally has the opportunity to put years of mystery reading to practical use. One by one her comrades, the Bingos, are dying. Is this natural attrition, or is there a sinister plot afoot?
ISBN 978-1-883523-84-2 $14.95

NIGHT DIVING by Michelene Esposito. *Night Diving* is both a young woman's coming-out story and a thirty-something coming-of-age journey that proves you can go home again.
ISBN 978-1-883523-52-7 $14.95

FURTHEST FROM THE GATE by Ann Roberts. *Furthest from the Gate* is a humorous chronicle of a woman's coming of age, her complicated relationship with her mother and the responsibilities to family that last a lifetime.
ISBN 978-1-883523-81-7 $14.95

EYES OF GRAY by Dani O'Connor. Grayson Thomas was the typical college senior with typical friends, a typical job and typical insecurities about her future. One Sunday morning, Gray's life became a little less typical, she saw a man clad in black, and started doubting her own sanity.
ISBN 978-1-883523-82-4 $14.95

ORDINARY FURIES by Linda Morgenstein. Tired of hiding, exhausted by her grief after her husband's death, Alexis Pope plunges into the refreshingly frantic world of restaurant resort cooking and dining in the funky chic town of Guerneville, California. ISBN 978-1-883523-83-1 $14.95

A POEM FOR WHAT'S HER NAME by Dani O'Connor. Professor Dani O'Connor had pretty much resigned herself to the fact that there was no such thing as a complete woman. Then out of nowhere, along comes a woman who blows Dani's theory right out of the water.
ISBN 1-883523-78-8 $14.95

WOMEN'S STUDIES by Julia Watts. With humor and heart, *Women's Studies* follows one school year in the lives of three young women and shows that in college, one's extracurricular activities are often much more educational than what goes on in the classroom. ISBN 1-883523-75-3 $14.95

DISORDERLY ATTACHMENTS by Jennifer L. Jordan. The fifth Kristin Ashe Mystery. Kris investigates whether a mansion someone wants to convert into condos is haunted.
ISBN 1-883523-74-5 $14.95

VERA'S STILL POINT by Ruth Perkinson. Vera is reminded of exactly what it is that she has been missing in life.
ISBN 1-883523-73-7 $14.95

OUTRAGEOUS by Sheila Ortiz-Taylor. Arden Benbow, a motorcycle riding, lesbian Latina poet from LA is hired to teach poetry in a small liberal arts college in northwest Florida.
ISBN 1-883523-72-9 $14.95

UNBREAKABLE by Blayne Cooper. The bonds of love and friendship can be as strong as steel. But are they unbreakable?
ISBN 1-883523-76-1 $14.95

ALL BETS OFF by Jaime Clevenger. Bette Lawrence is about to find out how hard life can be for someone of low society standing in the 1900s.
ISBN 1-883523-71-0 $14.95

UNBEARABLE LOSSES by Jennifer L. Jordan. The fourth Kristin Ashe Mystery. Two elderly sisters have hired Kris to discover who is pilfering from their award-winning holiday display. ISBN 1-883523-68-0 $14.95

EXISTING SOLUTIONS by Jennifer L. Jordan. The second Kristin Ashe Mystery. When Kris is hired to find an activist's biological father, things get complicated when she finds herself falling for her client. ISBN 1-883523-69-9 $14.95

A SAFE PLACE TO SLEEP by Jennifer L. Jordan. The first Kristin Ashe Mystery. Kris is approached by well-known lesbian Destiny Greaves with an unusual request. One that will lead Kris to hunt for her own missing childhood pieces. ISBN 1-883523-70-2 $14.95